A Long
Road to
Redemption

Chad Spradley

PAGE PUBLISHING, INC.
Conneaut Lake, PA

First originally published by Page Publishing 2021

ISBN 978-1-6624-6509-3 (pbk)
ISBN 978-1-6624-6510-9 (digital)

Printed in the United States of America

CHAPTER 1

He got the call just before six that morning. He didn't care about the time since he was up early anyway. Roger Taylor was never really one to sleep in. Even in his college days, he was usually up before everyone else he knew. What bothered him was that a body was found on a construction site right outside of Warrenton, still barely within the city's jurisdiction but almost crossing into the county sheriff's jurisdiction. Maybe the killer thought that dumping a body in competing jurisdiction would slow down the investigation. He dismissed the thought as being too much planning for most killers looking for a place to dump a body in a hurry. Taylor poured the rest of his coffee into a thermos, grabbed his light jacket, and headed out the door of his small one-bedroom apartment.

It didn't take him long to arrive since the morning rush wasn't close to starting. The uniformed officers had just finished taping up the scene as he arrived. Officer Barnes, a female officer with dirty-blonde hair and a nose that Taylor thought belonged on another face, gave him a look of disapproval as he lifted the tape she had taken time to so precisely place to close off the scene. Barnes was a good officer, maybe attractive, but Taylor wasn't interested.

The scene was pretty much a dirt lot with the skeletal frame of a building. They hadn't gotten very far on the project by the looks of it. They wouldn't get any further today either. He could see the construction foreman out of the corner of his eye, both answering questions and asking them. Doubtless, he wasn't happy about losing a day's work. Hate to tell him he would probably lose more than a day. Detective George Sullivan, Taylor's best detective and friend for the last seven years, was near the deceased, going through the routine of processing the body, taking photos, checking for identification, and all the other things cops did before a forensic team arrived. It could take a long time for them to show up in a small city inside a small county that neighbored a much larger county and city. Sullivan noticed Taylor's approach and stood up, giving Roger his first good look at the body. "Morning, Roger. Our victim's name is—"

"Manuel de Santos," Roger interrupted, "thirty-eight years old, originally out of Veracruz, Mexico. Truck driver by trade for the last nine years. Wife and three kids."

"Yeah, how the hell did you know that? He drove for—"

"I know who he drove for." Taylor turned to walk back to his car. Sullivan fell in behind him, not really following what just happened. The two detectives crossed the crime tape and stood by Taylor's Dodge Charger.

"You want to tell me what this is about, Roger?" Sullivan asked as he reached into his jacket pocket and drew out his cigarette pack. He politely offered Taylor one, knowing he didn't smoke, but he always offered. It was chilly this morning in early May. Sullivan wrapped his jacket around him, putting the cigarettes back in his inside pocket.

"Manuel was a confidential informant. I recruited him about two months ago. He was brought in on DUI and possession charges. When I heard who he worked for, I made him a deal. The charges go away if he spied on his boss for me. You know the drill." Sullivan nodded. He knew Taylor had tried a number of angles to get info on this company, and he had always come up empty. "He called me a couple of days ago and told me he had something for me. Wouldn't tell me over the phone. Said he would meet me when he got back from his run to Phoenix this week."

"So I guess you think that's why he's lying there with holes in his body, huh?"

"What do you think?"

"Tell you what I know. There are three gunshots. One in the forehead and two in the chest. Whoever did this looked him in the eyes while he did it. Cold. Colder than it is out here today."

"Damn it," Taylor said as he reached in his pocket to retrieve his phone. "Finish up here. I'll go break the news to the widow. Do a good job on this one, George, no mistakes." He got in his car and drove away toward the de Santoses' home across town. Somehow they did it to him again.

CHAPTER 2

Sidney Lewis was in her last semester at James Morgan University, where she majored in business. By all accounts, she was a very likable young woman, but a bit on the shy and naive side. Her father, Todd, was a native of California and owned a printing business in Warrenton, California. Her mother, Sophia, was an immigrant to the United States from Greece and was married to Todd for nearly thirty years. By anyone's account, they were a devout family, and Sidney remained active in her college's Christian ministry. On her last spring break before she graduated from college, Sidney and several of her friends traveled to enjoy the surf, sand, and a little nightlife in Santa Monica. On their last day there while her friends were getting ready to go out for the evening, Sidney decided to try for one more good wave before calling it a day. She loved the beach, and surfing was her passion; her tanned skin reflected that. The feeling of the wind in her long brown hair as she surfed was something she loved. She also loved scuba diving and spent the better part of a day diving near a coral reef.

"Hello, there," came a voice behind her. She was startled when she turned to see a young man with sandy-blond hair and a scruffy beard approach her. "I'm sorry, I didn't mean to startle you. It's just that you looked familiar from back there, and I wanted to be friendly."

Sidney remembered seeing the man on the beach earlier and thinking he was very attractive, and she couldn't help blushing. "Sorry, I don't think we've ever met." *Really? That's what you're going to start with?* she thought. She tried not to look as embarrassed as she felt. Sidney had never seriously dated anyone. A boyfriend was out of the question. Her friends always told her to loosen up and quit spending so much time with her nose in books.

He didn't seem to notice her nervousness though, and if he did, he wasn't letting on. "Well, that's a shame really. I'm Lawson, Lawson Pierson, and who might you be?"

His smile was so disarming to her. There were few people that she knew who could put her at ease, but this Lawson whatever he said his name was did so like a pro. A small voice inside her head told her this was too good to be true, but she dismissed it. "I'm Sidney Lewis. Good to meet you, Lawson," she said with a smile. *Oh gosh, Sidney, you're doing it again. Stop blushing,* she thought. "Um, where are you from?" *Where are you from?* she thought. *Really, Sidney, ask something interesting for once,* she thought again.

"Probably from no place you've ever heard of really. I'm originally from outside a small town called Warrenton, not that far from here actually."

"Warrenton?" she exclaimed. "I grew up there. I graduated just a few years ago. I mean, I'm about to graduate now. College. James Morgan University. About thirty miles from here. Did you go to school there? I don't remember you."

"Oh no, I graduated from private school, but we must have seen each other about a few times."

"Yeah, maybe."

"Look, my things are over there on the beach. What say we grab our stuff and catch up somewhere over dinner?"

"Oh wow, yeah, that would be great. Wait, no, I can't. I'm supposed to go out with my friends tonight. It's our last big time together before graduation, and we promised. I really want to really." *Calm down, girl, you sound desperate,* she thought.

"Tell you what, then. Why don't you give me your number, and I'll call you next week for that dinner. I know a really nice place near the beach."

"Yeah, um, yes, that sounds…yeah, that sounds great."

"You competitive at all, Sidney?"

"A little."

"All right, then try to keep up with me." He caught the incoming wave so naturally.

Sidney snapped out of her daze and caught the next one. She had to admit he was pretty good, but she was better. *Do I beat him or let him win?* she thought. She decided to try and beat him to shore, but he stuck with her the whole way.

"Hey, you're good," he said, flashing an irresistible smile.

"Thanks, you're not so bad yourself." Looking up, she could see one of her college friends waving and calling to her. She waved back and told him she had to go. They exchanged numbers and agreed to dinner next week. With that, she started back to her room. That night, her friends picked on her the whole night about finally meeting her Prince Charming.

Lawson was true to his word. He called her on Tuesday, and she agreed to go out with him that Friday night. She lived in an apartment with two of her friends off campus. She gave him the address and counted the hours until the appointed time. Her roommates teased her about never seeing her be so excited over a guy before. When the night arrived, Lawson was a few minutes early. Her roommate Donna let him in, and Sidney started to nearly panic. She checked herself in the mirror for the hundredth time and finally walked into the sitting area to find him holding several newly picked flowers. "I found these for you. They do not do you justice. You look amazing."

Oh gosh, here comes the blushing again, she thought. As they walked together, they chatted about the week they had and other small talk. Then she saw his car. "That's your car?" she said aloud without meaning to. She didn't know the make and model, but she knew by its looks it was very expensive.

"A small thing really," he said, trying to put her at ease. "I got it from a dealer in LA a couple of years ago. It gets me around town."

"Gosh, Lawson, I don't know if I should sit in it or not. I'm afraid I might break something." *Okay, why hasn't he left me by now with all those stupid comments?* she thought.

Lawson laughed. "Please, it's just a car. Let me get the door for you."

She had to admit he had an easy way about him. She half-expected him to take off like a fighter plane, but to her surprise, he drove like everyone else. They talked the entire way to the restaurant, which overlooked the ocean, and had valet parking. This was way more than she was used to, and it made her a little uncomfortable. He almost could sense her unease, and he reassured her that she had no reason to be shy. After they ordered their meals, Sidney's curiosity got the better of her. "So what is it you do for a living?" she asked him, hoping it wasn't too soon for that question. She could tell by his car that whatever it was, it brought him a very comfortable lifestyle. He didn't seem to mind the question, and she was relieved.

"Well, as strange as it sounds, I work for my father's trucking company. My job requires me to travel around meeting with our clients, mostly on the West Coast. From time to time, I'll visit places like Atlanta, Richmond, New York, and others in between."

"Wait, a trucking company?" she asked him. "Pierson Trucking Company? Oh gosh, yes, how did I not get that before?"

"I'm not really a celebrity, so it's okay. Actually, I'm glad. Some women see the car or the clothes, and all they can see are the dollars." He took a drink from his glass. "But that's not you, is it?" Lawson could see her shift uncomfortably in her seat. "That's a good thing. I can tell you are not like so many others. You're special. And I just went all weird on you."

"No, not at all," she said as she smiled back at him. The rest of the evening went by smoothly. They talked as if they were old friends. The date ended just after midnight. She shyly asked if he would like to come in, but he politely refused, saying he should return home, but he promised to call her. He took her hand and kissed it with a good night. She shut the door behind her, nearly out of breath. Donna was staring at her with a sly smile on her face. "Oh, shut up," Sidney said and went to her bedroom.

CHAPTER 3

Months passed, and the couple became inseparable. They spent weekends at the beach together, surfing and scuba diving. She moved back to Warrenton after graduation and took a job with a local business there in town. Lawson traveled a couple of times a month, but they always found time for each other. It wasn't long after before they were talking about marriage. On her birthday, Lawson took her to meet his parents, Leonard and Lauren Pierson. They looked the part of an older, charming couple living inside a house that made a city block in Warrenton look small. When she commented how beautiful the house was, the Piersons brushed it off. "It's been our family home since 1938," Leonard told her. "We take care of it, and I think it takes care of us. Please do sit and tell us everything about yourself."

Talking with his father, Sidney could see where Lawson got his charms. Leonard had a way of making you feel as if you were the most important person in the room. They laughed and smiled and found a way to make her feel at home. His gray-and-black hair perfectly matched that of his beard. He gave off a vibe of supreme confidence yet remained somehow approachable.

"Sidney dear, if you don't mind, I need to pry Lawson away from you for a while," said Lauren. "Lawson, there's some things in the back I need your help with that your father just refuses to do for me."

After they had gone, Leonard smiled and said, "Never mind her, she's far more capable than me in so many things. Please forgive me, but I heard Lawson say it was your birthday today. Is that correct?"

"Yes, it is. It's not exactly a major birthday year though."

"My dear, every year should be celebrated. I have something for you here. A small token to show my appreciation for making my son so happy." He handed her a long, wrapped box.

"Thank you, but you didn't have to do this." She began to open it and realized it was a hinged jewelry box. Inside was a necklace with a large diamond attached to it. "Is this real?" she asked without realizing she said it out loud.

"Of course. A friend of a friend owns a jewelry business where I buy all of my diamonds. I hope you like it."

"Mr. Pierson, I can't accept this."

"Nonsense, my dear," he said as he rose to his feet. "Now would you permit an old man the privilege?" He took the necklace from her hand. Sidney moved her long brown hair from her neck as he placed it around her. "There, but I must say that your beauty far outshines the diamond, if you would pardon an old man to say."

The evening was lovely, and she was all aglow by the time Lawson took her home. She invited him in, and they sat on her couch. He took her into his arms and kissed her. A feeling she could not explain washed over her, and she felt her resolve begin to melt away. They had agreed to take their relationship slowly. She had never been with a man and told him she wanted to wait for the right one. Now her guard was down, and she could feel her heart begin to race as if it would burst out of her chest. "Well, it's late," he said. He kissed her again and started to get up to leave.

"Stay," Sidney said in a voice she almost didn't recognize. "Please stay. I want to, but I'm not sure how…"

He did not say a word but took her into his arms. She felt her inhibitions melt away in the softness of his touch. Lawson put her at ease, gently taking away her nervousness, replacing it with a soft passion she had never felt. They became lost in each other as the moments seemed to pass slowly and much too fast at the same time as if every heartbeat inside her brought a new life of its own. The moment was like a river that swept her away, and as long as it carried her back to Lawson, Sidney longed to follow.

CHAPTER 4

The next afternoon, Leonard called a meeting with Lawson back at the family estate. He arrived on time because nobody wanted to be late for a meeting with his father. When he walked into the office, his father was already there on the phone with a client. He saw Lawson arrive and motioned for him to sit down. A few minutes later, Leonard hung up the phone and directed his attention to Lawson. "I trust the young lady had a good time last night," he began.

Obviously, there was more to this meeting than idle small talk about his date last night, but Lawson decided to play along. "Yes, Father, they did. Thank you for allowing us to come over. Sidney wanted me to thank you for her gift, but she feels like she should return it to you. I explained to her it would insult you if she did."

"Honestly, do you really think me so shallow to be insulted by something like that, Lawson?" he responded in his deep, monotone voice.

The door opened to the office again, and Jonathan Pierson, Lawson's younger brother, walked into the office. He was shorter than Lawson by several inches and did not have the same athletic build. He was recently married and managed two of the side businesses of the Pierson family. "Well, Dudley Do-Right finally showed up. Helping little old ladies across the street again?" teased Lawson to his brother.

"Were you born an ass, or do you have to practice, Lawson?"

"You know, little brother, I—"

"That will be enough," came the harsh voice of Leonard Pierson. "I will not sit here and listen to this again. I called this meeting because there are important decisions I have made in regards to our family businesses."

Both men turned their attention to their father. Their rivalry went back to their childhood with each competing with the other for their father's attention. Jonathan always felt he had to compete harder than Lawson for their father's approval. He carried pent-up frustration with him about how Lawson always seemed to find more favor with their father. Jonathan was a better student in school by far, but Lawson was an athlete, while Jonathan joined the marching band. His father never said it, but that choice disappointed him. Even though he married first, Lawson still remained their father's chosen son.

"It is time that we begin expanding your roles in the family businesses. I will continue, of course, to run our shipping operations, but Lawson will begin the process of taking it over from me and handle the day-to-day operations. You will, of course, continue to network with our current clients and take steps to acquire new clients as well."

The smile on Lawson's face sickened Jonathan. Every last ounce of restraint was required to keep from wiping that smile off his face. Leonard seemed to sense the tension in the room. Glaring at his youngest son, the man kept whatever protest he was about to make inside him. After a few more seconds, Leonard was ready to continue.

"Jonathan, since you seem somewhat reluctant to handle our main business, I have decided to sign our two minor franchises to you completely."

Lawson nearly came completely out of his chair. "What?" he said as he raised his voice. "How does he rate getting his own business—" The icy stare from Leonard seemingly froze the words in Lawson's mouth. His oldest son sat back down. "My apologies, Father." Lawson glanced at his brother with a look that Cain could recognize when he looked upon Abel. Jonathan gave a half smile as Lawson calmed himself.

"You two need to learn to work together as a team. Lawson is the perfect face of our operations, while you, Jonathan, are the brains behind the machinery. If you work together, I have no doubts about the future of this family."

"Father, I still think that we don't have to—" Jonathan began before being cut off by his father.

CHAD SPRADLEY

"I will not have this argument again either. Now leave us. There is a matter I must discuss with your brother in private. There are papers for you here in this envelope. Read over them and sign them so we can get the transfer of the businesses to you processed."

"Of course, Father," he said as he got up and left the office, taking the papers with him. Lawson watched him leave, still fuming inside. When the door closed, he looked at his father, but the stare that was returned was one that gave him instant pause. He wanted to say more, but he knew better than to take the initiative from his father, so he waited until Leonard was ready to speak.

"What are your intentions with this girl, Lawson?" he began.

"Only the purest of intentions, Father. I think—"

"Enough, Lawson. She is a fine match for you. I think you should consider marrying her. You will need a woman like that in your new role."

"What is that supposed to mean?"

"It means that it is time for you to grow up. I tire of hearing about your past indiscretions with women, the boorish entourage that follows you around carousing and drinking all of your money away, and these childish antics that I will not even begin to list. You are a Pierson, and that name carries great weight with it. Do you understand?"

"Of course, Father."

"I doubt that you do, so let me make this abundantly clear. You are on a very short leash here, my boy. This party life of yours ends now."

Lawson squirmed in his chair. "Father, I…" The look on his father's face made him change the lie he was about to tell. "I'm not like that anymore, Father. You're right, I've had my fun. Now it's time to get serious. Sidney is good for me. She's settled me down."

"Good. I hope you understand as well the gravity of the situation. I am grooming you to take my place, son. We move tons of cargo every year for clients who have very particular tastes. Those clients will not hesitate to find another method of moving that cargo if they believe you are not up to their ideals of…discretion."

"You can trust me, Father."

14

"Trust? I will be watching to make sure of this change you've spoken of so confidently," Leonard said, clearly dismissing Lawson from the meeting. The younger Pierson got up to leave when Leonard stopped him. "By the way, I will need you to fly to Dallas tomorrow. One of our clients is having an issue getting his deliveries on time. I need you to smooth out that problem."

"Anything in particular I need to do?"

"Promise him anything you have to. This is an important client and will be a good test of your readiness to handle the affairs of our business."

Lawson left the room to find Jonathan outside waiting for him. "So you're thinking this girl is the right one, huh?"

The question made Lawson want to punch his brother in the throat. He restrained himself from acting on his impulse and replied, "Jealous much, little brother?"

He wanted to leave it at that, but Jonathan stood in his way out. "I know you and who you are, Lawson. You're a user. You use people and discard them, and personally, it makes me sick. If you're not careful, it's going to catch up with you someday."

Lawson chuckled. "What would you know? All your life you've been jealous of me. Like Father just said, it's time to grow up. Now if you'll excuse me, I have a flight to get ready for in the morning." Lawson got in his car and drove away. He picked up his phone and dialed a familiar number. "Jordan, how are you, man? You got plans for the next couple of days? Good. Fly with me to Dallas tomorrow for a couple of days. Ha, you know it. Yeah, got to keep it more low-key this time, but yeah, same deal. Yeah, make sure the equipment gets set up like usual. Should be fun." He ended the call and drove to his townhome. Sidney was supposed to come over tonight, so he had to make sure everything was set up and ready. Tonight was going to be a special evening with just the two of them. Marriage was not something that was really on his mind right now, but maybe in a few more months, that would change. Not even Leonard Pierson was going to force him into marriage before he was ready. Tonight was not about marriage, but it might bring that one step closer.

CHAPTER 5

Sidney arrived at seven o'clock that evening. She looked stunning in the little sundress she was wearing. He kissed her as she walked through the door, and it seemed to make her blush. "So easily embarrassed even after months of being together," he teased her. She smiled back at him and said she couldn't help it that she blushed naturally. He invited her into the dining area of the spacious townhouse, which Sidney knew cost more to rent a month than she made in three months. He asked her about her day and pulled her chair out for her to sit down at the table. Once she was seated, he served a meal he prepared. "Okay, so I didn't really cook this. I actually planned on cooking a lasagna, but in typical Lawson fashion, I burned the hell out of it, so this is from the Italian café."

Sidney laughed at him. "Well, it's the thought that counts, right? I'm sure it's fine." She had to admit that the food was very good.

During the dinner, they chatted away about this and that. It was so easy to open up to him. She felt so at ease telling him so many things about herself. Likewise, he shared several interesting stories about his time growing up and about his travels. "Speaking of travels, Father is sending me to Dallas tomorrow."

"Really? For what?"

"Nothing really, just a scheduling and supply problem. I should be back by Thursday or Friday."

"Will I get to see you this weekend?" she asked him.

"Yeah, more than likely. Just a small problem, nothing to worry about."

After dinner, they went for a walk in the park near the townhouse. The park had a small scenic outlook where you could see the lights of the town at night. They found a spot on a bench and soon found themselves in each other's arms. She could feel her heart racing again, and she felt compelled to ask him a question. "Lawson, is this going anywhere?"

He seemed shocked by the question. "What do you mean?"

"I mean, after the other night, I just... I'd never, you know, done that before. I just want to know before I give my heart to someone that there's the chance that...that they feel—"

"I love you, Sidney."

His words froze her in place. No one besides her parents and best friend ever told her that. She stared at him wide-eyed, almost gasping for breath. Her knees grew weak to the point she didn't think she could stand.

"Well, please tell me I didn't just make a fool of myself with the too early 'I love you.' I mean, if—"

She pulled him to her lips and kissed him passionately. Slowly she moved her lips to his ear and whispered, "I love you too." Her whole body was trembling. If this was a movie, she hoped it never ended. No, it wasn't love at first sight, but after several months, now she felt it. Maybe she had known all along, but she knew now that he also felt the same. They returned to his townhome and could hardly keep their hands off each other. In the back of her mind, warning bells were going off telling her this wasn't how she was raised and not what she was taught in church. Yet everything he did felt so right. They made it to his bedroom in the heat of passion. As she moved onto the bed, she noticed Lawson pick up a small remote control. He pushed a button, and the lights in the room dimmed. She thought nothing more of it as he took her into his arms, never seeing the small eyes secretly planted all around them.

CHAPTER 6

Taylor pored through his case files, trying to find anything to connect the murder of de Santos to any of the case files he'd investigated over the last several years. The frustrating part of the job was getting a lead and to have it dry up nearly as fast as it came in. Two weeks ago, he tried to follow up with another driver. By the sound of it, he seemed ready to give up some information on illegal activity. Predictably, when they met up, the driver claimed he didn't know anything.

"Roger, want to go to lunch?" asked Sullivan as he approached Taylor's desk. He looked up from his files long enough to shake his head. "Come on, Roger, it's after one. You've been obsessing about those cases for days now. Let's go."

Roger exhaled loudly and stood up, realizing just how stiff his muscles were after sitting for so long. They took a table at a local restaurant near the back of the place. Roger sat at the table still apparently in a foul mood. Sullivan sat across from him, tapping the table louder and louder until it finally got Taylor's attention. "You got a drum solo you're prepping for, Sullivan?"

"Look at that, he can speak," Sullivan mocked him. "So now that we know you can talk, why don't we discuss what's bothering you?"

"It's this series of cases I'm working. I know that they're somehow connected, but I can't find the missing link."

"Roger, you've been doing this long enough to know that sometimes you can't solve a case no matter how hard you try. Hell, we got a whole vault of them at the station. It doesn't mean you're a bad cop."

"I know that, but it's there. I know it. I just need to find the missing link."

"Roger, how long have you worked this angle?" Sullivan asked. He hoped he could bring Taylor out of his malaise.

"Too long. Look, I get what you're trying to do, but this is like—"

"An obsession," Sullivan interjected. "Look, we're cops. We're not gods. We do as much good as we can, but sometimes the bad guys win, but we move on and get the next one. There's always going to be a next one, but you can't stop them if you obsess over the ones you didn't get."

Roger took a long drink from his iced tea in an effort to come up with something to counter Sullivan's argument. "Maybe you're right," he conceded. Sullivan was right about one thing; he was obsessing. He knew it was starting to affect his other case load. "I guess some of these can go on the back burner for now." That seemed to satisfy Sullivan, and surprisingly, it seemed to lighten his mood.

When they returned to the station, Taylor set aside the older cases and turned to his most recent case load. A car theft from a local supermarket was on the top of the open case file. Next was a domestic dispute for an address he recognized from at least two other reports and finally a theft of property from a home on Delta Drive allegedly involving a neighbor's kid. He took a deep breath and picked up the phone and dialed the first number in the car theft case.

Lawson and Sidney drove out to Santa Monica after lunch on a Saturday afternoon. They made their way to a hotel, and to Sidney's surprise, it was the same one she was staying at when she met Lawson. "How romantic, I didn't realize you knew where I was staying."

"I made a call or two to one of your college friends and got the name of the place. Let's get checked in and then hit the beach. What do you say?"

She kissed him. "Sounds like a plan."

As they were checking in, Lawson's phone rang. Looking at the contact's name, he excused himself to take the call. "Jordan, did you get the equipment set up? Good, good. I owe you one." He walked back over to the front desk and gave the person behind the counter his card. A minute or two later, they had their keys and headed to the room. When they got on the elevator, Sidney asked him who called. "Oh, just office business really. Nothing too important. I told them to handle it because nothing was going to spoil my weekend with my girl."

They changed and made their way to the beach. It was late afternoon, so they sat and relaxed on the beach for about an hour. As the sun began to set, Lawson turned to her and took her by the hand. "You know, right over there is where we first met," he told her. He could tell that impressed her.

"I can't believe you remember that. I thought you were some weirdo guy when I first heard your voice."

"You thought I was weird?"

"Well, not after I saw you, no, but you have to admit it was pretty strange how we met."

"I admit it was unusual, but admit it, Sid, it's worked out pretty good, right?"

She smiled coyly at him. "Yes, it has."

"You know, I was going to wait and do this tonight at dinner, but this seems to be the right place and the right time."

"Time? Time for—" She stopped midsentence as he rose to his feet and dropped to one knee, holding a diamond ring. Before she knew it, she was blushing and short of breath. In her mind, she pictured herself gasping like a fish out of water.

"Sidney Marie Lewis, you've made me the happiest man alive, and I want to make you even happier not just today but for the rest of my life. Will you marry me?"

"Oh gosh, oh gosh, oh gosh. Yes. Yes, a hundred times, yes." She held her finger out, and he placed it on her finger perfectly. Out of the corner of her eye, she caught sight of an old couple watching what transpired with happy expressions on their face. The rest of the night, Sidney was giddy. After dinner, they went dancing and walked along the moonlit shoreline near the hotel. The ground beneath her feet felt more like a cloud, and she never wanted the feeling to end. That night, they ignited the flames of passion like they never had before all the while watched by tiny eyes.

CHAPTER 7

Finding a date for the wedding proved to be more difficult than Sidney thought it would be after the proposal. Lawson's travel schedule grew heavy with his expanding role at his father's company. He told her that he was being groomed to take over for his father and that he had to take a far more active role. This new role was a complication and a blessing. On one hand, she was happy for her husband-to-be, but she was seeing less of him. When they did get together, he was not interested in talking about setting a date. It struck her that he seemed as if he was avoiding the subject altogether. On one particular night, he grew angry with her for bringing the subject up. The reaction surprised her, and she sat there quietly for several minutes, not wanting to make eye contact with him. Lawson apologized and explained that he was stressed out from work. He did not mean to take it out on her, and of course, they should talk about a date later.

Time passed on, and they still did not set a date. A number of coincidental events began to arise any time he agreed to set a date. It was starting to appear to Sidney as if he was again avoiding her so that he would not have to pick a date. In a way, she understood his reluctance with his new responsibilities, but at what point did his behavior cross over to avoidance? Another thing she noticed was that he was taking less interest in her physically. While she didn't really mind the abstaining from night surfing, as he called it, he didn't sit with his arm around her as much when they were together. He had stopped holding her hand when they were out in public. While none of that by itself necessarily meant anything, taking all of it together was concerning to her. She even tried to bring it up to him once, but it drew the same excuse of him being stressed or exhausted from work.

The fighting started to occur more often as well. There were every couple of fights now and again, but his reluctance to do much in the way of wedding planning worried her. Sidney started to suspect that something was wrong, and their arguments seemed to prove it. She wanted desperately to reach out to him, to help him through whatever it was that was bothering him, but the thought that she might be the problem worried her more than anything. She decided to try to work it out once and for all the next time they were together. That opportunity came on a Sunday night before Lawson's trip to Seattle. She cooked his favorite meal, three-cheese lasagna and all the fixings. Lawson seemed to be in a better mood when he arrived. The couple sat down and enjoyed their meal together and settled in for what Lawson thought was going to be a quiet night.

Sidney prepared herself for the moment at hand. What she planned was far short of an ultimatum, but she wanted a meaningful conversation, something that they had not done much of in the last month or two. "Lawson, we need to talk about the wedding."

"Oh god, Sid, not this again. I told you when my workload lets up, we'll talk about it."

"Lawson, there are things that have to be done in order to get ready. There are reservations that have to be made, there's premarital counseling—"

"Counseling? You know I don't like that kind of stuff. Why do we need that?"

"Because Brother Paul won't marry us until he has two counseling sessions with us."

"Well, why does it have to be him? My father knows several ministers. We could just use one of them."

"Because Brother Paul is the one who baptized me when I was twelve. He taught me so many life lessons as my youth minister that I want to have him marry us. It's only for an hour each session. And he won't try to talk us out of marriage or tell us how hard it is or anything like that. He just wants to be sure we understand the commitment we're making to God and man."

"Okay, fine, call him up and make the appointment if you want to. Just text me the date and I'll be there."

"We also need to set a date so that we can reserve the venue. My church has a calendar that—"

"Stop," Lawson interrupted her. "My family estate is where we need to get married. My father and brother were both married there. Churches are fine, but it's our tradition."

"Fine, that's fair. You need some input too," she said, clearly disappointed. They were making progress. Sidney began to think that she was starting to worry over nothing. If she could get him to commit to a date, then the rest would take care of itself. "But we have to pick a date. Lawson, people are starting to wonder when our marriage is going to take place. We both have family coming in from out of town and all those other arrangements that have to be made."

"Sid, fine. Let me get back from Seattle. I will be back late Thursday night. Why don't we plan on meeting on the yacht Friday night, just me and you. We'll sit down and set a date. Sound good?"

Suddenly he was back to being his old, charming self. Maybe he was right, and the stress was getting to him. She herself was having a rough go at work as well with a client who was not submitting the proper paperwork to close out his mortgage. So she understood he was stressed, and maybe she was to blame for being too pushy. "That sounds wonderful. I'm sorry if I'm pressuring you. I just want this to be perfect. I want it to be something we will remember our whole life. And I'm sorry that you're having a hard time at work."

The tension in the room died down. "I guess I haven't been very attentive to you either. Don't worry, I'm going to make it up to you this weekend. Just us. And why don't we plan on going diving as well. Would you like that?"

"You know I would. I haven't been in months. I would love to go diving or anywhere else with you. I love you and just want to make you happy."

"Same here. Love you, Sid," he said with that sly smile of his. "Now I got an early-morning flight, so I got to go. I'll call you when I get settled in." He kissed her and left the apartment.

The conversation went much better than she thought it might. She was relieved that he was finally coming around to the idea of marriage. It's not like she wanted to run off and elope, but she wanted to make sure he understood her side of the issue and that things needed to move forward. Friday, then, would be a big night for them, and they could settle this once and for all. Once that happened, she could start planning their dream wedding. She walked back to the sitting area of her apartment to collect the drinking glasses and dessert dishes from the evening. As she took hold of the glasses, she spotted a small object lying on the floor. Sidney took the glasses and plates to the kitchen sink and returned to the sitting area. She picked up the object and saw that it was an ordinary flash drive. Strange, she thought that she had put all of them away, but apparently, this one had somehow gotten left out.

Thinking nothing more of it, she took it over to her laptop computer and set it down on its closed top. Sidney thought that she should be more careful with those. She was one of those people who kept every paper she had ever written in school, backed up all her personal files many times over, and kept business records to take home on the rare occasion she worked from her apartment. She chided herself again for not paying attention and thought it pretty lucky that it didn't get stepped on while Lawson was here. Calling it a night, she turned out the lights and went to bed to read a book for a while. After completing a couple of chapters, she turned off the lamp on the nightstand and drifted off to sleep. It was a peaceful sleep, and she felt as if a heavy weight was lifted off her. Tonight, she believed that all was right with the world.

CHAPTER 8

As promised, Lawson called Sidney on Monday from his hotel. He told her that things looked promising and that there was a slight chance that he could be home earlier than he thought. After he disconnected the call, he drove to the meeting. It was a terribly boring conversation with a group of men who clearly had nothing better to do with their lives than sit in board meetings and whatnot in their expensive suits. He sat there half-paying attention to their concerns while the small team that traveled with him handled the details. Finally, he could take no more of it. "Why don't we just cut the crap," he finally spoke up. "None of this is being recorded. It's just us in here, right? All these fancy euphemisms and code words are really not necessary. You want the trucks to keep rolling, and you want your supplies to arrive on time, right? Just when have we ever failed to deliver that for you? We can get as technical as you want, but at the end of the day, we know what's really going on."

"Mr. Pierson," a balding man, who clearly had no life outside of the executive suite, spoke, "the matter is not so clear-cut. There are growing expenses, money transfers, various sundry details that must be ironed out if we are to continue doing business. Our clients—"

"Want their things as fast as possible. They're worried about the bottom line, the profits, right?" He got up and walked to where the man was sitting and got uncomfortably close to him. "That's what we want too, Tom. It is Tom, right?" He smiled his winning smile, but there was something dark behind that smile that not only Tom could see but the entire room could see as well. They grew silent as if hushed by an unseen hand. "You can always try to ship your merchandise with somebody else, but that means changes. It means possible screwups, and honestly, who wants that with such high-value cargo?" He let the question hang for a moment. "Not to mention your customers, as you call them. Your real customers aren't people who put up with screwups for long now, are they?" He gave a small laugh that was both charming and sickening at the same time to those who heard it. "You should know that my father raised me to be firm but fair. He also raised me to know when someone is trying to bullshit their way to get more out of you than what is due." He got up and walked slowly around the room, smiling, making eye contact with each person sitting there. "Tell me, are your profits down? No? Are we always on time and deliver as promised? We are, aren't we? I see no problem, then. So shall we sign the contracts now, or should we wait until we have a stop in your supply chain?" Lawson stopped and looked back at the visibly shaken and sweat-covered balding man. "What do you say, Tom? We got a deal? Of course, we do, don't we?"

Tom nodded and wiped his brow.

"You see, easy enough. Oh, do calm down, Tom. Here, I'll buy you a nice lunch. You like a good steak? I know just the place."

That evening, he first called his father. "Father, the deal is done. There are a few details to work out, but we're good."

"Very good. Did you find them compliant?"

"Let's just say I gave them the old Pierson charm."

"Good, finish up there and return as soon as possible. I want you to settle this wedding date as soon as possible."

"What's the hurry? There's plenty of time for that."

"Because, son, your engagement is big news, and this needs to be a spectacular event befitting a Pierson. That requires planning."

"Did she talk to you about this? Because that's exactly what she said."

"Of course not. She doesn't need to. Set the date quickly."

"Yes, Father. We're supposed to take the yacht out on Saturday. I promise by the end of the weekend we will have a date."

"Good. See that you do." And Leonard hung up.

Lawson changed in his room and then made his way to Tavern on the Rocks, his favorite Seattle hangout. He dialed Sidney's number to check in on her before going into the tavern. They talked for a few minutes about their days and how much he missed her. Before ending the conversation, he said that he loved her and couldn't wait to see her Friday evening. Walking through the door, he put his phone in his pocket and made his way to the bar. He ordered a drink and began to survey the bar's occupants. At the far end sat a blonde woman with slightly curled hair. He made his way over to her, smiling as they locked eyes. "You must be Ashley," he said, taking the seat next to her. "I must say, your picture doesn't do you justice."

"You must be Lawson. Great to finally meet you face-to-face. Are you going to be in town long?"

"Long enough," he said. "You want another drink?"

"Sure," she said as she finished the cocktail and sat the glass on the bar.

He ordered another drink and turned his attention back to Ashley.

"So how long have you used the dating app?"

Lawson gave a sarcastic laugh. "Dating app? I don't know that's what I would call it, but a couple of years off and on. You?"

"About three months. Like you, not very often, but it's nice when you want some no-strings-attached attention, right?"

"My thoughts exactly," Lawson said as he finished his drink. They stayed at the bar about an hour before taking a cab to his hotel room.

CHAPTER 9

Sidney hung up the phone after Lawson's call. She was glad that he thought about her and called. It was a short conversation, but she had brought some work home with her, so that was fine. Lawson was flying home tomorrow evening, and they had plans for Friday, so she could wait. After making a sandwich, she fetched her laptop, forgetting about the flash drive she sat on top of it a few days ago. She picked it up and took it with her back to her sitting room. Making herself comfortable, she decided to get to work. Curiosity got the better of her though, and she decided to see what was on the flash drive. She put it in the USB port and clicked to open it. What she saw puzzled her. She could see it contained a number of files that looked like business files. What really got her attention was what looked like a number of video files. She didn't remember loading any videos recently. To solve the mystery, she clicked on the first one. Instantly she recognized the room as Lawson's bedroom. She then watched in horror as the two of them came onto the screen. The memory of that night came rushing back to her. Sidney felt a knot forming in the pit of her stomach as she watched her and Lawson's lovemaking. Worse still, the camera angle changed several times, meaning that there were multiple hidden cameras in his room.

Sidney gasped and turned off the video. She counted fourteen other videos on the drive. The next one was taken from the hotel room they stayed in the night of their engagement. She told herself to stop, but something inside her told her to click one more file. When she did, it was again Lawson's bedroom, but the woman in the video was not her. Closing the video, she slammed the laptop closed so hard she thought she might have broken it. Tears began to stream down her face uncontrollably. She felt physically and emotionally sick, but worse still, she felt betrayed. In their time together, she gave Lawson the best of her. He was the only man she'd ever been with, and she gave him her whole heart. Now her heart was lying in pieces. Leaving everything sitting where it was, she went to her bed. The realization that her bed was the place she first gave herself to him made it impossible for her to stay there. She got a quilt and blanket out of her closet and went back to her couch.

When she got there, the laptop still sat on the cushions, where she left it. Moving the computer, she grabbed the flash drive. Her first thought was to destroy it. However, a voice inside her said she should keep it. The sight of it made her sick all over again, so she took it to her bedroom and placed it in the top drawer of her chest of drawers. She then returned to the couch and pulled the blanket and quilt over her head and cried. The next day, the Thursday before Lawson returned, she called in sick to work. She'd never taken a day off before since she started her job. Today, all she wanted to do was lie on her couch and shut out the world. What was she going to do? Lawson would be home tomorrow, and he was expecting her to meet him on his family's yacht just outside of Warrenton. She had to think of something. Was this the end of their marriage before it even started? How could this have happened?

Sidney must have lost track of time because she was startled to hear a knock on her door. "Sidney," came the voice of her mother, "Sidney, open up. It's Mom." She slowly got up from the couch and opened the door for her mother. "Sidney, honey, your office called me and said you were sick. Is everything okay? Are you not feeling well? Have you eaten enough? How's your stomach? Do you need to go to the bathroom?"

"Mom, I'm fine, just please stop asking me health questions."

"Well, what's wrong? Are you constipated? Because if you are, I can go get you some medicine that will fix that in less than an hour."

"No, Mom, please no. I just don't feel well, and I would like to be alone right now."

"It's your fiancé, isn't it? I knew it. Did you two get in a fight? I told your father I thought he was too good to be true. You know, nobody is that clean. When I was in school, there was this guy who tried to seduce me, but I told him that—"

"Mom," Sidney said, almost screaming. "Mom, please, I appreciate you coming, but I want to be alone."

"No, sweetheart, please. You look terrible. Tell me what I can do for you. Tell me how to help."

"I don't think you can, Mom," she said as tears began to fall again. "Can I just lie on the couch with my head in your lap while you play with my hair like you did when I was little?"

Sophia agreed, and she sat down. Sidney laid her head on her mother's lap as Sophia ran her fingers through her daughter's hair. The tears didn't stop, but her sobbing did. Sophia whispered kind words to her daughter. It occurred to her that she'd not seen Sidney like this since she had her heart broken in high school. This was different. She could tell her daughter's heart was broken, and as much as she wanted to fix it, she knew this was something that would have to run its course. Whatever it was, she would tell her when she was ready.

Late that afternoon, Sophia talked her into eating something. She cooked a small spaghetti and brought it to the couch. Sidney picked at it before eating about half of the meal. She thanked her mother for coming by and cooking for her. Sophia didn't pry any further, as bad as she wanted to. They passed another hour watching television. As she got up to leave, she asked her daughter, "Is there anything you need?"

Sidney told her there wasn't and that she was feeling better.

Sophia thought that wasn't the whole truth, but she didn't press her anymore. Her mother pulled her close and embraced her. "I love you, baby. Whatever you're going through, I'm here for you when you're ready. When I get home, your dad and I are going to pray for you."

"Thanks, Mom. I love you too. Be careful going home."

She shut the door behind her mother and went back to the couch. Looking at the clock, she realized that in less than twenty-four hours, she was supposed to meet Lawson. Sidney considered canceling on him. She also thought about calling him up right now and breaking things off with him. Another part of her wanted to throw the ring in his face. Every emotion available flowed through her. She was angry at him for doing this to her. She was heartbroken for giving her love to him and having him use it that way. Mostly, she was depressed and disappointed. They dated for over two years, and she felt as if he had played her for a fool. Yet at the same time, she still loved him. Even after all she had seen on that flash drive, she still loved him. How could she still love someone like that after all she just found out? It didn't make any sense. Did she really want to try and save their relationship? Unbelievably, she did. They had been through so much, and she had given so much to him that she couldn't let him go without trying.

Her phone rang as she was lost in thought. It was Lawson calling to check in. She picked up the phone and started to answer it but could not bring herself to talk to him just yet. The call went to voice mail. Thirty minutes later, she listened to it. He said he was calling to check in on her before he went to bed because he had an early-morning meeting before flying home. He wished her good night before signing off. The next morning, she called in sick again. She spent the entire morning going over what she would say and then changing it over and over again. Everything that passed through her mind seemed to fall short of what she wanted to say to him. After lunch, she started to pack her bag for the yacht. She picked up her phone many times to tell him she wasn't coming and never wanted to see him again. Each time, she decided not to give up on him. He deserved a chance, if nothing else, to set things right. Tonight would be one of the most important times in her life.

CHAPTER 10

The night was already off to a bad start by the time she arrived. Walking on the pier, she saw the large yacht berthed in a spot barely large enough to contain it. The yacht was a multideck vessel able to accommodate several people, which was exactly what she saw when she got there. Lawson spotted her from the rear deck and yelled down to her, "Hey, Sid! Look who showed up. Come on aboard and grab a drink."

She waved at him and smiled, trying to hide how angry she was that all those other people were there. *So much for just the two of us*, she thought as she started up the gangplank. A crewman that she didn't recognize took her bag and escorted her to the cabin she and Lawson shared. After the man left, she looked herself over in the mirror and calmed down. Making a scene was not what she wanted, so she decided to try and play the part of the gracious hostess.

As she made her way to the party, she greeted everyone she passed. Most of the people were Lawson's friends and their dates, wives, or whoever they were. Lawson called her over and greeted her, "Sid, how are you? Work go all right today?" He asked her in a voice that sounded like he had been drinking for a while.

"I didn't go today or yesterday. I've been sick."

"Oh, is that why you didn't answer your phone yesterday? Poor thing. Feeling better today?"

"Yeah, I'm fine. Can I talk to you in private for a second?"

"Anything for you. Guys, excuse us for a moment." The two stepped to the rear corner of the boat. "What's on your mind?"

"Lawson, why are all these people here? It was supposed to just be us?"

"I know, but I ran into Carl and Steve in the coffee shop this morning, and I asked them to join us, and well, one thing led to another."

"Lawson, we need to talk later."

"Hey, I know. Don't worry. Soon as everyone goes to bed, we'll talk."

"Goes to bed? Did you invite them to come with us tomorrow?"

"Well, yeah. Be kind of rude not to, don't you think?"

"Sure. Sure, whatever you think, Lawson."

"Great, this is going to be fun."

The night was anything but fun for Sidney. As hard as she tried, she didn't feel like being social. She disappeared several times into her cabin, trying to stay focused on the night ahead of her. Second thoughts about what she planned to do crept into her mind. Would he even be sober enough to bother talking about this tonight? She couldn't just pretend that nothing was wrong the whole weekend either. It would be much better to get things in the open before the boat launched tomorrow morning.

Festivities began to die down, and she decided to find Lawson. When she found him, he was saying good night to an old college friend, Steve, she thought, and holding a half-empty bottle of scotch. The way he was stumbling around suggested that he was too drunk to have a serious conversation tonight, so she decided to put him to bed and leave in the morning with the excuse she was still too sick to dive.

"Lawson, come to bed. It's late."

"Oh, there you are. Where've you been all night?"

"I'm not feeling well. I think I may go to the doctor tomorrow."

"What? No, something's bothering you. Come on, Sid, tell me."

"Later. Right now, let's go to bed."

"No, you've been a first-class bitch all night, and I want to know why."

"You're drunk."

"And you're being a bitch. What is going on?"

"I found your flash drive Wednesday night," she said to him in as calm of a voice as she could manage.

Lawson was having difficulty standing. "What flash drive?"

"The one you've been loading videos of us having sex along with other women and you having sex. How could you do that to me?" she finally burst out. This was not how she wanted to have this conversation, but it was out in the open now. She felt her heart beating in her throat, and she felt her eyes starting to water.

"Come on, Sid, I just wanted something to remember our times together, that's all."

"What about those other women? You lied to me," she said. "You told me these were all just business meetings, but you've been having sex with who knows how many others. And you even did it in the bed we shared."

"Look, what's the big deal? It's just sex. You know I love you. Isn't that enough?" he responded. He poured the second glass of scotch since she came out to the deck. The scotch seemed to be having a greater effect on him.

She wanted to end the discussion and just leave, but despite the thought, she pressed onward. "No, it's not enough. You don't cheat on people you love. And you don't film them having sex with you without them knowing." She felt the anger, frustration, and heartbreak building up inside her. "Tell me you haven't shown these to anyone." Lawson turned his back to her and began to pace unsteadily. "Oh god, you did."

He ran his hand through his hair and turned back to her. "So what if I did? They're my friends, and they won't tell anyone. Why are you so mad?"

"Me? You're trying to blame me for this?" The tears now began to fall freely. "How could you blame me for this? I love you, but how can I ever trust you again?"

"I knew you wouldn't understand, and that's why I never told you. If you can't understand that, then we're pretty much through," he said and turned to go.

"Lawson, stop," she said as she reached out to grab his hand to keep him there. "How can you walk away from me after all I've done for you."

Lawson turned and pushed her with a force that completely surprised her. He pushed her hard toward the rail of the boat bordering the pier below. "What the hell is your problem? We're done, but at least I got a few memories of us to watch," he said with a sickening smile on his face.

Sidney caught herself on the railing. Regaining her balance, she slowly walked toward him. She pleaded with him, "Lawson, please. Please don't walk away. We were going to get married. At least get rid of the videos." She was visibly trembling as she continued to walk toward him. Things had gone horribly wrong. He had never gotten violent with her before. It must have been the alcohol. Maybe when he sobered up, he would see things differently.

Lawson turned to her again and quickly closed the gap between them. He dropped the bottle of scotch and grabbed her just below the shoulders, digging his fingers into her muscles. "I thought I made myself clear. We're done. I'm a Pierson. Just who the hell do you think you are?" He forced her back to the boat rail, forcing her so hard into the rail she thought he was going to push her over. "I should just push you over the side and let you bust your head on the pier. You best keep your mouth shut and hand over that flash drive, or that's exactly what will happen."

"Lawson, you're hurting me. I didn't bring it. I swear it's at my apartment. Please let me go."

He let go of her and turned his back, searching for the bottle of scotch. "Is that right? It's at your apartment? That's too bad, Sid. You know, you were really good. I probably could have married you. Maybe you could have even joined me on a business trip or two." He found the bottle and picked it up, discovering it was empty. He turned the bottle upside down, grabbing it by the long neck. He raised the bottle to his eyes. "Yeah, I'm going to miss you, Sid. Like I said, a lot of memories though." Lawson tightened his grip on the bottle as he looked over his shoulder at her. There was a look in his eye she had never seen before, and it frightened her. It seemed to her as if he were looking through her than at her, like a shark looked at a fish before it struck, blank and uncaring.

That last comment, the blank look in his eyes, and how he held the empty bottle scared her more than she could ever explain. Sidney was not a violent person. She'd never even had a parking ticket, but that last comment and the ominous way he held the empty bottle was more than she could stand. Almost without a thought, she grabbed a scuba tank from the storage rack and hit him in the back of the head. Lawson instinctively grabbed the back of his head and saw blood on his hand. He stumbled around in his drunken and suddenly dazed state. "You bitch," he muttered. Lawson staggered as he tried to turn toward her. He slipped on the scotch he spilled and lost his balance. He fell down to the deck, hitting his head hard against a heavy wooden deck chair.

Sidney stood there with a shocked expression on her face. She ran her fingers through her hair and began calling his name, but Lawson did not respond. Panic-stricken, she ran to him, careful to not slip and fall like Lawson just did. She shook him, trying to get him to give a response, but Lawson just laid there. Looking down, she saw that the sundress she wore had blood on it. His head was freely bleeding despite her efforts to stop it. She checked his breathing, finding it was short and shallow and becoming fewer in number. His eyes were open, staring blankly at nothing in particular. Checking his pulse, it was slow and then became undetectable. Lawson was gone. Sidney began to gasp for air in a panic. Almost without thinking, she put the scuba tank away to its proper place. She walked as calmly as she could to her room and took off her blood-stained clothes. She got in the shower to clean the blood off her. "Oh god, what have I done? What have I done?" she thought out loud. "I should call the police and turn myself in. I should explain it was just an accident. I didn't mean to kill him."

Exiting the shower, she dried off and put on her wet suit almost without thinking. It was only a matter of time before Lawson's body would be discovered. She was having trouble focusing on what to do. She paced back and forth trying to decide what to do. Then she did the only thing she could and called the police. She told the dispatcher that her fiancé was injured and possibly dead. The dispatcher told her to stay on the line and remain calm and that the police and ambulance were on the way.

It was nearly five that Saturday morning before they got there. The paramedics were first on the scene. They tried to revive him, but it was no use. Lawson was dead, and it was her fault. The guests began to wake from all the commotion on the back deck. Officers kept them back, but there was no hiding the fact Lawson was dead. Most stood in stunned silence, while others cast judgmental glances at Sidney.

Movies and TV had it all wrong when the police investigated. They made it seem like everything happened so fast, and the villain always confessed in the end and revealed their plot. It was nothing like that when the police began to ask questions. "Which one of you is Sidney Lewis?" a female officer, Barnes, she thought, asked. She really didn't have to answer because people were turning to look at her.

"I'm Sidney. I called you," she said, and the officer motioned for her to come over.

"Ma'am, we're going to need to ask you a few questions. Is there somewhere we can talk in private?" Sidney suggested the dining area next to the galley as a place where they could talk uninterrupted. "Ms. Lewis, our detectives are still always out, so I just want to ask you a few basic questions. What's your relation to the victim?"

"He's my fiancé. We were supposed to set our wedding date this weekend and go scuba diving," she answered, still trying to calm down.

"I guess that's why you're wearing a wet suit, then."

"Yes, that and my clothes had blood on them, and I showered and put this on before you got here."

"You showered? Before or after you called us?"

"I… I… I showered before I called you. I was scared, and I had blood on me. I was freaking out."

Barnes wrote down what Sidney was telling her. It was then that she decided she might want to wait about telling what happened. It didn't matter because the detective arrived, and Barnes went out to meet him before he came in to talk to Sidney. She was getting nervous about keeping her story straight and explaining what happened. Maybe they would believe that it was an accident, and this would be over soon.

"Ms. Lewis, I'm Detective Sullivan. I understand you are the one who found the body, is that right?"

"I did it. It was me," she said, trying to stay brave. "We got into an argument, and he tried to push me over the side. I was scared, so I hit him with a scuba tank. I wasn't trying to kill him. I just got angry when he broke up with me and told me how he'd shown those videos he secretly made of me to his friends. He pushed me against the railing and held that bottle like he was going to hit me with it. I swear I never meant to kill him."

Sullivan looked at her in disbelief. "Wait, so you two were arguing, and he shoved you against the rail? Then you hit him?"

"No, well, yes. You have to believe me. I didn't want to kill him. I swear. I didn't even want to talk to him about the videos because he was so drunk, but he wouldn't let it drop?"

"You keep saying videos. What videos?"

"Lawson was secretly recording videos of us having sex."

"And he got mad when you confronted him?"

"Well, yes. I told him to go to bed, but he just kept after me."

"That's when you hit him."

"No, he attacked me. Then he had that scotch bottle, and I thought he was going to hit me with it. I was scared, scared of what he might do."

Sullivan thought for a moment and decided he'd heard enough. "Well, okay, sit tight. You're under arrest for the murder of Lawson Pierson." He got up and called Officer Barnes into the room. "Officer Barnes," Sullivan began, "Ms. Lewis is under arrest. Take care of things while I head up to the scene."

Sidney sat in disbelief. She wanted to scream to him that was not what happened. Why didn't he understand that this was all an accident? Why didn't he see that she was attacked by Lawson? Then again, what did she expect to happen? *I just killed my fiancé. Of course, they are going to arrest me. It's their job. God, what have I gotten myself into?* she thought.

"Ma'am, I need you to stand up, please," Officer Barnes told her. "Turn around and place your hands behind your back."

Sidney did as she was told. Her heart sank with the feeling of the metal cuffs going around her left wrist and then her right. How she kept it together she didn't know, but she didn't want to cry as she walked past all their guests. That was the worst part. She tried not to look at them as the officer walked her out in cuffs in front of everyone. One of Lawson's college friends yelled, "Murdering bitch! I hope you rot in prison." The others just stood there, not believing what they saw. It was almost a relief when the officer put her in the car and drove away.

Sullivan watched as Sidney was led away down the pier to the waiting car. He surveyed the scene and took a few photos with his phone before the crime-scene investigators arrived. It would still be a while since he had yet to call them, but he knew he couldn't wait much longer. He made a few notes about the scene and the body, then called out the crime scene unit. After the call ended, he walked over to where one of the officers, Keller, he thought, was interviewing the witnesses. "Is there a Jordan Byrd here?" A small-framed, black-haired man raised his hand, like he was sitting in a classroom. He motioned him over and took him down to the dining room. "I need to know if Lawson had any of those cameras in his room."

"What? I don't know what you're talking about," Jordan answered, his head throbbing as the hangover really began to sit in.

"Cut the crap, Byrd. You know damn well what I'm talking about, so unless you want to explain to Leonard Pierson why you let his dead son's reputation get slandered, answer the question."

"Yeah, okay, yeah, there are four cameras in—"

"Then get in there and get rid of them before the crime-scene unit arrives."

Jordan wasted no time in removing the cameras. When he was finished, he reported back to Sullivan. "They'll search his house next," Sullivan told him. "Do you have a key to his house?" Jordan nodded that he did. "Good, then get down there and remove the cameras. Then if I were you, I would go find a place to hide out for a while. A long while." Now came the part he dreaded the most. He got out his phone and dialed. "Mr. Pierson, I'm afraid I have some bad news."

Taylor arrived at the docks just as a police car drove away with a young woman in the back. At the time, he gave no thought to that.

He had a scene to examine before the crime scene unit arrived. He boarded the boat and asked a uniformed officer where he could find Sullivan. When he found Sullivan, he was emerging out of the dining room with a disheveled young man. "Morning, George. Who's that?"

"Roger, good morning. One of the victim's friends. Hungover as hell, so not a lot of help."

"So who's our victim, and where are they?"

"Rear deck. It's Leonard Pierson's oldest son, Lawson."

"Oh god. You know how far off the crime scene people are?" he asked as they both started moving to the rear deck.

"Who knows. I've locked things down here for now."

When they got to the back deck, he saw that the body was covered. He pulled it back and began his examination. He noticed that there were two head wounds, one to the back and one to the side of Lawson's head. It was hard to tell; but the wound to the side of the head, at first glance, appeared worse than the one on the back of his head. The autopsy would have to determine if he was right, so it was impossible to say for certain with just a look. "We got a suspect?" Roger asked as he pulled the covering back over the body.

"Yeah, the girlfriend. Apparently, they got into some kind of confrontation, and she beat his head in."

"Maybe. Tell you what, keep things locked down here until the crime-scene unit arrives. I'm going to look around and then interview our suspect."

"Roger, this is my case. I should interview the suspect."

"Afraid I'm going to pull rank on this one, George. Sorry." Taylor could tell that did not sit well with Sullivan. George was a good cop, and he believed Sullivan would do a good job, but Taylor needed to take the lead on this one. "Look, I'll keep you in the loop. This is going to take both of us more than likely."

Taylor snapped a few photos with his camera and took notes on what he saw. He did not want to stay too long because he needed to interview the suspect as soon as possible. Walking back to his car, he tried to put together what he thought happened. He knew better than to prejudice in his mind what the truth was in reality nor did he want to jump to conclusions about how the Piersons might get involved or even be involved. What he did know was that the clock was running, and it was only a matter of time before the press got wind of the death of Lawson Pierson, and he knew once they did that it was likely to become a media circus.

CHAPTER 11

The police station was smaller than she thought it would be. They drove through a secured door that led into a fenced-in area. Officer Barnes let her out into what was essentially an enclosed garage. Through the door, there were a handful of people working the intake. Some wore police uniforms, while others wore medical scrubs. They removed her cuffs and took her picture. Next, a female wearing scrubs took her into a separate room to search her, which wasn't hard since she was wearing a wet suit. Surprisingly, this was not a strip search but a thorough pat-down search. She returned to the booking room and sat at a small desk as the arresting officer took down her information. It felt strange to tell a complete stranger her entire life history. She thought about her apartment and her belongings. Sidney began to wonder if she would ever see all that again and just as quickly shamed herself for that selfish thought. She was fingerprinted at the desk using a touchpad, and then the officer told her to walk over to a solid gray door on the other side of the room.

The officer opened the door with a key and told Sidney to step inside. Sidney saw that you could only turn to the left or right as there was no passage forward. She was told to turn to the right. For the first time, she saw three jail cells. Things really started to feel real now for her. Tears started to well up inside her, and while the thought of being locked in a cell without being able to leave frightened her, she was ready to release this pent-up emotion. "We're going back to the cell all the way down," the officer told her. Sidney walked down the short hallway, noticing that there was no one in any of the other cells. She stopped in front of the cell door as the officer inserted the key and opened the cell. "Step in, please."

With only the slightest hesitation, Sidney obeyed. She thought, *These are my last seconds of freedom for the rest of my life.* As soon as she was inside, the door closed loudly behind her.

"I heard why you're here, and while I don't agree with what you did, he sounded like a real jerk. The detectives won't be here for about an hour or so. Enough time if you need to get it all out and compose yourself, if you know what I mean. I don't think anyone will be in here for a while, so you can get a little loud." She then handed Sidney a handkerchief. "Keep it." She gave Sidney a quick, sympathetic smile and then left.

As soon as the door to the cells closed, it happened. Sidney hadn't cried since the day she found out that Lawson had cheated on her. She began to sob uncontrollably. *How did I let it get to this? Why did I hit him with that scuba tank? I just thought it would put a knot on his head, not kill him. But when he fell, he hit the deck chair too, and then he died. Why didn't I call for help sooner? Why didn't I just tell the truth to start with? I waited too long. Now they think I wanted him to die. Stupid, stupid, stupid. Now I'm going to live the rest of my life in a cage. I was supposed to be a good person, with a family. Now I'm a criminal. I ruined everything.* All these thoughts flowed through her mind as the tears freely flowed.

The wait was more like two hours before a guard returned. "Ms. Lewis," a male guard called to her, "I need you to come with me. The detectives are ready to talk to you." Sidney got up and offered her hands to be cuffed again. "That won't be necessary, ma'am," he said as the door slid open. He led her into a small room with a single table and two chairs inside. "Have a seat there. They'll be with you shortly." And he left the room.

After a few minutes, the detective entered the room. "Ms. Lewis, I'm Detective Roger Taylor of the Warrenton Police Department. You've had a busy day today. Why don't you tell me about it."

"Where do you want me to start?" she sheepishly replied.

"Well, let's start with the last time you talked to the deceased. What was your exact relationship to him?"

"He was my fiancé. We've been dating for over two years."

"Okay. Was there any abuse? Did he ever beat you?"

"No. I thought everything was fine between us until a few months ago when he started putting off our wedding date. He kept wanting to go out with his friends and drink and party, and I didn't want to be part of all that. I just kept hoping that he would settle down. We were going to set our wedding date last night, but he invited all of those people."

"So you got to feeling he was never going to marry you?"

"No…well, maybe, yeah, but that's not what we were arguing about."

"What was it, then?"

"We argued earlier this week about setting a date. He left my apartment after that. When he left, I found a flash drive. I thought it was mine, and I put it away for a while. I went back to see what was on it on Wednesday and found it was Lawson's, full of videos he secretly took of us having sex. It also had more than a dozen videos of him having sex with other women as recently as two weeks ago."

"So why did you go to spend the night on his boat?

"We were supposed to go scuba diving with friends today, so he invited a few couples to spend the night on the boat with us. After everyone went to bed, I told him I wanted to speak with him on the back deck."

"You were going to confront him about what you found on that flash drive?"

"Yes. He was drunk, so I changed my mind about talking to him and just tried to put him to bed. He wouldn't let it drop though. Told me I was being a bitch to his guests. When I told him about the flash drive I found, he asked me why it was such a big deal that he'd been having sex with those women. He even said that he's shown the videos of us to his friends. One of them was even on the boat with his girlfriend. Next thing I know, he broke up with me and shoved me into the railing. I tried to stop him from walking way, but he grabbed me and threatened to push me over the side. He's never talked to me like that before. Then he had that bottle, and I thought he was going to hit me with it. I was scared, so I reacted."

"Okay, stop right there. Have you called a lawyer yet?" Taylor couldn't say why, but he believed every word she was saying. In the back of his mind, he thought she might be able to help him in his investigation of the Piersons' shipping business. It had to be done in the right way though, so a lawyer needed to be in on his plan.

"No, I've been locked in that cell and haven't used the phone."

"All right, well, I don't normally do this, but I want you to stop there. You need to call a lawyer right now and get them here. That's what I'm going to advise you. If what you say is true, I can help you, but I think you need a lawyer. Now you want to keep talking, I'll listen, but remember, everything you say can and will be used as evidence against you."

"Okay, thank you."

"Don't thank me yet. You're facing serious charges. I'm going to be completely honest, you're looking at the possibility of life without parole. You should also know you're not going home today, all right? You're going to be staying with us at least overnight. You will have to go before a judge to set bail for this type of crime, if he even sets bail. More than likely, he will, but Judge Corley is not in today, so you'll have to wait until tomorrow. Till then, you'll have to sit back in the cell."

"Okay. Can I call my parents?"

"Yeah, we'll let you do that. Soon as you've made your calls, we'll have to get you dressed in a uniform. Officer Barnes, the one who arrested you, will do that when you're done. After you talk to your lawyer, we'll speak again. Understand?"

"Yes, thank you."

Shortly after the detective left the room, Sidney was allowed to use the phone. She called her parents and let them know what happened and where she was. Her father told her that he would call the family attorney, an old college friend of his and golfing buddy. Understandably, Todd and Sophia were devastated. They told her to stay strong and keep quiet until the lawyer arrived. As soon as they could, they would come and see her. Once she hung up the phone, Officer Barnes walked up to her. "Okay, Ms. Lewis, come with me, please."

She followed her to a room with a curtain and stepped inside. Again the door shut, but this time, Officer Barnes was inside with her.

"All right, this is the embarrassing part. I need you to strip completely down including your undergarments and place them in that bag on the wall."

Sidney noticed the white bag hanging there, and the realization suddenly hit her she was about to be naked in front of a total stranger. She took off her shoes and placed them in the bag. Then a wave of shame washed over her that Barnes seemed to notice.

"Look, I've done this a hundred times, and it's not a lot of fun for me either. It's just part of the job, and I'm the only female officer here today."

That seemed to make her feel a little better, but starting to unzip the wet suit was one of the hardest things she had ever done. She peeled it off and, at last, placed it in the bag. Next came the bikini top and finally the bottoms. There she was completely disrobed, trying her best to cover herself. That didn't last long. Sidney was put through a series of searches, each more embarrassing than the last one. She had never been overly shy about her body since she usually wore a bikini to the beach, but everything important was always covered. The idea of being nude in public, though, was different altogether. That was one of the things that bothered her so much about Lawson taking those videos and showing them around. She felt exposed. Exposure was exactly what she was going through now as well. She didn't blame Officer Barnes. It was her job, but she felt humiliated nonetheless. When it was over, Barnes gave her an orange uniform to put on. At least that part was like in the movies.

The walk back was not as dramatic as the first time. She again waited by the cell door and heard the familiar clang of the door as it shut behind her. No tears this time, just a resignation that this might be how things were going to be for a long time to come. She sat down on her bed and tried to pass the time as best as she could. One of the first things she started to notice about being in jail was that time seemed to pass slowly. She was still by herself, so she decided to try and get some rest.

CHAPTER 12

District Attorney Jim Cooper was in no mood to be patient this morning. Since the news of Lawson Pierson's death reached him, he had taken call after call from Lawson's family telling him he better do his damn job. *Piersons think they own every damn thing,* he thought as he walked into the station. "Butler," he said as he walked into the police chief's office, "did that girl do it or not?"

Ashton Butler was in his sixth year as police chief in Warrenton. He knew Jim Cooper could be a real jerk, but today he seemed even more so. "Yes, come in. Why don't you have a seat, Mr. Cooper." The chief was also not in a good mood. The phone hadn't stopped ringing from the media, Pierson's family, and everyone else trying to get the story, half of them glad the bastard was dead and the other half wanting to put this girl away for life or worse. A media circus was in the making with sex, lies, and videos, the whole thing made for TV. Why the hell did it have to happen in his town?

"Cut the smart-ass crap, Butler. If that girl killed Lawson Pierson, then you better do everything you can to lock her up good."

"That's not my job, sir. That's yours. My people investigate, and from what Detective Taylor told me, there's no way a first-degree murder charge will stick."

"I don't care about that. I got Leonard Pierson breathing down my neck about elections, funding, and all that crap. Now you tell me whether or not I can tell him this girl is going to rot in jail or not."

"Really? Is that all you care about? Forgive me, but I thought justice was what we were about. You ever heard of serve and protect? Even the accused have rights in this country. Now I'm going to do my job. Did she kill him? Yeah, she did. Was it premeditated or overly heinous? No, a crime of passion in the heat of the moment. Bastard might have even pushed her first."

"She tried to hide it, didn't she?" Cooper replied, starting to calm down just a bit. "She went all night without calling the cops or seeking medical help, right?"

"Yeah, looks like." Butler's voice also began to relax. "She's a scared kid, Coop. You look at her for two seconds, and she looks like a damn rabbit in a room full of coyotes." He flung a file down hard on his desk and sat down in his chair. "I hate cases like this. Always hoped I'd never have one."

"What did he do to her?" Cooper knew the Piersons' good name covered a lot of secret sins, but Leonard Pierson was not a man to let something like the death of his son go.

"Typical stuff. Filmed them during sex without her knowledge and showed all his buddies. Led her on about marriage and kids and all, and she's too young and dumb to see through it until now."

"God Almighty knows," sighed Cooper. "What do we know about her?"

"Not a damn thing. Clean record. Not even a parking ticket."

"Damn it, Ashton, why couldn't she have been a money-loving slut? Would have been a hell of a lot easier."

"Yeah, well, she's not." Butler leaned forward and looked Cooper in the eyes. "You really going to throw the book at her?"

"You tell me, Ash. You think she deserves it?"

"She broke the law. Killed a man while he was walking away from her. It ain't right. Was she in the right frame of mind? No, she wasn't. Would she do it again? No, I don't think so, and her attorney's going to bring all of that out at trial. Hell, you might even get a sympathetic juror to hold out long enough for a mistrial."

Cooper let out a long breath. "I'm going murder in the second. It's the only thing that will satisfy the Piersons. She'll serve twelve to fifteen years."

"Manslaughter would be better. I think it qualifies under—"

"No," Cooper said, cutting off the chief, "she hit him in the head with his back turned. Whether she meant to or not, she killed him, and there's no self-defense. I hate to lock up Cinderella like that, but that's what's got to happen. The Piersons are creeps, but they did lose a son. Even creeps are entitled to justice."

"You really think that's going to make them happy?"

"Hell no, but that's what they're going to get. I'll get things set up for the hearing tomorrow, then reach out to her lawyer. Who is it?"

"Luke Brady."

"Oh dear god, could they have found a worse attorney?"

"It's not a rich family, and I think he's been a friend of her dad's for years."

"They would almost be better with a public defender. All right, let me get moving on this. And I don't want the press to know any more than they have to know. Tell your officers to keep their mouths shut on this one. I don't care what those reporters pay them."

"I'll do my best."

"Yeah, you do that," Cooper said as he marched out the door.

CHAPTER 13

It was late that morning when Sidney was brought into the same small interrogation room as before. There sat a medium-sized man in a suit and tie with dark-rimmed glasses. "Sidney, how are you holding up? Oh, I'm so sorry I couldn't get her sooner. Your parents called me this morning, and I tried to get here as fast as I could."

"It's nice to see you again, Mr. Brady. I guess I'm okay," she responded.

"I know it's been a tough day, but we need to talk about your case. I've not spoken to the DA yet, but they're going to push for first-degree murder, I think. They won't get that to stick, of course, but second degree is very likely, and you've probably already guessed the Piersons are going to come after you hard for this."

Sidney hadn't really thought about that. She had only met Lawson's parents a couple of times, but she knew they were very influential people. "What?" She paused. "What am I looking at? Will I be able to go home?"

"Well, not today I'm afraid. Because of the severity of the crime, you have to have bond set by a judge, and unfortunately, court is adjourned today, so it will be at least Monday morning."

"But you think I can get bailed out?"

"Can, yes, but will Judge Corley allow it is another thing. The most important thing is, we need to prepare your defense, so you need to tell me everything that happened."

Sidney began to recount everything to him. She told him all she could remember and about the flash drive and the other women. "Well, that's a heck of a story. Where is the flash drive now? Please tell me you didn't take it with you?"

"No, it's safe in—"

"Stop. Write its location on this," he said as he produced a small notepad. "These guys think I'm a bad lawyer, but I do know a thing or two. Not to mention a lot of my cases are nearly unwinnable. These rooms are not supposed to be bugged, but never hurts to be too careful."

Sidney wrote down the location of the flash drive and handed him back the notebook.

"Now I need to know, are you locked up by yourself?"

"Yes."

"Okay, good. Don't say anything to anyone about your case without me here, and I will tell you what to and not to answer. If I say don't answer, then don't. If you get a cellmate, don't say a word about your case especially if they move you to county jail. You're going to have to be less trusting and more paranoid if you're going to get out of this."

"What do you think will happen to me?" she asked.

"Well, that's hard to say. The Piersons are going to want to lock you up for life. I doubt that will happen, and I'm going to do my damnedest to see that it doesn't." He looked at her closely. "But you need to be prepared for the real possibility of a long prison sentence. I will take this all the way to trial, but at the end of the day, your best bet may be to try to work out a plea deal. If this trial becomes a media frenzy, the DA may want to get it over quickly, which means he may be willing to work with us. Maybe."

She sat there in silence for a while, running over everything in her head again. "I don't want to go to prison. I just wish I'd never met him now."

"I understand, but we can't change what happened. We can only shape how this plays out now. Focus on that and leave the rest to me. Get some rest, and we'll talk again after I meet with Cooper."

"Okay, I will."

"And remember, be polite but don't talk about your case."

"I won't. Thank you."

Sidney must have drifted off because she was startled by the cell door opening. "Ms. Lewis, DA Cooper and Mr. Brady are in the conference room waiting for you," said an unfamiliar male officer.

Sidney got up and followed him into the conference room. Cooper sat on one side of the table, and Brady sat next to an empty chair meant for her.

Cooper began, "I think you know that you are in a lot of trouble, young lady." He started to lean toward her ever so slightly. "This isn't something you're just going to walk away from. After consulting with Detective Taylor, the DA's office intends to charge you with second-degree murder."

"That's ridiculous, and you know it, Cooper," answered Brady. "My client has already told you that she didn't intend to kill Mr. Pierson, and we intend to prove self-defense. Not only that, the extenuating circumstances of what he did to her, his level of intoxication, and the heated method of their exchange makes this a clear manslaughter charge at the most."

"She may not have had intent, but she tried to hide her involvement in the crime and did not call for help immediately after he fell. That's murder two if ever I've heard of it."

"And you've never had to deal with all that she has over the last several days. I can make a clear case for manslaughter just based on her mental state at the time and, with her record, have her out of jail before the ink dries on her parole papers."

"That's not going to happen," Cooper replied. "This whole thing will end up being a shit show by the time a trial is over. So against my better judgment, I have a proposal."

"We're listening."

"She pleads to murder two. Sentence is twenty-five years and serves fifteen of them."

"You have to be kidding."

"Like hell I am. I take this to trial, I'll push for twenty-five to life."

"No jury in the world would go for that especially once we show the contents of that flash drive to the world."

"All right, we're done here," Cooper said. "My offer is good until trial. After that, all bets are off. You want a shit show, you'll get one, but it will cost you in the end. You better think about that, young lady." Cooper left them.

"As much as I hate to say it, you may want to seriously consider that offer."

"Why? You just said that you could plead insanity or manslaughter."

"I was trying to get him to budge. He's a real jerk, but he's not wrong. Even with the events of this week, there's no guarantee a jury will buy it. And knowing Leonard Pierson, he's liable to buy the jury."

"Can he do that?"

"Not legally, but that won't stop him."

"So that's it, then? I just waste away in a cage for the rest of my life?"

"Look, I told you I would do everything I can to not let that happen. Sometimes, though, you have to lose a battle to win a war. Just because you take the plea doesn't mean we stop fighting. I wish I had better news."

"So how long do I have to decide really?"

"Cooper wants to arraign you the day after tomorrow. Legally they can hold you for seventy-two hours before I can file habeas corpus and try to get you out. I'd say you have until then. If you do decide to take the deal, then make sure you don't sign anything until I've had a chance to read over it." He could tell the news was not what she hoped for, and he wished that he could do more. "Sidney, I need you to stay strong. These next several days are not going to be easy. I'm going to do everything I can to prepare for a trial, but I have to be honest, we are up against tough odds. Leonard Pierson runs this county, and that alone makes him dangerous. Just know I believe your story, and I will continue to fight for you no matter what. I owe that to your dad. Speaking of which, I'm going to see them as soon as I leave here. Anything you want me to tell them?"

"No, just let them know I'm okay."

"I will. It will probably be tomorrow before I get back, so remember what I told you. Stay positive, and I'll see you tomorrow."

CHAPTER 14

Brady and Sidney's father, Todd, arrived at her apartment. Thankfully, the police still hadn't arrived because the door was still locked. He hoped they weren't too late to get there before Pierson's people either. As soon as the door opened, he breathed a sigh of relief because nothing had been searched yet. "Okay, Todd, she told me that the flash drive was hidden in her underwear drawer. There's not really a good way to do this, so do you want to search for it, or do you want me to look?"

Todd thought for a second about that question. On one hand, he didn't want Brady searching through her underwear, but neither did he want to do it either. "I guess I will," he said hesitatingly as he moved toward her bedroom. Finding the chest of drawers, it didn't take him long to find the flash drive. He handed the drive to Brady unsure of what to do next. Brady found her laptop and powered it up.

"We have to be sure it's the right one," Brady told him as he put in the password that Sidney gave him. "Don't worry, you don't have to watch them." It didn't take long before the flash drive was authenticated, and they knew it was the correct one. "All right, let's get back to your place, and I'll give you both the rundown on the case. Oh, and make sure we leave everything the way we found it."

They somehow avoided talking about Sidney's predicament on the drive back to Todd's home. He wouldn't say it, but Brady had known Todd long enough to know when he was upset and trying to put on a brave face. He didn't press the issue in the car. Better to talk to both Todd and Sophia together so he could answer their questions at one time. The men went into the home after they arrived and found Sophia sitting on the couch softly sobbing to herself. When she saw them, she hardly acknowledged their presence. Todd sat next to her and put his arm around her shoulders. Brady could tell this was not going to be easy.

"I know you both probably have a lot of questions, so I'm going to try and talk you through this. Hopefully, that will answer some of them," Brady began. He took a deep breath. "Honestly, things don't look good for her. After talking with the DA, he's already offered a deal to her. If she doesn't accept it and goes to trial, he's going after a twenty-five to life sentence." Brady saw that the news shook Sophia greatly. Todd continued to play the strong man, but he knew Todd too well to believe it. "Look, I believe her. I've known Sidney all her life, and she would never do something like this without good reason. But I also know who is pushing all of this behind the scenes."

Todd looked up with a mix of sadness and anger. "How much do you know about this Pierson guy?" The question was not one of recognition since everyone in Warrenton knew who the Piersons were but one of familiarity. "How do you know so much about him?"

"First off, I don't know him very well personally. We've met a few times in the course of business. What I know about him personally comes from a lot of different sources. He's a man that can be as charming as anyone, but there is a cruel side of him that few know about. Rumors have it that he runs a number of criminal enterprises, but nothing ever sticks to him. The rumor is that he practically controls the DA's office and even has judges in his back pocket. None of that can be proven, of course."

"What does that mean for my baby girl?" Sophia spoke up.

"I don't know. Like I said, the DA seems out for blood, and I think it's likely that Pierson's influence is behind it. Basically, they are holding all the cards right now." He could tell this wasn't giving them much comfort. Honestly, he didn't feel too confident either. "I promise you both I will fight this as long as I have to and do whatever I can to bring her home. That deal, though, may be the only way to keep her from spending a large part of her life in prison. There is also a safety aspect. If Pierson doesn't get his way, he may try to come after her. If he does, I shudder to think what he will do to her."

"Luke, is there anything we can do to help?" Todd asked. Brady could hear the helplessness in his voice.

"You can pray. Stay positive especially when you talk to her, but don't build up her expectations too much. Hope for the best but expect the worst. The bail hearing is Monday morning, and we'll know a little more about what to expect then."

They talked for a while longer before Brady got up to leave. Todd walked him to the door to question him further. "Luke, you seem worried. Tell me the truth, do you honestly think you can win in a trial?"

Brady wanted to go into the whole speech about how unpredictable trials were and that anything can happen. He wanted to tell him he could prove her innocence and that she acted in self-defense, but Todd was his oldest friend, and he didn't want to lie. "Todd, it's not unwinnable. Hell, under normal circumstances, I would probably say she stood a good chance of being cleared. But to say she's gotten mixed up with the wrong people is an understatement. They have resources, influence, and they know enough things about the right people that it makes it hard to fight back. Sarah and I never had children, and I love that girl as my own, so I will do my best."

"I know you will, Luke. Thank you."

With that, he left their home, hoping he could do what he promised them.

CHAPTER 15

Monday morning, Sidney was taken across the street to the courthouse. The Warrenton Police Department was not originally across from the courthouse. Years ago, the county built a newer, larger courthouse across from the police station. The old courthouse was still there but was essentially now used for the issuing of licenses and other county business while trials were held in the new building. Many times on court days, anyone held at the police station was simply walked across the street shackled and under guard. That was exactly what they did with her. Sidney's case was the fourth to be called that day. "Court will now hear the bail request of Sidney Lewis," announced the bailiff. She was brought forward, released from her handcuffs, and seated next to Luke Brady. They talked over a couple of details before Judge Corley began.

"Mr. Cooper, how do the people move on the matter of granting bail to Ms. Lewis?" the judge asked.

"Your Honor, the people ask that bail be denied on the grounds of the serious nature of the crime and the high media attention this case is starting to gain. We also believe the defendant may be a flight risk."

"Defense, what say you in rebuttal?"

"Your Honor, while we do not refute the serious nature of the charges, my client is looking forward to her day in court to fight these charges. She is not a flight risk since her entire life is here in this very town. Her family is here, and she would not abandon them. She is also a person of high moral character."

"The court finds that due to the serious nature of the crime and the high media attention this is likely to garner that the defendant shall be denied bail."

"Your Honor, you can't be serious!" exclaimed Brady. "My client has never once been in trouble with the law and has no history of violence. How can she be a flight risk if there is literally nowhere for her to run to?"

Judge Corley banged his gavel hard. "Mr. Brady, another outburst like that and I will find you in contempt of court." The judge looked over at Cooper and could easily see the satisfaction on his face. "Mr. Cooper, do the people have any further recommendations to make?"

"Yes, Your Honor, the people request that the defendant be held here at the Warrenton City Jail instead of the county facility, again due to the high-profile nature of the case."

"More like so you can keep an eye on her, Cooper."

Judge Corley banged his gavel hard again. "Brady, you are fined $250 for contempt."

"Your Honor, I protest this decision. My client—"

"A $300 fine. Another word and you can join her in the city jail for the rest of the day. The court agrees to the request of the prosecution, and the defendant will be held in the city jail, pending trial. Bailiff, call the next case."

Brady felt the sting of the judge's rebuke. The realization really sank in at the near-hopeless situation that confronted the Lewis family. It was obvious now that if they went to trial, they could only expect more of the same. It made him sick how one family so completely controlled the comings and goings of this county. He spoke some encouraging words to Sidney as the bailiffs arrived to escort her back across the street. After they had gone, he seethed in anger at the near-hopeless situation and felt frustration for not knowing what he could do to help Sidney. What Pierson didn't know was that Brady had a few secrets of his own.

CHAPTER 16

Night in jail was a strange thing. There's no sunlight, clocks, windows, or anything that let one knew it's dark out. The lighting stayed the same with its florescent glow. Lights out was going to be at 10:00 p.m., so it had to be sometime before then. Sidney was exhausted, and sleep was starting to take her. Before the lights were out, she drifted into a fitful sleep. She didn't know how long she'd slept, but something wasn't right. Somehow a light was on. She cracked open her eyes, and it seemed that the light was concentrated in her area alone.

"I guess you think I'm the most evil man on the planet by now," came a deep and gravelly voice. She knew that voice all too well. "Frankly, I don't blame you. Let me assure you, you're surrounded by monsters here. The worst of them aren't in these cages though." Leonard Pierson stood just to the right of her cell door. He was dressed in a charcoal-gray suit impeccably pressed and tailored. His brushed-back gray-and-white hair was perfectly placed. He had piercing blue eyes that seemed to look through her rather than at her. His unmistakable salt-and-pepper beard was neatly trimmed, his face seemingly set in a permanent scowl. He was a tall and imposing figure to be sure. "By now I'm sure everyone you've talked to has warned you about me. They're not wrong."

"How did you get in here?" she asked, somehow more frightened than she'd been all day.

"I had such high hopes for you. Make no mistake, I know what kind of man my son was. I was constantly deleting those perverted videos of his. You'd be surprised how few of them you were actually in. I thought that you might convince him to grow up. I gave him every opportunity to God only knows. I gave him a job that would satisfy most, and he turned it into an orgy of perversion."

He reached behind him and pulled up a chair. "So I gave up on him and started prepping his brother, Jonathan, to take over the family business. You know, I really should thank you for taking care of a potentially bad situation for me."

"Were you going to kill him?"

He laughed. "Kill him? Young lady, you don't get to where I am in life by going around killing people." Then he got up and approached her cell. "But there are things far worse than death. Believe me, when I am done with people, death will seem a release." He backed away and sat back down. "You've put me in a bad position. While I'm not that upset Lawson is gone, I can't let his death go unanswered. On the other hand, I know you have some very incriminating evidence on that flash drive that could prove embarrassing, to say the least."

"What do you want from me? I didn't mean to kill him. Please, I just want this to stop."

"As do I, so I come to offer you a choice, some small rays of hope. You take the deal Cooper made you, and I'll make sure that you only serve twelve years. Do your time and I promise to disappear from your life. And all you have to do is tell that hack of an attorney of yours to hand over that flash drive."

"What if I want the trial?"

"Trust me, you don't because you won't win. Remember, there are things worse than death. Think of where you will be, locked away for your whole life, constantly worried if today is the day that Leonard Pierson makes all those horrible things happen."

"Look, I just want this to be over. I'm not someone who can harm you. Why don't you just leave me alone?"

"Because, Ms. Lewis, you are nobody, and I can't be outdone by a nobody. Return the drive, take the deal, and quietly do your time, and then this all goes away. Sleep on it."

With that, Leonard Pierson stood and disappeared down the hall. Sidney mulled over what just happened in her mind. She was guilty, that much she knew. Pierson's threats were the markings of a bully but a bully that held all the cards. Sidney knew what she had to do. It scared her to think about life in a prison, but at least now she knew it would one day end. The only thing left was to face the inevitable truth and accept the deal.

The next day, she talked again with Brady about her situation. He agreed with her that it didn't look good. He also told her that while he couldn't prove it, he was certain the facts were being purposely distorted against her. She then told him about Pierson's visit to her that night. "It doesn't surprise me, considering everything that's happened. I hate to say it, but they have us backed against the wall."

"If I do take the deal, when will it happen?"

"That depends on a lot of factors, but pretty soon, I think. They haven't set an arraignment hearing yet, but based on what's gone on these last days, it won't take long."

"Will I get to say goodbye to Mom and Dad before I go?"

"I don't know, sweetheart, I really don't. None of this is going the way it should. I am so sorry."

"I'm scared, Mr. Brady. I'm scared to take the deal, and I'm scared not to take it."

"I know. Believe me, I wish I could do more. But I will keep trying. Like I said, I will be with you every step of the way no matter what."

He left the station and made his way to his car. The first person he called was Jim Cooper to inform him that Sidney would take the plea deal. The second person was Leonard Pierson to inform him that once the plea was officially in place, he would deliver the flash drive outside the court in public. Brady felt hollow as if he had let down his best friend and his entire family. Now was not the time to dwell on his failures but to begin to enact his contingency plans.

Detective Taylor walked into the station after watching the events of the Lewis case unfold. The feeling that things were amiss in the case bothered him. His efforts to return to the crime scene had also been blocked not by any official reason but through a number of events that were too coincidental. He began to get the feeling he was being stonewalled and purposefully kept from the investigation. "Chief," he began as he entered Butler's office, "I need to speak with Ms. Lewis about the Pierson murder."

"No can do, Taylor, the investigation is closed as of a few minutes ago."

"What? How?"

"She's taking the deal made to her by Cooper. Investigation is officially closed."

"Chief, that's insanity. There are so many things wrong with the case against her that the defense should have a field day with the prosecution. Why would she do that?"

"I don't know, Roger, but it's not our job. DA says shut it down, so we shut it down."

"Since when do we take orders from him? We have a duty to—"

"Don't lecture me on our duty, Taylor. I know what's expected of us. It's over. I know you've been trying to bust the Piersons for years. You even got that FBI buddy of yours to investigate them a few years ago. I know how bad you want them and that you thought that girl could help you. I even hoped you were right. It's over though. It's time to let it go."

"Damn it, Chief, they are going to slip away again. How can we just sit here and let it happen?"

"Roger, you have to let this go. Live to fight another day. This one is a dead end. Let it go."

Taylor stormed out of the office and sat at his desk, seething. He looked at the official reports on the case and noticed a number of inconsistencies. Details jumped out that didn't coincide with the notes and pictures that he took at the scene. Yet there was nothing he could do. Why did she take the plea? He left the office to do some investigative work on an open case, but the real reason he left was he wanted to be alone to think. Brooding might be a better way to put it. Without evidence and without the ability to collect that evidence, there was little he could do.

CHAPTER 17

"All rise," the court bailiff called out, "the honorable judge, Lilian North, presiding."

The judge walked in and took her seat on the bench. "Be seated, please. Bailiff, call the first case, please."

"Yes, Your Honor. People versus Sidney Lewis."

"Thank you. I understand that there is an offer of a plea agreement. Is that correct, Mr. Cooper?"

"That is correct, Your Honor. The people have made an offer."

"Defense, is your client prepared to accept this agreement?"

Brady looked at Sidney. She gave him a slight nod. "Be strong," he said to her. "Your Honor, Ms. Lewis is prepared to enter a plea of guilty and accept Mr. Cooper's plea agreement."

"Defense, please approach the bench."

Sidney and Brady rose and walked to the judge's bench. It seemed like the longest walk of her life. "Ms. Lewis, do you understand what you are agreeing to today? By pleading guilty and accepting this deal, you will agree to serve twelve years in the Helen Palmer Prison for Women?"

"Yes, Your Honor, I understand and agree with the terms of the plea."

"Are you sure? You have the right to a trial. Are you certain this decision is your own and is not being forced upon you by any person?"

"Yes, Your Honor. This is my decision."

"Very well. Would you like to make a statement before I officially pronounce sentence?"

"I just want to say how sorry I am to everyone that I have affected. I'm sorry to my parents for letting them down because they raised me to be a good person, and I failed to live up to that. I sincerely apologize to the Pierson family for taking their son away from them. I loved Lawson. I betrayed that love with my actions. I wish that night never happened, and I will spend the rest of my life regretting it and trying to make amends. I guess that's all I have to say."

"Ms. Lewis, in light of your acceptance of the plea bargain agreement reached with the state, the court is satisfied that you have made this decision willingly and of sound mind. It is therefore the judgment of this court that the agreement be honored and hereby imposed. Sidney Lewis, having pleaded guilty to the crime of second-degree murder, it is the judgment of this court that you shall be taken from this place and incarcerated in the Helen Palmer Prison for Women for a term of no less than twelve years and not to exceed twenty-five years. The defendant is hereby remanded into the custody of the Department of Corrections to begin her sentence. Bailiff, you may remove the prisoner."

As the courtroom cleared, Luke Brady made his way outside to wait on his intended target. He did not have to wait long as Leonard Pierson made his way out surrounded by press, answering questions as he went. He eventually locked eyes with Brady and began the process of breaking away from the press. He approached him deliberately and slowly. "I believe that you have a piece of my property," Pierson said. "I would like it returned now as per our agreement."

"Of course, Mr. Pierson, but before I hand it over to you, there are some things I need to talk to you about."

"You do have the drive, don't you?"

"Oh yes, I do, and I am certainly going to give it to you before I go see Sidney off, but there are some technicalities we need to iron out before I simply give it to you and let you ride into the sunset."

"Technicalities?"

"Oh yes, sir, you see, most people think I'm a poor lawyer when actually I'm more of a second-rate lawyer. Thing is, it's my job to make sure that my clients are taken care of and well represented for as long as I am retained by them."

"Yes, yes, get on with it."

"Of course, sir. You see, Sidney is in a bad spot right now, and while it's going to be a long time before she needs it, she will need to make a living when she's released."

"Well, I hope you find her something suitable. The flash drive, if you please."

"Oh no, sir, not yet. By the way, did you enjoy your little midnight visit with Sidney the other night? It's kind of funny that we started out with serving fifteen years, but today it's down to twelve. I wonder how that happened?"

"We all know what is at stake here, Brady. Give me the drive."

"Oh yes, oh yes, I will. Absolutely, sir. Like I said, Sidney is going to need a job, a decent-paying one when she's released, and you're going to make that happen."

"And why the hell would I do that?"

Brady removed the flash drive from his jacket pocket. "I don't want you to blame Sidney for this. I swear she is so naive at times. I mean, she fell for all that good-boy crap from your son after all. You see, she told me where to find the flash drive the day she was arrested, and I've had it ever since. Now this is the part that's going to interest you. See, Sidney didn't get past all those videos, and really, who could blame her, but that's why I'm the lawyer. Second rate, right?"

Pierson was starting to feel his temper rise. "Are you going to give me the drive?"

"Please be patient, sir, because like I said, this is your part. You see, I watched the videos looking for things I could use for her defense, and may I say your son had a great taste in women. However, there was one file that didn't have any video. Some really interesting reading about some of the things Pierson Shipping and Transportation Company have been hauling all over the country. Very interesting, indeed. Your son must have had a terrible memory, with all that drinking and late-night sex partners, one named Jim, if I'm not mistaken. It's okay, sir, he didn't seem to mind. So I made a copy of the flash drive for my records."

"You did what?"

"Might want to keep your voice down, sir. There's still a lot of press around. So here's the deal. I'm keeping this copy safe as an insurance policy for Sidney. In twelve years, she walks out of that prison a free woman with a convenient job offer waiting for her. Nothing too fancy but enough to support her and maybe a future family, who knows? If anything should happen to her in jail or if you make any attempt to harm me to recover my copy, the people I have entrusted with this copy will send it far and wide. Every government agency from the FBI to the Food and Drug Department. Hell, the president might even get a copy. Every media outlet will have it, and somehow, I don't think the Pierson shipping empire will survive that."

"So that's your game? And just how exactly do I avoid all of this?"

"The day Sidney walks safe and sound out of prison and into a new job, the drive vanishes."

"And just what do you get out of all this?"

"Two things really. First, my client will be taken care of once this is over. Second, I get the pride of knowing that I beat the great Leonard Pierson at his own game."

"And how do I know the drive has been destroyed?"

"As long as she leaves prison alive, and well, you won't have to find out. Do we have a deal?"

"Fine. She's not worth the trouble anyway. Now give me the drive."

"Here you go, sir, as promised. Now as long as you keep your promise, this will all go away." Brady handed him the flash drive and turned to go. He walked about ten feet and turned back around. "You know, people say I'm a bad lawyer, but I've learned a thing or two. What do you think?"

Pierson did not say a word. He turned around and made his way to his car and drove off. Brady turned to walk back inside to see Sidney one last time before they transported her. She might never know what he did for her today, but at least he could say he did all he could for her. The next several years were going to be hard, but at least now he believed she would survive. He was not so sure about that this morning. Now at least it was not a total loss. She would suffer, but at least there would be a new life waiting after she paid her debt to society.

CHAPTER 18

In contrast to the events of the last several days, the waiting for transport to the prison was actually a welcome relief. With the exception of the few minutes she had to say goodbye to her parents and the visit with Luke Brady, things greatly slowed down. It was odd talking to her parents with her hands locked behind her. It was also odd that she was now sharing a cell for the first time with other women, four of them, in fact, all waiting for transport to the same place. Still, it was kind of nice to know a lot of the uncertainty was over. Basically all that was left to do was wait.

The next day started at 5:00 a.m. when they brought in a bagged breakfast. Inside was a bologna sandwich, a small apple, and a small milk carton. They were told that they would be changing into a different uniform for transport and leaving in about two hours. It would only be a two-hour drive to the prison, so they were told to use the bathroom before they left since they would likely not stop until they arrived.

Sure enough, after about an hour and a half, a couple of officers arrived and called each woman out one at a time and changed them into their new uniform and returned them to the cell shackled hand and foot. Sidney was the third to be called, and the whole process was repeated on her. After a brief search, she was changed and shackled and returned to the cell she shared with the others. When the last girl returned, they were told they were leaving in about ten minutes. In fact, the wait was far less, and soon the women were taken in a single line to a waiting van with caged interior doors. The first two were seated to the left while Sidney and the lady behind her were seated to the right, separated from the first two by a solid metal divider. Neither really knew what to say to the other, so they rode in almost complete silence except for the occasional small comment when the van hit a bump or turned a little too fast. The lady next to her looked to be in her midforties, and from some of her comments, this was not the first time she had taken this ride. Sidney had been told by Brady to not ever ask why some were in jail and, likewise, not offer to tell anyone why she was there.

True enough, about two hours after they left, the van pulled through the gates of Helen Palmer Prison for Women. She could not see well through the windows of the van as to why the guards did not immediately open the doors and let them out. "They check the bottom of the van for bombs and shit," said the woman next to Sidney. Apparently satisfied, the van doors opened, and the women were told to follow the sidewalk to what must have been an intake building. The door buzzed, and they were told to go inside. All four were placed in a large caged cell that reminded Sidney of a backyard fence except this fence went all the way to the ceiling. They were locked in there over an hour before the guards came for any of the new inmates. Each of them was called one at a time by alphabetical order. At last, she was called and led from the holding area. They led her to a small room, where her shackles were removed. "Place everything you're wearing in this bag," she was ordered by a female guard, who looked and acted like she had rather be anywhere but here. After she was undressed, she went through the same type of invasive searches as in the police station. "Get used to this, inmate, 'cause if you sneeze wrong, we search you."

Once she was dressed, Sidney was taken to another waiting and holding area. Another hour passed as the four new arrivals sat and waited. "All right, ladies, on your feet. Follow that yellow line and wait at the end for your name to be called."

After more waiting, her name was called, and she was taken to a station with a nurse who asked her several personal questions and performed a few routine medical procedures like taking her blood pressure. After that, she was put back in a holding area again. It must have been evening because a different set of guards arrived. "Okay, ladies, follow me."

The women did as ordered and arrived at a desk with a camera.

"You were supposed to have done this by now, but we'll do this now instead, I guess. When I call your name, come forward."

Again, Sidney waited her turn. She stood in front of the camera and was issued an identity card with her picture.

"This way."

She was led to a room with a shower and told to undress again.

"Here's your soap and shampoo. Scrub yourself down and dry off. You got five minutes."

When she was dressed, the officer led her through a long hall to another building. Just inside the door, she was issued bedding, toiletries, two pairs of extra socks, and undergarments and led to a cellblock. "Stop here." The guard opened the door and told her to step in. She hardly waited for her back foot to clear the door before she started to close it. "Lights out in two hours, ladies." And with that, she walked away.

Sidney looked at her cellmate, a young, red-haired woman who looked about her own age. She smiled slightly at the girl, who seemed to look at her with suspicion. "Um, hi, I'm Sidney."

"Do you fart a lot, Sidney?"

"What? "she responded, more than a little taken aback by the question.

"I asked if you fart a lot. So do you?"

"Um, not any more than anyone else, I guess. Why do you want to know that?"

"Because I've been here for six months with this forty-something woman who farted so loud at night it would wake me up. You know what's worse? She slept on the bottom bunk on her stomach, so guess who had to breathe that all night? So I've got to share this cell with you for the next seven years, and I would like to know if I got to deal with that again."

"Oh. Um, sorry."

"Look, newbie courtesy goes a long way around here. You got to do what you got to do on the toilet there, but a courtesy flush or two is not just appreciated. It's pretty much required."

"Okay, right. So do I—"

"Look, fix your bed up there, and step on the back of the bunk to climb up. Never step on someone's stuff and never sit on their bunk or pillow. If I say you can sit down here with me, you can. Otherwise, sit up there."

"Sure, okay."

"I'm Jillian. Jillian Porter. One of the guards told me to expect you and that you'd be here longer than me, so I wanted to get that out of the way." Jillian relaxed and calmed herself. "You got a lot to learn, but I'll help you. And no, I'm not trying to sleep with you. Frankly, after my last boyfriend, I think I'm swearing off sex forever."

Sidney made her bed and crawled into a ball. She felt a tear start to roll down her face and wiped it away. She tried not to sob, and when that didn't work, she tried to keep it quiet because she didn't want to make a bad impression on her cellmate. However, she must have cried louder than she thought. It didn't take Jillian long to stand up. "Okay, come down here." She climbed down and stood next to Jillian's bunk, trembling as she stood there. "Sit," she said, patting the mattress. Sidney sat down, nervously shaking. Jillian gently placed her arm around her, which caused Sidney to flinch. "It's okay, it's not like that. Let it all go if you need to." Sidney did not need any prompting. She cried as hard as she ever had since that night Lawson died. "Look, you're going to be okay here. It's not like in the movies. Mind your business and don't stare at people. Never give a guard or anyone else attitude. Always show respect. Oh, and don't criticize the food even though it sucks. Yeah, there's a lot of bad people here who will take advantage of you, but most of us just want to do our time and get out. Really, the first week or two is the worst. It's not that bad once you adjust."

"It's not?"

"Look, this isn't summer camp. Life is tough here. There's a lot of things to get used to, but I'll help you."

"Why would you do that? You don't know me?"

"First of all, I got to live with you. Second, you know they do psychological profiles on you, so they try to pair you with people you have characteristics in common with."

That brought a small smile to Sidney's face. "Look, I don't know why you're here, and it doesn't matter. We're cellmates, so let's take care of each other. We all need support after all."

"Yeah. Thanks. It's been a while since someone was nice to me. I just can't believe I'm here. I've never done anything wrong before, and I'm still here for twelve years for something I didn't even mean to do."

"Common story here. Just don't go around saying that to anyone 'cause they're liable to take that as a sign you think you're better than them, and that can lead to trouble. Believe me, you don't want trouble."

"No, I don't." She was finally calming down, and dried her eyes. "Thanks, Jillian. I hope I'm a good cellmate."

"Don't mention it. Try to get some sleep. They'll get us up at five thirty in the morning and do a roll call. It will be seven before we get breakfast. You should have showered, so we won't get to do that until tomorrow. Don't worry, when it's our turn, I'll go with you. It's weird being naked in front of a bunch of people you don't know, but you'll get used to it."

"Great. Good night, Jillian. I'll try not to fart," Sidney said, which brought a laugh from both of them.

CHAPTER 19

Even though her mattress was thin and hard in all the wrong places, it was probably the best Sidney had slept in a long time. The morning wake-up call happened at exactly 5:30 a.m. "You still alive up there?" came the weary voice of Jillian. "No matter how long I've done this, it still sucks," she complained.

"I'm alive," Sidney responded. "Believe it or not, I slept better than I have in a while."

"Don't get used to it. It can get pretty loud around here sometimes at night. Oh, and hey, you need to go ahead and comb your hair and go to the bathroom. They do a count of us, and we have to be standing where we're easily seen."

"I can wait if you want to use the toilet first."

"Courtesy, you're already catching on."

About half an hour later, a guard came by with a clipboard and made his mark and moved on. Jillian said, "Stick close when we go to breakfast and sit right in front of me if you can. Now whatever you do, don't criticize the food no matter what it's like. Also, don't whisper ever around here. Makes people think you're talking about them. Oh, and don't try to listen in or join in folks' conversations. If someone wants to talk to you, they'll say something directly to you. Got it?"

"I think so. Anything else?"

"Yes, about last night. Look, that was your freebie. You can't cry over everything here. It makes you look weak, and you already look scared to death, no offense."

"I am."

"Yeah, we all know that, but do your best not to show it. Believe me, people heard you last night, but it's your first night, so it's to be expected, but it stops now. You're going to have to learn to be tougher. I'll help you, but I can't be with you all the time, so you've got to learn some things on your own. Basically, if you think what you do might get your ass kicked, don't do it."

"I think I got it. Should I introduce myself when we sit down?"

"No, usually someone will ask me who you are, and that'll be your cue. You don't want to seem too anxious, but you don't want to come off like a snob either. Try to say just enough, and don't add any details about why you're here."

The two were allowed to go to the cafeteria about thirty minutes later. They made their way through the line and sat near the end of one of the tables. Sidney noticed that the inmates tended to sit in groups by their race and affiliations within their race, usually gang affiliation Jillian told her later. Breakfast consisted of a small bowl of cereal, juice, coffee, eggs, and a small biscuit. It reminded Sidney a lot of the lunches she had in school. It certainly wasn't the worst she'd ever eaten, but it was far from the best. She did her best to eat what was on her plate, but the thought of food was far from her mind.

"Okay, Sidney, listen," said Jillian. "After breakfast, you've got to go with me to my work assignment. Everyone here technically has a job, but there's too many here for everyone to do a job. Basically, we have to clean a section in our block all day. It won't take long, but we got to try and stretch it out best we can."

"What do we do once we finish?"

"Clean it again until they tell us we can stop."

"Sounds fun. Is that what I do from now on?"

"Well, maybe. Neither of us has been here long enough to build up any trust, so until then, we get the crap jobs. Oh, and the warden may want to talk with you at some point too if you have a college degree or a certain job skill they might need. You go to college?"

"Yes, I graduated a couple of years ago with a business degree."

"Well, maybe then you'll get lucky and get an office job here. Probably will be a while, so till then, we clean."

Prison life was very regimented, and every second of the day was scripted and planned exactly like the one before. After breakfast was back to the cellblock to bathe, brush their teeth, or take care of any hygiene needs. Once that was complete, they began their work detail, and true to form, they had cleaned their area in about an hour and a half, so they started over. Lunch was a bologna sandwich, a small cup of beans, a scoop of canned fruit, and an orange-flavored drink. The afternoon consisted of time in the cellblock, sitting around watching the communal television or reading and writing. At around four, they were allowed in the prison yard until evening meal at 6:00 p.m. That meal consisted of a piece of baked chicken, more beans and canned fruit, a flavored drink she thought was orange again, and a piece of vanilla cake. After the meal, they returned again to the cellblock for their evening routine, which was almost exactly like the afternoon routine.

Jillian had left Sidney several times so that she could interact with some of the other inmates. Most of the interactions were just small talk from women who ranged in age from eighteen to sixty and older. There was no real stereotype she could identify in them. Some were like the people most would assume would be in prison. Others did not look the part at all of someone who should be in prison, more or less like herself. Surprisingly, after the initial fear of Jillian walking away passed, she began to feel a little bit of confidence build in her. She was still scared, but she was starting to learn how to deal with it. About an hour before they had to return to their cells, Jillian came back. "Hey, you making out okay?" she asked.

"Yeah, so far. It's easier than I thought it would be, not that I think I'm just the life of the party or anything."

"Good," Jillian responded. "Come on, there's someone who's asked to see you. Her name is Jo, and she's pretty much the one who runs this block. There are three people you don't want to piss off. Kitchen personnel, commissary workers, and Jo."

The two walked a short distance to where Jo and a group of others were standing around. She was an African American with sharp facial features. She was in her late forties, and while she was in the same two-piece orange prison uniform, she looked slightly different than the others. She stood out, and Sidney could tell she demanded respect, and the others gave it to her. When she saw them, she said something, and the others disappeared. "You must be the new girl," Jo said in a matter-of-fact tone. "I like to meet all the new arrivals soon as I can. I'm Jo. Not ma'am, not sir, just Jo. What's your name?"

"I'm Sidney Lewis, good to—"

"Let me explain a few things to you, Sidney Lewis. I run things here. You got a problem with one of these girls you two can't solve, you come to me before you throw hands. Someone takes your shit, you come to me. We don't talk to guards here, and we don't snitch no matter what you see. Some bitch stabs someone, you didn't see shit. Got it?"

"Yes, ma… I mean, Jo."

"That's good. You do your part. You keep your nose clean, we'll get along fine. I run this block like family, and family takes care of its own. Cause trouble and you'll deal with me. Get it?"

"Yes, Jo."

"See, Jill, a fast learner. Do your part, and all this will eventually be over. Now come here." Jo embraced her, as if she was a child. "That means you're in the family now, and you'll stay in it as long as you don't betray it." With a slight nod, they knew the conversation was over, and so they walked back to where they were.

"Told you don't mess with her. She's got nothing to lose because she's here forever, and she's not kidding when she says she runs this place."

"Do the guards know that?"

"Know it? Hell, they encourage it. Less for them to do."

"Does she know everyone here?"

"Most of them. I'll explain more after lockdown, which is in a few minutes."

Five minutes before 9:00 p.m., a guard announced lockdown and to return to their cells. Sidney stepped in and sat on her bunk. She reflected on the day and realized that most of her time was spent waiting for something to happen, which nothing did. Most of her day was spent simply passing time. She wouldn't call it boredom, but more than likely, she would see it that way in the coming days. She and Jillian made small talk that night but nothing overly insightful. More or less, it was what they might have called girl talk in college. When the lights went out, she noticed how uncomfortable the mattress was. As she lay there, she thought, *One day down, only eleven years, eleven months, and twenty-nine days left.*

CHAPTER 20

The next morning started just the same as the previous one. With the exception of slightly different pieces of advice Jillian told her, everything happened almost exactly the same. The food was the same. The time spent in the cafeteria was the same. It was almost no different. In some ways, it reassured Sidney that life had finally gotten into something of a normal routine. Yet at the same time, the thought that this was going to be how life was for a very long time frightened her. She and Jillian sat in the same area as before and made small talk. They were joined by the same two inmates as yesterday. One—who was twenty-nine, with short brown hair, and slightly overweight—was named Rebekka Miller. The other—who was a short, red-haired thirty-two-year-old woman who wore dark-rimmed glasses—was named Sarah Billingsley. Sidney was friendly but avoided going too much into detail about herself and nothing about her case. Though she didn't ask how much time the other two had, she could tell that they were not going to be leaving anytime soon.

Once breakfast was complete, it was time to return to the cellblock. After the head count, they had a while before going to their workstation. "Okay, girl, it's our turn to hit the showers, so grab your stuff and let's go," Jillian said.

"Um, Jillian, do we have to right now? I mean, can't we wait until later when there aren't as many, you know, people looking?"

"Hey, trust me, you want these people to see you bathe today. It proves you aren't someone who's going to be nasty. Come on, I'm going too."

"Jillian, I've—"

"Come on, there had to be a dozen people who saw your keister when you were brought in. What are you afraid of? You got a third boob growing under the other two or something?"

"No, but I've only been searched by one or two guards and never in front of others."

"Oh, come, Sidney, it's not that bad, and no one wants to stare you down. Now grab your stuff and move your ass. We're on a schedule."

Jillian grabbed her by the wrist and started leading her to the shower area. The room was a complete bath area with sinks and toilets separated by a small cinderblock wall between them that offered a clear view of the person's face seated next to the user. The showers were located directly in front of the toilets, so those sitting there could easily see anyone in the shower. There was no privacy whatsoever. The bath area was designed for easy observation by any correctional officer that wanted to look in. Though males were supposed to announce their presence, some were better about that than others.

When they arrived, Jillian looked over at Sidney. "Okay, hang your clothes there, put your shower shoes on, and let's go." Jillian unhesitatingly started to undress. Sidney was much slower and reluctant but eventually managed to get undressed. It was then she noticed they were not alone in the shower. Two much older black women were already in there washing up. One looked up and saw Sidney's hesitation.

"Honey, you can come in here. We ain't gonna bite," the first one said. She must have been in her mid to late sixties.

"Yeah, you got nothing to worry about. Jo don't allow nobody fightin' in here. She wants everybody clean, and you can't get clean if people is fightin'," said the other lady, who also looked to be in her sixties.

"You see, Sidney? Now come on." And with that, Jillian grabbed her by the wrist again and led her inside. Once she was inside, Sidney began to relax a bit more. The water was not much above lukewarm, but it was good enough to get the job done. The soap-and-shampoo combination was supposed to have no scent to it, but somehow that made it smell worse. Again, it was just good enough to do the intended job but not much else. It seemed like the shower lasted forever, but the whole thing was done in about ten minutes.

After they dried off and put their uniforms back on, they made their way back to their cell to get ready for work. "See, I told you it wasn't that bad," Jillian teased her.

Sidney gave her a disapproving look. "Okay, yeah, you did. It wasn't bad."

"You have to get used to doing things in front of people that you once did when the doors are shut. When I was at my former job, I would walk down two flights of stairs to a small bathroom down the hall to go number two. I thought I was being so smart until I came out one day and my boss was about to walk in. Now it don't bother me a bit. Matter of fact, some of the best conversations of the day are in the bathroom. That would have never happened on the outside."

Sidney laughed despite herself. "Jillian, I don't think I could do that. I mean, I'm not potty shy, but I don't know about carrying on a conversation while going."

"Give it a few weeks and you'll be surprised what you'll be doing. Come on, let's not be late."

The rest of the day followed the exact routine as before. The meals, the breaks, everything happened the same way as yesterday. By the time they returned for lockdown, Sidney was starting to feel the routine of the place begin to sink into her. By no means did she know all that she needed to, and by no means was she an expert, but she knew what the next day's schedule would bring. She stretched out on her bunk and tried to get to sleep. It was a lot to take in for such a short amount of time, and she hoped she was doing okay. Nobody gave her a prison report card to tell her how she was doing. As she closed her eyes, the thought ran through her mind, *Eleven years, eleven months, and twenty-eight days to go.*

CHAPTER 21

A week passed, and the routine of the place stayed exactly the same save for a few changes on the weekend. Prisoners were allowed to attend worship services on Sunday at designated times. Sidney and Jillian attended the same generic Protestant service since there was not one specifically for Baptists like Sidney or a Methodist like Jillian. The chaplain was a retired minister named Nathan Gossett. He was not employed full time at the prison and apparently did not receive any money for his services. His messages were not very exciting, but Sidney could tell he truly believed what he was saying. After that, Sunday was pretty boring, mostly sitting around watching the few approved TV shows or playing checkers and cards or just talking until lockdown that night. On Monday after the usual routine, she and Jillian were cleaning their area when a guard approached. "Lewis, seventy-four," he called out her last name and last two numbers of her prison number. "Lewis, seventy-four, get over here!" he yelled again.

She walked over to where he was standing, "Yes, sir."

He more or less looked through her. "Come with me."

They walked completely out of her building and down a side-walk. "Where are we going?" she asked.

"Did I tell you to say something, inmate?" he responded. So they walked in silence the rest of the way to the administrative building.

When they arrived at the door, the guard buzzed them in. There were a few desks in the room and several offices. She saw a couple of inmates working around the desks and taking files and what she assumed were records of some sort. Clearly, they were office workers. They walked to the end of a hall with several chairs near a closed door. "Sit there and no talking," the guard told her. She waited about an hour before the door opened.

"Lewis?" asked the woman who'd opened the door.

"Yes, ma'am, that's me."

The middle-aged woman with her hair in a bun on the back of her head regarded her briefly. She was not in a uniform, so she must have been someone who worked here by choice. "Come in, please, and have a seat. The warden will be with you in a few minutes."

She did as she was told and took a seat near the door. In the room was a small metal desk and several filing cabinets. The secretary had no pictures of family or anything else. It was as bland and dull as the cellblock with the exception of the much more comfortable chairs. Again, more "Hurry up" and "Wait" as another hour passed. When the door to the warden's office opened, a man in a suit came out still finishing whatever thought he made as the two men left the office. He gave a slight smile, apparently satisfied he'd made his point, and walked out the door. Warden Beck looked more like a high school principal than someone in charge of some of society's most dangerous women. "You must be Ms. Lewis," he said in a surprisingly warm voice.

"Yes, sir, Sidney Lewis, number—"

He stopped her. "That won't be necessary here, Ms. Lewis. Please come in."

She did as she was told and stepped into his office. There again were no distinguishing decorations or pictures, but the office was much nicer than anywhere else.

"Please sit down."

Sidney sat and felt out of place in his office.

"I apologize for not sending for you sooner. Generally, I try to meet with as many of the new arrivals as I can. Most of the time I meet with them as a group, but sometimes I do meet individually, especially those who have certain skills and education I think may be useful. I see here that you are a college graduate, is that correct?"

"Yes, sir, I graduated two years ago from James Morgan."

"Yep, the Patriots. I went to Southwestern California. We beat you guys three years in a row while I was there. You go to any of the home games?"

"Yes, sir, most of them. I missed one my sophomore year because I had the flu. I especially liked the night games."

"I bet. Best time to have a football game is at night especially early in the season when it's still summer." He seemed to be doing his best to put her at ease. Sidney told herself not to get used to this but to enjoy it while it lasted. "Are you getting along with your cellmate? What's her name? Um…"

"Jillian Porter, sir. Yes, she's great. She's helped me a lot."

He began, "Well, good. Showing you the ropes I hope. Just don't let your guard down. There's a lot of dangerous people you share a cellblock with, but stay out of people's business, and you'll be fine. So guess you're wondering why I called you here. Well, the truth is, I have a job offer for you. After looking at your record, I think you'll fit nicely. Our librarian is getting out in a couple of months, and we need to replace her. Don't get too excited. You're not going to be the head librarian, but do a good job and maybe one day. Interested?"

"Yes, sir, thank you."

"Well, not like I was going to give you much of a choice, but thought I would at least be polite and ask. You start soon as you walk out the door. I may also need more office workers here in a few weeks. Is this Jillian person someone who can fill one of those jobs?"

"Yes, sir, I think she would do fine."

"Good, I may call her in here later, then. By the way, your job pays $25 a month. You can use it at the commissary or save it, whatever."

"Yes, sir, that's very generous. Thank you."

"Hardly, but there it is. I'll have the guard escort you to the library, but before that, Mrs. Morris outside will have you fill out some paperwork. Got to be official and all."

"Yes, sir."

"Oh yes, before you go, I forgot that I have something for you. Another reason I called you here." He handed her a small envelope about the size of a greeting card.

When she opened it, her heart nearly stopped. Inside was a small card with a golden script letter *P* on the front of the card. Inside it, she read the unmistakable message: "Hello, Sidney, I hope you are doing well in your new life. Remember our little deal. Do your time, keep your mouth shut, and all of this will one day be a memory. Leonard Pierson."

"Just so you know, I have no affiliation with Mr. Pierson, and I have not read the card. Whatever he wants with you is yours to know alone. Have a good remainder of your day." With that, he opened the door, and Sidney left to take care of her paperwork. As soon as she stepped out of the office area, the man in the suit that Sidney had seen when she first arrived stepped back into the office. "You heard all of that, I take it?" Warden Beck asked him.

"Of course, Mr. Pierson will be pleased. You do understand that he will be very unhappy if any harm comes to her while she's here."

"Why is he so obsessed with her? She killed his son. Why didn't he just kill her?"

"Mr. Pierson's reasons are none of your concern, Warden. Needless to say, what is your concern is to make sure his wishes are carried out." The man in the suit turned to go and then slowly turned back to the warden. "By the way, Mr. Pierson suggests that you stay out of the casinos for a while. If you run up any more debts, those nasty people who he paid off might just find a reason to visit you again." With that, he left and shut the door behind him. The man walked out of the gate and made his way to his car. He started it, but before he left, he called his boss. "Mr. Pierson, your message has been delivered, as ordered."

"Did you make my intentions toward the girl clear?"

"Yes, Mr. Pierson, the warden will do as told."

"Good. Call me when you get back. I may have another errand for you."

"Yes, sir. May I ask, the warden is right. Why not just kill the girl and be done with her?"

"I never had any intention of killing her. A king does not waste his move killing a pawn. She also tried to help my son grow up, so that has to be worth something. She stays where she is, and that's all."

"As you wish, Mr. Pierson."

"Oh, and, Goldman?"

"Yes, sir."

"That had better be the last time you question my decision in this matter." Pierson hung up the phone. Bernie Goldman was right. It would be so much easier to kill her and be done with it. Even behind bars, that would be easy to do, but even without the evidence that Luke Brady had against him, he couldn't bring himself to do it. Why he didn't really know. Maybe it was pity for her or maybe a small measure of gratitude for what she tried to do for Lawson even if she did kill him. But he knew even that was not true.

When the coroner's report came in, what Pierson found surprised him. The blow to the back of his head would not have been fatal. It cut his head deeply and would have required stitches, but nothing more. In short, had he not pushed her into the rail near the scuba tanks and not been heavily intoxicated, he would not have fallen and hit the side of his head, which was what actually killed him. Pierson knew that at worst, Sidney Lewis should have been charged with manslaughter and might have a case for self-defense in the eyes of some jurors. Of course, the scandal that would have been created would have brought far too much attention and simply could not be allowed. Sympathy for the innocent could only go so far.

So he bullied her into her plea bargain agreement. Easily enough, it was done. Cooper, it turned out, was far easier than Sidney. That man had no character and even less backbone. He knew obsessing about a twenty-four-year-old girl was not like him, but something about this even seemed wrong to him. Still, she had to pay a price for killing Lawson, accident or not. Just as well to let the state do it. Even so, a small part of him actually wanted to make that price as painless as possible for her. A small courtesy or an old man having a soft spot for a pretty young woman who by all rights should have been his daughter-in-law, he couldn't say. Lawson's death did solve a major problem in putting Jonathan in charge of his company. Whether it was sympathy, blackmail, revenge, or something else, one thing was clear. Sidney Lewis wasn't going anywhere.

CHAPTER 22

Shelia Lee—the name was Americanized by her grandfather after they moved to California from South Korea after the war—could always tell when a big story didn't make sense. By all rights, the story of an heir to a shipping fortune getting killed by his fiancée should be bigger news than this. Not to mention the fact that the case moved so fast through the courts that there was no way justice could have been served. Shelia had covered crime stories for nearly six years, and in that time, she'd never known a defendant to take a plea that fast or a prosecutor to offer one that quickly either. Even if she confessed, which according to the official report she did, what kind of investigation could have taken place? All the other stations might have moved on, but something didn't feel right. There must have been a bigger story. Her curiosity only deepened when the autopsy report was slow in being released. She knew that coroners took their time, but in this case, it should have been much faster. All she knew was that Sidney Lewis, by all accounts someone who wouldn't hurt a cockroach, killed her fiancé in a heat of rage. Still, her reporter instincts said there was something more to the story, something they weren't telling.

Shelia tried calling Luke Brady's office, but he did not return her call. She then tried the DA's office, but again, nothing. All Leonard Pierson's statement said was that they were satisfied that justice had been done and were still mourning their son. Even her police contacts told her nothing. She was certain that somewhere, there was a cover-up of some kind, but why? This case should have gone to trial next year at the earliest, but this young woman had taken a plea and swept away to prison in a matter of weeks. True, some cases were open and shut but not this open and shut. Thinking back, she remembered that a reporter at another news station started doing a report on the Pierson Shipping Company, but he was forced to give up on it. Months later, he left the station for a job in Oklahoma. It was not unusual for reporters to have stories that go nowhere, but this was different. Supposedly he had good leads. His information about things going on with the Piersons ranged anywhere from drug running, human trafficking, to a possible terrorist link. None of that could be proven, of course, but she'd heard the stories. Most just thought it was an example of a journalist out to bring down someone who was rich and powerful, but Shelia began to suspect there was more to the Pierson name than just a wealthy man who supported charities and other good causes, and she knew just the man to ask.

"For the Tiger Sharks in the third, no runs, no hits, two left on. At the end of three, it's the Coyotes two, Tiger Sharks one," said the field announcer. Roger Taylor continued to fill in his scorecard, marking the third inning results.

"So you still keep a scorecard, Taylor? Can't you just sit back and enjoy the game?"

"It helps me relax and pay attention. Surprised you remembered I did this," Taylor replied. "We were together long enough. You should remember."

Shelia smiled. "How've you been, Roger? It's been a while."

"We're not together anymore. It should be a while."

"Now don't be like that. We had something good."

"Yeah, you could get your crime stories for free instead of paying for them like you do now."

"You know it wasn't like that. Come on, we were good together."

"I thought so. Wasn't enough though, was it?"

"That's not fair, Roger. I just… I just had to make tough choices careerwise. It was never a matter of love."

"Guess love's not all you need, huh?"

She really didn't want this argument again mostly because he was right. It was a hard decision, but she chose her career over Roger. She couldn't deny that. Her big break came with a studio in Sacramento as a junior reporter. Roger had just made detective and couldn't move with her. They tried to make it work, but within a year, it was over. Now she was the crime reporter in Santa Monica and had moved back closer to Warrenton. Roger resisted giving her inside information on cases at first, but he usually couldn't say no to her. His information and connections gave her leads into many of the stories she had worked on over the years.

"So what do you need now, Shelia?" he asked her before taking a sip from his overpriced beer.

"Tell me about Sidney Lewis."

Hard as he tried, he couldn't stop himself from nearly choking. "What the hell?" he said as beer trickled down his chin.

"I could ask you the same thing."

"Where's this coming from? She confessed, and she's locked up. End of story."

"That's bullshit, and you know it," said Shelia more forcefully than she intended. "All this wrapped up so quickly. No way."

"Shelia, it's over."

"Over? Are you covering something up, Roger? I can't believe you of all people would do that. Not the Roger I know."

"It's not that simple, Shelia. Now let it go."

"Roger, did that girl really kill Lawson Pierson or not?"

"Yes, damn it, she did. She confessed the whole thing. Pierson wanted to keep this out of the news to avoid a scandal so his family could mourn his boy. She got a good deal, so just drop it."

Shelia could tell he was holding something back. She also knew he probably wouldn't tell her anything more here. "Yeah, a good deal. Twelve years for killing the heir of a shipping empire. Sure, keep telling yourself that." She got up and started back up the stadium steps. "Enjoy the game, Roger."

"I'll do that. Have fun in Sacramento."

Shelia climbed the steps to the tunnel and walked out of the stadium. When she got to her car, a smile crossed her face. It would be after 11:00 p.m. before she would know for sure, but she knew the truth was there. Shelia also knew that Roger just told her far more than most of the people sitting around them knew. "Have fun in Sacramento" was what he told her when she moved several years ago. Now the phrase had a whole different meaning. She drove back to the studio and submitted her report for the evening news. Once she finished recording her piece, she drove to a small bar in Warrenton called O'Brien's. It was a nice place and popular among the locals, and by 11:00 p.m., it was just crowded enough to not attract attention. She made her way inside and soon found who she was looking for, already waiting for her. "I thought I would have to wait longer than this. Must be really good."

"Don't flatter yourself. The game was a blowout. Vasquez gave up six runs in the fifth, and we couldn't touch Gordon's fastball. It's good to see you again, Shelia."

"Same here, Roger. Now what have you got for me?"

"Look, you can't take this to air yet, Shelia. You got to promise me that. This girl's life may be in danger."

"Roger, I promise, but I have to know why."

"Look, Sidney Lewis really did kill Lawson Pierson, that's true. Like you said, there's more to it than that." He looked around, but as far as he could tell, no one was listening in on them. "Apparently there's a flash drive floating around somewhere showing Lawson's hidden sex tapes of them and other girls he met on his business travels. She confronted him, they argued, and she hit him on the head with a scuba tank."

"So it's a jilted lover thing? Why all the secrecy?"

"That's the thing. There's no flash drive."

"So she's lying?"

"No, I don't think so. I think the sex videos are the least of Pierson's worries. He's secretly been investigated several times, but nothing can ever stick, but I think Lawson got careless. I think there's evidence on that flash drive Leonard Pierson doesn't want people to see."

"What makes you think that?"

"Like you said, it's all too simple. Cooper's been in Pierson's pocket for a while now. So if Pierson said move on this, that's what happens. This whole thing has Pierson all over it, and that girl got herself right in the middle of it."

"So what do you think happened?"

"I don't know. When I got to the boat, Lawson's body reeked of alcohol, and there was an empty bottle of scotch on the deck. My guess is, they argued, and he might have shoved her or something toward the boat rail near where the tanks were stored. Then she hit him in the head and killed him."

"How many times did she hit him?"

"Once. Funny thing is, from what I could see, there were two wounds. One on the back of his head. The second on the side of his head. My guess is that he fell and hit his head on the corner of the deck chair."

"My god, how hard did she hit him?"

"That's the thing. The official autopsy report doesn't mention the second wound, and while I can't swear it, that first wound didn't look severe enough to kill him. Scuba tanks may not be overwhelmingly heavy, but someone her size would still have a hard time to swing and kill him in just one swing."

"What did she do after that?"

"Went to her room, took a shower. She let several minutes pass before calling for help. Put on her wet suit and tried to pretend nothing was wrong. Not very smart, kinda think she panicked. She was an emotional wreck the whole time. Sullivan didn't even ask her any questions about the crime before she confessed."

"She confessed on the boat?" Shelia said in a surprised voice.

"Yeah, she did. Said she wasn't raised to lie. She was a scared kid really. I don't usually feel bad for criminals, but for some reason, this one's got me stirred up."

"Roger, do you really think she should have been charged with murder?" she asked him.

"Honestly, no. Manslaughter, yes, but murder, no. When I heard she agreed to a twelve-year term, it bothered me. Why would Brady go along with it if he really thought he could win on a lesser charge? Literally with the extenuating circumstances surrounding this case, I thought she could be out of jail in less than two years. In fact, she told me he tried to push her over the boat rails. She might have won on a self-defense case."

"But the Pierson name is involved," Shelia interjected.

"Right. And where is this flash drive? It's nowhere to be found, and now that she's pleaded to murder, no one is interested in finding it." Roger sat back and took a long sip of his beer.

"And Pierson goes on doing what he does." Shelia heard rumors for years about secret cargos on board Pierson's trucks, but no one could point anything at Leonard Pierson himself.

"Yep. You ask me, Brady struck a deal to keep her alive even if it means she rots in prison."

"So what do I do with this? You can't expect me to sit on this forever."

"Shelia, that's exactly what you should do. I'll keep looking into this, quietly looking into it. Maybe there's some way to help this girl I don't know. Look, she's not innocent, and maybe she belongs in jail. I don't know yet, but something just doesn't sit right, like there's something more I can't see. Just don't push too hard on this one, okay?"

"Fine. I won't push, but keep me in the loop. I got a feeling when the truth comes out, this is going to be big."

CHAPTER 23

Sidney's first day of library duty was more tiring than one would think about a library. She spent most of the day looking for books or returning them to the shelves. When she wasn't doing that, she swept the floor and emptied the trash. Very little of her time was behind the counter. The head prisoner in the library was a Hispanic woman named Rosa. She was a short-timer with only a couple of months left on her sentence. Another inmate named Jeanette Flowers was picked to take her place once Rosa was released. That meant Sidney was supposed to be Jeanette's replacement. Until then, she did anything the other two told her to do. That night after dinner, she sat around one of the tables playing checkers with Billie West, who was in the middle of a three-year sentence for a DUI that injured a pedestrian. Billie was an interesting person with a talent for art. She had a number of tattoos on her arms and one that she said Sidney might see if they were in the shower at the same time. Billie asked Sidney if she had any tattoos, to which she replied that she did not and that they weren't really her thing.

"How the hell did you get that card again?" came a shout from a table across from Billie and Sidney.

"You tell me. You dealt them," came the response.

"Nah, tell me where you got them hid," replied a slender black woman, whom Sidney didn't know.

"I ain't hid no cards, bitch," shouted another black woman who up until then had been playing cards but now stood up ready to answer the challenge to come, and it didn't take long. Suddenly the smaller woman crossed over and landed a punch on the other's left cheek. The fight was on.

Inmates got out of the way as fast as they could. While some of the younger inmates cheered them on, most of the others got out of the way as best as they could. The guards would be responding in a matter of minutes if not seconds. Until then, fists began flying, and it looked as if the smaller girl was getting the better of it. However, things took a turn when the larger inmate managed to strike the other's nose, knocking her back. That was about the time the guards rushed in. They ordered everyone to lie down on their stomachs. It took some doing, but they finally got the two subdued, cuffed, and hauled out. Everyone else was ordered into lockdown.

Jillian walked into their cell, clearly agitated. "Going to miss my show tonight because of this," she said.

"What was that about?" Sidney asked her. "They not like each other or something?"

"Probably nothing. They were gambling for soup packets. That skinny girl's a sore loser and a hothead. Those packets are $2 a pack, so probably nothing more than that. So how was your first day in the library?"

"It was good. I was surprised how many books are actually in there. It's a small place, but there's more than there appears. Jeanette told me Rosa was a lawyer at one time."

"Yeah, that's what I heard. Supposedly she got caught smuggling drugs into jail for one of her clients. Don't know if it's true, but that's what I heard."

"Hard to picture her as a lawyer."

"We all did something before we got here, just like we did something to get us here. You think you're going to like it?"

"Yeah, I think so, not like I got a lot of choices."

"Nope. By the way, I appreciate you putting in a good word for me. I start in the office next week. That's unheard of for someone who's been here for such a short time. What did you say to them?"

"He asked me if we were getting along and if I thought you would do a good job. Of course, I told him you would as long as he didn't mind giving you lots of smoke breaks."

"Whatever, girl, I don't smoke or vape." Jillian sat down on her bunk and motioned for Sidney to join her. She took a spot near the foot of the bunk and relaxed. "Seriously, Sidney, it's good to see you smiling." It surprised Jillian to say that. When Sidney first walked in, Jillian tried to keep her distance and not get too personally involved. There was just something about the new girl, though, that changed her mind. It wasn't really sympathy, but perhaps something like it. Maybe it was because she seemed so out of place here. Whatever it was, she was glad she ignored her first instinct.

"Thanks, I owe you. I don't know how I would have made it otherwise."

"You'd found a way. Just not as easily if I hadn't been here," Jillian said with a sly smile.

It was true. Sidney had been locked up for just over a month now, and she could sense a change in herself. She felt more confident, more certain about herself. It's not that she liked being in prison, but it was forcing her to grow up more, to be less trusting maybe, but also to be tougher than before. Sidney never wanted to be the toughest on the block, but she believed she was starting to find her place. Life was hard here. Doing the same thing day in and day out was tough mentally. It was hard to keep her mind focused at times because there was mostly a lot of time passing separated from her parents, practically the only ones on the outside who had not turned their backs on her. There was no doubt her days were going to be hard. It's not fun there at all. Slowly, though, she was learning to make the best of it. Sure, life was better on the outside, but she couldn't be there now and more than likely not for over a decade. Still, she was going to make the best of it. If nothing else, she was safe from Leonard Pierson, and that was worth something.

CHAPTER 24

Visitation day finally came for Sidney. Her parents were allowed to visit only twice a month, and due to the distance between them, this was the first time they were able to visit. Before she was brought into the visitation room, the guard reminded her that she was allowed to hug them when she first saw them and then right before they left. The duration of the visit was to be kept at two hours, and once that was over, she had to return. Sidney told the guard she understood, and he let her into the room. Her father, Todd, and mother, Sophia, were waiting for her at a table in the middle of the room. They were warned beforehand that they were not to move around the room, but the sight of her daughter was almost more than Sophia could stand. They both rose to their feet but resisted the urge to run to her. Sophia did her best to be strong as she embraced her daughter. After embracing her father, the group took their seats at the assigned table.

"How are you holding up?" he asked her, not really knowing what to say to break the ice.

"It's hard, but I'm adjusting. I miss you all. Is everything all right at home?"

"Oh yes, we cleaned out your apartment and have your things in a new storage building we had built behind the house."

"Dad, you shouldn't have done that."

"Nonsense, dear, they're your things, and you're going to need them when you get out," her mother joined in the conversation. "How are they treating you? Are you eating okay? You look like you've lost weight."

"Mom, I'm okay. Really."

"Sweetheart, you can't be happy here. This place is dangerous, and I can only imagine what it's like in there."

"Mom, really, I'm okay. It's not like I have a choice here. Look, I'm going to be here for a long time, and I have to try and make the best of it. I got a job in the library, and my cellmate and I get along great."

"You're not sleeping with her, are you?" her mother asked, whispering the word *sleeping*.

"Mom, not like that, no. Neither of us has any interest in that."

Her father cut in, "We pray for you every day, Sidney. We pray for your safety and that you will get to come home sooner than that judge said."

"Dad, I don't think that's going to happen."

"Well, I talked to Luke, and he thinks that you have a good chance at an appeal," he replied, almost sounding like he was holding on to some faraway hope.

"Of course, he's going to tell you that, Dad, but the judge gave me a minimum of twelve years." Sidney knew they meant well, and maybe they were being too optimistic, but they had to hold on to something. She didn't have any brothers or sisters, so it was hard for them to accept their only child was locked up for so long. It was hard for her too. Being kept away from her family was one of the worst parts of this whole experience. The routine, the orders to go here and there, and the lack of privacy she was getting used to, but the separation was something almost impossible to overcome.

"Just so you know, Sidney, we are going to give Luke a power of attorney over our estate in the event we pass on before you're released," her dad said after an uncomfortable silence.

"Dad, don't say that."

"No, it's a good idea. Luke and I have been friends since we were in college. I trust him, and it's only in case your mom and I are both gone before you get out. Honestly, you can't do anything with the estate until you get out anyway. He wrote into the contract that as soon as you are released, his power of attorney ends. There's no other family we can turn to, so what choice do we have?"

"Your father just wants to be careful. We're in our sixties. I want to live to a hundred, but you never know. We just want you to have something after your release, and this is the best way to do it."

"Okay. I trust Mr. Brady to handle that, but I don't like this talk about you dying and all."

"Sidney, it's a fact of life," her father said. "We never got a chance to go over all of this stuff with you before, so we just need you to know where our personal effects, investments, bank accounts, and all are located, just in case. He's done all the legal work for the business over the years, so it's just one more thing."

"Mom, Dad, I just want to say I'm sorry. I should have seen through Lawson sooner. I messed things up bad. As stupid as it sounds, I loved him. I'm just sorry I've put you both through this, just sorry for everything."

"Oh, baby girl, it's going to work out. I promise you it will. Even if it takes twenty years, we are going to get through this. Your father and I support you no matter what. We're here for you. That's what we Greek women do. We support our families no matter what. You stay strong."

"I will, Momma, I will."

"Oh, before we go, I brought your Bible. They said you could have it once they searched it. Imagine that, searching a Bible," Todd said sarcastically.

"Dad, people use all sorts of things to smuggle stuff in here."

"That's what they told me too. No respect for the Bible these days."

The time passed, and a guard announced that the time for their visit was nearly over. "We love you, sweet girl. Be careful and stay safe," Sophia told her as they rose to their feet and embraced.

"I will, Mom. I love you."

"We're praying for you. We still don't know why you didn't fight this harder, but we're praying every day that the Lord will bring you home to us. I love you."

"Thanks, Dad. I love you and will call soon, okay?"

"Okay, sweetie. Tell your roommate we're praying for her too," he said as his voice cracked a little. Todd was a tough man, but seeing her in this place and leaving her pushed all that toughness to its limits. He embraced his daughter one last time and turned to go.

With that, the visit was over. As she started the walk back to the cellblock, she began to miss her parents. Her dad had two brothers growing up, but one died three years back. The other lived near Seattle. It was a small, close-knit family, and this must have been tearing them up as much if not more than it was her. It was amazing to her just how lonely she felt surrounded by dozens of people at any given time. After being admitted into the entrance to her building, the guard escorting her said she would have to be searched again. Two female officers took over for him and started the search process. Though she was past the embarrassment part, it frustrated her to no end because one of the officers continually told her to expose herself more or cough harder. Sidney thought it was excessive, but she complied as best as she could and finally got the approval of the officer. She got dressed and was finally admitted back into her block.

Later that afternoon, she got a couple hours of yard time. She spent most of her time in the yard walking with a couple of the ladies she met over the last several weeks. Jillian was there as well and warned her to not walk too close to inmates grouped together. She also warned her to stay as much as possible within her race. She explained that even if you were someone who was very tolerant of other races on the outside, it was important on the inside to hang around within your own race. Sad, though, it might be, but it was just the reality of prison life. After yard time ended, they spent the remainder of the day in the cellblock. Sidney watched television, while Jillian played cards with a couple of other inmates. When they returned to their cell for lockdown, Sidney asked Jillian how she made out that night. "Won three cookies, but that's all. How was your visit with your folks?"

"It was great to see them again, but in some ways, I wish they hadn't come. So tough saying goodbye. They are the only ones that will come and see me. Everyone besides them has pretty much turned their back on me."

"I know how you feel. My dad is coming next weekend. My mom sends a letter to him and encloses a photograph. She says she can't stand the sight of me in a prison uniform. I miss her, but I understand why she doesn't usually come."

"Sorry to hear that, Jillian."

"It's fine. She comes on holidays and all, so it's fine."

"My dad and I were always close. My mom and I used to fuss a lot when I was a teenager, but she's great, and we get along fine now. Gosh, I miss them. I miss my church, my apartment, my car." She stopped suddenly and felt a wave of embarrassment. "I'm sorry I'm complaining. Didn't mean to."

"Hey, it's okay in here. In front of the others, don't complain, but you live here. This cell is your home, just like it is mine. Out there, no, don't complain. Just be thankful we're in a two-person cell instead of being in a dorm room full of bunks."

"Oh, that would suck. You ever been in one like that?" Sidney asked.

"Yeah, the county jail I was in for the first three months was like that. It was small and overcrowded, and I half-expected it to be like that in here. I mean, it sucks in here, but it really sucked in county. What about you?"

"I was held in city jail for most of the time. The courthouse was just across the road from where I was held, so I spent most of the time by myself."

"What? How did you manage that?" Jillian asked, a little surprised.

"Sorry." She hesitated. "I can't discuss that. I took a plea is all I can say."

"Okay, I won't ask, but it sounds like things moved awful quick."

"You could say that. I start worrying every time I think about it, but my attorney said he's still working on my case, so who knows?" Sidney replied, sighing after she spoke.

"You're all right, Sidney. Honestly, I hate the reason why, but I'm glad we've met. I know I act tough, but it's good to have a friend."

"Same here, Jillian. I would have been lost without you. Oh gosh, let's get some sleep before I cry again."

"Yeah, me too. Good night, Sidney."

"Good night, Jillian."

With that, the day ended, and with the morning, the routine repeated itself.

CHAPTER 25

It was late as Shelia began to go through the information available on the Lawson Pierson murder. Everything was so cut and dry—a rich heir to a fortune, a jilted lover who snapped, a quick confession, and a swift move to put the killer away. If this were a TV show, it would be a great episode, but something wasn't sitting right with her. Was rejection enough to cause a young woman who had no history of violence to snap? Somehow she didn't think so. This whole thing with the missing flash drive bothered her. How could such a valuable piece of evidence not be used in her defense? Worse yet, why had so few heard of its existence in the first place? The police should have made every effort and more to locate such an important piece of evidence. It was almost as if almost everyone dismissed it as a story cooked up by a desperate defense.

She decided to start by doing a little homework on Lawson Pierson. On the surface, he seemed like the picture the prosecution painted him to be, so she had to look a little deeper. If it was true that he was a womanizer, then that information would open up some new doors in pulling apart the facade he'd carefully built. That was easier said than done. Lawson was certainly wealthy, but it wasn't like he was a movie star. Sure, there were society pieces in the local news, but it's not like he was always making a scene. It was probably also a waste of time to try to track down any of the women he'd supposedly been with over the years. Then again, maybe one of his friends could provide information on that subject, but she would have to figure out a way to get close to one of them without arousing suspicion.

The next thing that bothered her was the differences in the official report and the story Roger told her about what he saw on the scene. If what he told her was true, and she had no reason to doubt that it was, then there was a major corruption problem in the Warrenton Police Department. It also meant that the district attorney's office collaborated with the Piersons in order to put Sidney away without the normal due process of law. Why would Sidney herself go along with that in the first place? Given that she did hit him on the head with a scuba tank, why were there two wounds when she said in the official report that she only hit him once? If she was telling the truth, which wound was the cause of death? Was it possible that she hit him once, and then the second could have been self-inflicted in his fall? Possible, yes, but that's not what the official cause of death was listed as. Officially, Sidney hit Lawson in the back of the head, killing him, but that just didn't make sense. For whatever reason, this young woman took a plea that had landed her in prison for at least twelve years.

What if there was a flash drive with exactly what she said there was recorded on it? That could change a lot for her. Okay, so maybe not murder but manslaughter. She would almost certainly get locked up but probably for far less time when one took into consideration the extenuating circumstances of the case like the mental stress and the intoxicated nature of Lawson that night. Then again, almost none of her side of the story made it into the official account. It's as if the prosecution was allowed to build whatever case it wanted to, and the defense was fine with signing off on it. End of story. Maybe then the place to start was with Luke Brady, the attorney, or maybe from the source herself. No, Brady would be able to shine more light on her case than she would. Some of his decisions were odd, to say the least. Why would he agree to a plea on a case that could make his career, especially one that in her estimation he had a chance to win? It was time for some answers, and Luke Brady might be the only one who could provide those answers.

The next morning after checking in with the studio, Shelia went to the office of Luke Brady. When she arrived, he was still meeting with a client, so she waited about a half hour for the meeting to end. A man in a suit came around the corner carrying a briefcase. He gave a nod to the secretary and walked out the door. Another ten minutes passed before Luke Brady came around the same corner. "Hello, I'm Luke Brady," he said as he offered his hand. "Please come on back."

His office was nothing like she pictured. She thought it would be a disorganized mess with files and books scattered throughout the office. However, it was immaculately clean when she saw it. Everything was in its proper place, and his desk had several files neatly arranged to one side, giving him plenty of workspace. "I bet this isn't what you were expecting, was it, Ms. Lee?" he asked.

"How did you know my name? I haven't introduced myself yet," she asked in reply.

"Oh, come on, Ms. Lee, I watch the news. I bet I even know why you're here." He shut the door and took his seat behind the desk. The look on his face was as good of a poker face as Shelia had ever seen. "You're here to ask me about Sidney's case, aren't you?"

"I guess it makes sense that you'd know," she said as she took the seat across from him. "Tell me, Mr. Brady, why didn't you make more of a defense?"

"You get right to the heart of the matter, don't you?" He leaned back in his chair and exhaled in what was a mixture of frustration and relief. "I can't go into a lot of detail, you know. We are filing an appeal and going through various legal maneuvers for my client."

"I'm sure you are, but how do you expect to appeal? She took a plea deal, and you can't usually appeal those."

"Usually, yes, but there are some legal measures you can take, and I'm sure you're not here to listen to a lot of legal terminologies."

"Then tell me this. Why would an attractive young woman with everything going for her kill her fiancé after a lover's spat? It's not like people don't argue from time to time. Why was this time different?"

"I can't discuss that with you. Like I said, we have a number of options that we are pursuing, and I don't want to jeopardize my client's chances by having this released in the media."

"Look, Mr. Brady, believe it or not, I would like to help if I can. I just want to know the truth."

"The truth is, Ms. Lee, my client is in a difficult spot. She made a terrible mistake, and she's paying for it. What the state and I have at issue with is how long she has to pay for it."

"Are you saying that she was forced into taking the plea deal?"

"I'm not saying that at all. What I am saying is that there are some things I believe may help my client out in the long run. My job is to look after the interests of my client and try to work the legal system in her favor."

"I understand that, but what is it you're looking for, or what do you have that you think is going to help?"

"As I said, I cannot go into that."

"Is it the missing flash drive?"

"What flash drive?" he asked.

There it is, she thought. That made him nervous. She could tell by the look on his face that he was covering something up. "The one that was mentioned in the interrogation but has mysteriously vanished and was never mentioned in court."

"How did you know about that?"

"I have my sources." Shelia decided to lay it all out on the table. "Honestly, according to my sources, this just feels like something that was forced upon her. She may not be completely innocent, but somehow I don't think this adds up to a murder charge. Something is missing here, and I'm trying to understand what it is, and I think you can help. I also think I can help you."

"I told you I can't let this get into the media. It could damage her chances and put her in great danger."

"Mr. Brady, I promise I won't publish any of this until it's appropriate to do so."

"Why? Why would you do that? It's your job to publish stories as a crime reporter."

"It's my job to get to the truth. I've done this job long enough to know when things don't add up, so if I can help get to the truth, that's what I want to do."

Brady thought for a moment. His resources were limited when it came to conducting investigations, and here was a well-known reporter offering her services. On the other hand, could she be trusted? If she went forward with what she found out, it could put Sidney in serious danger. And then there was Pierson. Without a doubt, he was looking for a way to recover the copy of the flash drive that he made. Sidney needed allies to be sure, but could he trust Shelia Lee?

Luke finally broke the silence. "So how about an exchange of information then? You tell me how you came to know the information about this case, and I'll tell you what I know."

Now it was Shelia's turn to consider her options. A reporter's sources were sacred, and if you ever disclose them, they more than likely were gone for good. Brady was asking for a sign of good faith. A small-town lawyer trying to find the resources to defend his client could certainly use the help. Also, this story, once it played out, could be the biggest of her career. She decided it might be worth the risk. "Roger Taylor. A couple of nights ago, I met him at a baseball game to discuss my suspicions about the case. We met later at a local bar, and he shared information on the case. He believes she's being railroaded but doesn't have the proof to keep investigating. As far as the DA and the police are concerned, this is a closed case. He can't officially investigate, but I can. That's why I'm here."

"Yes, but why? What do you get out of it?"

"I won't lie, it's a big story especially when it comes to the Piersons. Once this all shakes out, it will make for a hell of a news special, a book or TV movie type of stuff, but for starters, maybe it will help someone who needs it. So tell me, does she need it?"

Brady hesitated, then said, "Yeah, she needs it. Sidney isn't completely innocent, but I needed to protect her. We were backed into a corner by a powerful name and prosecutor who took his orders from that powerful man. Sidney took that plea on my advice and a promise to keep fighting."

"So tell me what you know. What happened that night?"

"I'll tell you, but I need some assurances that this won't be reported on before it's safe. I need to know that I can trust you."

It was now Shelia's turn to be defensive. "I'm not sure I can give you any assurances that will satisfy you," she began. "I could talk about journalistic integrity and all, and I doubt that would convince you at all. So I guess you have no reason to trust me other than my word." She gave a small laugh then continued, "I wouldn't trust me either, I guess."

Luke regarded her for a moment. He was now faced with a big decision. If he tipped his hand now, it could spell disaster for Sidney. However, if he didn't do something soon, the case would go nowhere. Could he trust the woman sitting in front of him or not? Was Roger Taylor also someone he could trust? A good cop on a corrupt force? Was that even possible? The weight of the decision hung heavily upon him. He took a deep breath and made his choice. "According to Sidney, Lawson Pierson had multiple videos of her and various other women having sex in his bedroom and on his business trips. To say the least, she was shocked by what she found. On the night he died, she went to confront him, but they were not alone like he promised her they would be. Though Sidney didn't drink that night, Lawson was intoxicated. When she confronted him, he confessed to the whole thing and tried to act like it was no big deal. She then said he rejected her and tried to walk away. When she reached for him, he pushed her against the boat rail. That's when she grabbed the scuba tank and hit him. According to her, he stumbled around for a while before falling and hitting his head again on a deck chair."

"So why didn't she call an ambulance for him?"

"She told me he was dead, and she panicked. Yes, she thought about trying to hide her involvement, but she couldn't bring herself to lie, so she confessed what she did. Sidney's not a master criminal. She admitted what she did. It was stupid, and she should have called for help immediately, but she didn't. That's why she's in the mess she is in."

"What happened next?"

"The DA charged her with murder in the second. He offered her a fifteen-year sentence if she would take the plea. I advised her to seriously consider it. That night, Leonard Pierson himself secretly visited her and told her to take a twelve-year deal and turn over the flash drive to him. In return, he would leave her alone."

"So what exactly are you trying to do? She took the deal. Just what are you hoping to happen?"

"Sidney is safe where she is right now, but if we could find a way to tie Pierson's influence to the case or find a way to bring him down, then we can let the truth be known about her case. If we can, maybe, just maybe, we can get her out of there much sooner." He exhaled a long, frustrated breath.

"Problem is, the coroner's report doesn't mention a second head wound," Shelia said.

"No, but it's in the original report. I was there when Taylor interviewed her, and it should still be in the record. I believe the coroner's report has been changed to reflect what the DA and Pierson wanted it to say."

"Roger said he can check in the records to see if the original is still there. Should be easy enough if it still exists at all. He's not really a stranger in that office after all. Roger also told me what he discovered at the site, and he verifies that he observed an injury to the side of Lawson's head," Shelia recounted.

Luke reflected on what she told him for a moment. He then responded, "There's also Pierson to contend with. He's hidden his involvement in a number of criminal enterprises very well. If we could tie him to any of them, it may give us the opportunity to bring him down and help Sidney in the process. As long as he is watching, it's too dangerous to try to free Sidney."

"There's one thing that I don't get," Shelia started. "Why didn't Pierson just have her killed? It would make things a lot easier for him."

Luke paused for a second. It's too soon for her to know that he made a copy of the drive. If she was playing him falsely, then at least he still would have his trump card. "I don't know. Maybe he doesn't want to risk it. A lot of things can go wrong when you kill someone. In the end, he's content to let her remain in prison. So let's do what we can to help her."

"Roger is behind you too. He told me he would keep looking into the case as quietly as possible. If there is something there, we'll find it."

With that, Shelia took her leave. Brady felt a tinge of regret for not telling her that he had a copy of the flash drive. There was little he could do with it without alerting Pierson he was trying to move on the information. That would put Sidney in great danger. However, if a third party were to be steered in the right direction, it might just be enough to keep her out of the way of Pierson's wrath. It was a risk to trust her and Detective Taylor. By all accounts, Taylor was a good cop, but trusting that any further investigation would go unnoticed was risky. So was trusting a reporter and a rogue, but what choice did he have? He needed allies, so did Sidney, whether she knew it or not. He just hoped he was doing the right thing.

CHAPTER 26

Months had passed, and Sidney continued to adjust to her new life. By no means was it either easy or desirable to be locked away from society. Sidney accepted that she deserved to be here. Life was regimented and pretty much the same one day after the next. Yet the routine could be deceiving. There was always the danger of violence at any time. There was also the possibility of random searches, shakedowns of her cell, lockdowns for various reasons, and any number of other factors that made life in prison so stressful, yet often boring at the same time. One could never fully relax even at night. She could never fully trust anyone either. Jillian had become a friend to her, but still, she felt like she couldn't fully trust her. It was normal in some ways not to trust anyone. Even unintentionally, Jillian might say the wrong thing to the wrong person, and that could lead to trouble. One could never fully confide in anyone in there. Constant vigilance was needed even around your closest friends on the inside. It's not that Sidney believed that Jillian would betray her, but it was best not to put that to the test.

Nearly a year had passed when one morning Sidney awoke early to use the toilet. No sooner had she finished and crawled back into bed when the lights came on. Soon, guards opened the cell doors to do a surprise shakedown. The inmates were required to exit their cells while half of the officers watched and the other half searched. When the guards came to her cell, Sidney couldn't help but feel a little violated to have her meager belongings rifled through.

"Hey, hook that one up," the male guard who was searching the cell said.

"Which one?" responded the guard standing next to Jillian and Sidney.

"The brown-haired one. Lewis."

"Me?" she asked surprised to hear her name called out.

One of the guards grabbed her and cuffed her behind her back before she could react. "Why are you doing this?" she asked.

"Quiet, inmate," was the only response she got.

"Hey, why are you doing that?" demanded Jillian.

"Shut your mouth, Porter, or you can join her."

The guard emerged from the cell with a plastic ziplock bag. Inside the bag was a small kitchen knife. "Yeah, found this near the brown-haired girl's bunk. Go take her to seg to cool her heels." Sidney protested that it was not hers, but neither guard seemed to care. "Wait a minute, that's not mine. I've never seen that before." Her pleas fell on deaf ears.

"Yeah, right. Let's go, inmate."

"It can't be hers. There's no way she'd be able to get a knife," pleaded Jillian.

"You trying to take possession of it, Porter? That what you want? Get your ass back in there and clean up the cell."

Sidney was taken to the segregation area. It didn't look too different from the cell she called home. However, she knew that here, you were locked down for twenty-three hours a day, and if you were ever brought here, it was unclear how long you would stay. She was shoved into the cell still cuffed and locked in. "Hey, aren't you going to take these off?" The guard ignored her and walked away. There she sat alone. It was far from quiet, but there was no one to talk to here. She knew there was at least one other person, but she couldn't see her, and there was no way to communicate. So she tried her best as she could to make herself comfortable.

Hours passed and no one came. Her arms and hands started hurting a long time back, but no one had been by to take off the cuffs. She waited trying to be patient, but it was getting difficult. At long last, someone finally came into the segregation area. "Excuse me," she said, "excuse me, can you please come here?"

The guard walked over, acting uninterested in her. "What do you want, inmate?"

"Sir, can you please take off these cuffs? They're hurting my arms."

"I'm not authorized to do that," he told her.

"Sir, please, what can I do? It's not like I can go anywhere."

"You haven't been searched yet, so I can't release you."

"Sir, please. I need to use the restroom. Please take them off."

"Sounds like a personal problem to me. Figure it out," he told her and walked away.

It was difficult, but she managed to get the task done. She felt angry over her situation. She had no idea where the knife came from. Could it have been Jillian's knife? Sidney couldn't believe that Jillian would do such a thing, but just because it was hard to imagine didn't mean it wasn't true. What would she do? Would she tell them it was Jillian's? The number one rule here was not to snitch, but this could land her in a lot of trouble.

The sound of footsteps broke off her thoughts. She recognized Officer Ferguson as he made his way to her cell and ordered the guard present to open the door. Gerald Ferguson was the supervisor of the guards in her block. He was a man in his fifties and had been at the prison for over ten years. He was no nonsense but did his job well. He was respected if not well liked by the inmates. "Turn around and let me take those off you. Why haven't you taken them off by now?" he asked the other guard.

"No one told me to. I thought someone was going to come and search her."

"Well, here, take these cuffs. Can you do that?" Ferguson undoubtedly had a long day already. "Lewis, where in the hell did you get this?" he said as he showed the knife still in the bag.

"Sir, I swear that's not mine. I don't know where it came from. You got to believe me."

"Doesn't matter what I believe. The knife was found near your bunk, and that makes it yours. So tell me, where did you get it?"

"I told you it's not mine. I've never seen it before and would never be in possession of something like that," she pleaded with him.

"Any particular reason you decided you needed a knife? You had any problems with another inmate?"

"No, I swear it's not mine," she said again, beginning to feel frustration building inside her.

"You know you're not making this easy on yourself. Just having this is enough to extend your sentence by ten months, and that's if it doesn't get used. God help you if you were holding it for someone, and they end up using it. You'd be charged as an accessory, and that could mean years added to your sentence."

"It's not mine. I keep telling you that. Why won't you believe me?" Sidney said, raising her voice.

"If it's not yours, is it your cellmate's? Were you holding it for her?"

"No, it's not mine or Jillian's. It can't be. She wouldn't."

"How do you know? This place is full of killers, child abusers, thieves, liars of every kind. You really think she wouldn't roll over on you? Better sit here and think about it. We're going to investigate, and you don't tell us where it came from as far, as we're concerned, it's all on you," he said as he turned to leave.

With that, he left her all alone. She took her meals in the cell that day and the morning breakfast. She didn't sleep much that night. There was strangeness of the solitude and the worry she had about being there longer for something she didn't do. If it really was Jillian, how could she have done that and let her take the fall? Even if Jillian was to blame, Sidney knew she would not blame her. She wouldn't snitch mostly because she didn't know who to snitch on. At some point in the day, a guard came to take her for an hour of outside time. She went through a door and into a small, enclosed area with a basketball. There was no hoop, just a basketball. Sidney spent the hour pacing back and forth bouncing the ball. She passed a thousand thoughts in her head as she paced. After the hour passed, it was back to her cell.

The next day was like the last one. Breakfast and lunch were served in her cell. Sometime after lunch, Warden Beck came in to see her. He was not in a good mood to say the least. "Well, you've had an exciting week. I thought you understood what was expected of you. I even gave you a preferred job, thinking maybe you could be trusted. This is how you show appreciation for what I've done for you?"

"Warden Beck, sir, I'm telling you that is not my knife. I don't know how it got there or who put it there, but it wasn't me or Jillian."

"You know I'd love to believe you. I really would, but it was found near your bunk. How do you explain that?"

"I can't. But I swear it's not mine. I would never keep a weapon. Why won't anyone believe me?"

"Because I'm the warden of nothing but innocent people. No one does anything. It's always someone else. That's why. We're still investigating. Until we're done, you're in here. I hope for your sake it isn't yours." He turned and left the segregation area.

Again, Sidney was on her own. She began to despair. Would she ever get out of this place? Why did she agree to take the plea? Lawson was dead because of her, but it was an accident. She never meant to kill him. She made a whole host of bad choices, and she would have to accept that and pay for it, but where did it all end? She slept restlessly again that night. Breakfast and lunch were in her cell again followed by her hour outside. After returning from outside, she was allowed to take a shower. It had been three days since coming into the seg unit. The loneliness of the place was starting to get to her. Sidney felt so isolated it hurt, not a physical pain but something deeper, as if she could almost feel every second tick by with no end in sight. She must have drifted off because when the guard called her name, it startled her. "Lewis, I said roll up your stuff and let's go. You're going back to your block."

"My block?"

"You got crap in your ears? Yeah, your block, unless you just like it here that much."

"No, okay. I don't have anything to take. No one ever brought me anything except food."

"Yeah, cry about it, won't you? Let's go."

"What about the knife?" she asked.

"Decided it wasn't yours. Didn't find your prints on it. Did find another inmate's prints though. Stockdale is her name."

"Stockdale? The skinny black girl?"

"Yeah, that's her. Confessed to the whole thing when we confronted her with her prints. Seems she was spooked by some guards and ditched it in your cell. Important thing is, you and Porter are in the clear."

"Where did she hide it in the cell?"

"Can't tell you that. Security reasons. Let's just say no one will use that spot again."

When Sidney returned to her block, Jillian met her and gave her a long embrace. "I'm so sorry, Sidney. So sorry, girl."

"I'm all right. I'm all right."

To her surprise, Jo walked up to them as well. "You back from your little trip?" she asked.

"Yes, I'm back."

"You say anything?"

"No, not a thing. I denied the whole thing, but I didn't blame anyone."

"You did good, kid. You all right?"

"Yeah, I'm fine. Stupid bitch tried to play me, that's all."

A hush fell over all those close enough to hear her. Jo stood there for a moment, taking in what Sidney had just said. She broke the silence with a great laugh. "Did y'all just hear that? We going to put some street smarts in this girl yet."

CHAPTER 27

Since her incarceration, Luke Brady met with Sidney at least once a quarter. Mostly, it was a short visit to update her on the status of her case and how things were going from a legal point of view. Sometimes he would bring news from her parents, and they often talked about her father and if anything was new around her hometown. There was a designated area that granted more privacy for an attorney and client to speak without other people listening on the conversation. When she arrived, Brady had already unpacked his briefcase and had a stack of papers in front of him. "Sidney, good to see you again," he said as she was escorted in. "How are you holding up?"

She smiled just a bit and took the seat directly across from him. "I'm managing things pretty well right now. How's my case coming?" When she agreed to take the plea deal, he explained that an appeal would be almost impossible but that he would continue to fight for her through other means. What that meant exactly, she couldn't say, but he must know what he's doing.

Brady shifted a bit in his seat and pulled off his glasses. "Not going to lie to you, not a lot has changed. I have a team of investigators trying to punch holes in the case against you so as to sink the prosecution's case. They covered their tracks well though. That being said, I think there's an angle we can explore that might yield some results, but it's going to be a long process. Probably means you're going to be here for a while."

"I expected that. I never meant to kill him. I just wanted him to hurt like I did." She thought that she had said that a thousand times. There was a feeling of frustration that she got every time she said it now. To her, it seemed no one cared. She was now just one of the many that society had written off. She tried not to think about that conversation with Leonard Pierson, but when he told her that there were worse monsters outside of the cages, she was starting to believe him.

"I know, and I'm doing everything I can to try and get you out of here as soon as possible. If nothing else, get your sentence reduced." He flipped through the papers from his briefcase, trying to find anything that might be useful. He didn't want to give her false hope about getting her released, but she needed to know that the investigation was still active. "Just remember to keep all the information about your case to yourself. Don't tell anyone about anything we discuss."

"Don't worry, I won't. That was one of the first lessons I learned here," she said in a detached voice.

"Look, I know it's not much. Things are moving forward, I promise. In the meantime, try to stay positive, keep yourself as busy as you can." He was giving her the normal useless advice, and he knew it. Sidney was stuck, and it was partially his fault. He was the one who said she should take the deal. His reasons might have been good, but they were far from perfect, and he couldn't help but fault himself. Under normal circumstances, maybe he could have gotten a better deal for her, but Pierson had Cooper in his pocket. Of course, no one told her to hit the bastard in the head. She had fault here too, and he had to keep that fact in perspective as well. He decided to change the subject. "Hey, your dad told me he and your mom were going on a cruise next month. Did he tell you?"

"He did," she responded. "Mom told me she would take a lot of beach pictures for me." She thought for a second. Brady meant well, and he had been a family friend for a long time. It wasn't fair to take her frustrations out on him, especially since it was her fault she was here, no matter what someone else did or didn't do. "The beach is the biggest thing I miss in here."

"You're going to get there again someday," he tried to assure her. He left that day wondering if he should have trusted Shelia and Detective Taylor with the information on the flash drive. He also kept another secret. It was true that he gave Pierson the flash drive, but the one he kept was not a copy but the original. Not only that, he didn't copy every file. There were things he knew about Leonard Pierson that few others did. Maybe the time was finally right.

CHAPTER 28

Police work could be an exciting time full of dramatic moments, armed officers swooping in and arresting the bad guys, searching vehicles, and finding large amounts of drugs and weapons and other contraband. The reality was that most police work was nothing like that at all. Sure, there were those heart-stopping moments, but a lot of investigations took place sitting at a desk. It's a lot of looking at pictures, going through files, and reading documents trying to find inconsistencies in what people said and what the evidence revealed. It looked so easy on television. The investigator looked in a file or two and quickly spotted what they were looking for to solve the case. In truth, investigations could take years. That's where Taylor was now. He became suspicious of the Pierson shipping business years ago when one of his trucks was found loaded with a large shipment of drugs. That in and of itself did not mean that the entire company was a front for shipping drugs, but it was the inconsistencies that he found in the driver's story. Like so many leads, though, ultimately the investigation went no further than the driver. Sure, drivers often took on illegal cargos without their bosses knowing. It's remarkably easy to slip in extra cargo or hide illegal substances in legal cargo. When one considered how many large trucks were on the highways at any given time, it's easy to just blend into traffic.

Maybe that's what attracted Taylor to continue to investigate Leonard Pierson, but after so many years of finding nothing, he was close to giving up. There was just enough there to keep him interested, but not enough to bring charges. It was frustrating. He knew something was there, but there were just no breaks in the case. Then came Lawson Pierson—handsome, charming, a young man who seemed to be in line to inherit a ready-made fortune. Lawson had just stayed under the radar of Taylor until he began to take a greater role in his father's business. The detective's impression of Lawson was that he was not as sharp as his father. He didn't seem the part of the untouchable crime boss. He was too high profile. He lived the life of the spoiled rich kid who refused to grow up, and he was sloppy. Taylor's few informants told him about how Leonard lectured him time and time again on why he needed to take business matters more seriously. For a while, he seemed to do just that.

Entered into the story Sidney Lewis, the ideal girlfriend for a guy like Lawson. She was young, pretty, and naive and didn't ask a lot of questions. Sidney wasn't stupid by any means, but she was completely taken in by Lawson. By all accounts, Leonard wanted his son to marry her so that he would settle down and slowly become the face of the company and eventually take it over from his father. It looked like again Leonard got what he wanted, but Lawson must have drifted back into his old ways of behavior. Then he literally pushed her too far. According to her statement, on the night he died, he was drunk and pushed her hard against the boat railing. She grabbed the scuba tank from the storage rack by her feet and hit him over the head. That much he knew. What he also knew was there was a second head wound on the side of his head. Sidney stated she only hit him once and that he staggered and then fell, hitting his head on a deck chair. If she had called an ambulance then, she probably wouldn't be in the mess she's in now, but she didn't. True enough, she confessed to the crime, but the investigation was essentially abandoned. In a matter of weeks, she was arrested, convicted, and locked away. The case was closed, and that was that except there's more to it.

The official death certificate mentioned nothing about the wound on the side of his head. The record of the investigation mentioned nothing about Lawson shoving her against the railing. There was also no mention of the missing flash drive full of sex videos of her and those other women. Basically, the reports were written in a way to make Sidney look as guilty as possible. Taylor had no problem locking people up if they were guilty no matter who they were. He'd made a career of doing exactly that, but this was something entirely different. Sidney was by no means completely innocent. She made some terrible decisions that night. However, Lawson did his fair share to bring about his fate as well, yet that was neatly erased from the record.

That was the part that got him the most. If the evidence obtained in the investigation was tampered with or manipulated, then that spoke to a bigger problem in the department. He suspected that there was a mole in the department and probably a lot of officers potentially on the Pierson payroll. It bothered him to no end that people he worked with day in and day out were actively working against him. To Taylor, there were few things worse than a corrupt cop. In such a small department, it hurt to think who it might be. No matter who it was, it was bound to be someone he knew, and that thought bothered him to no end.

So what's the play here? he thought. A big part of the investigation was interviewing witnesses and suspects. That was done, but with the exception of the notes he made, the interview video and transcripts were nowhere to be found. This was a cover-up if he ever saw one. He decided to first try to find the original death certificate. Luckily for him, he knew that the county coroner wasn't trustful of computers and kept a hard copy of all his records. Next, he would go interview Sidney. She might not know anything about the illegal activities of the Piersons, but she could shine some light on Lawson. Surely she knew the places he traveled and the people he knew. Lastly, he needed to talk with a friend of his in the FBI. If the Piersons were transporting contraband across state lines, then the feds were probably investigating as well.

That afternoon, he drove over to the medical examiner's office on the other side of town. When he arrived, he found Brian Meeks busy examining the body of a hit-and-run victim from last night. Meeks had started working for the county about the same time as Taylor became an investigator. They knew each other well and worked on a number of cases together over the years. Meeks was quirky, to say the least, but he was a good man who took great pride in his work. "Brian, is the county going to get any work out of you today, or you just going to stare at that corpse all day?" Taylor knew that would get a reaction out of him.

"You should show some respect for the deceased," he responded without looking up. "This poor fellow never saw it coming. Just crossing the street, minding his own business. You got my toxicology report on the driver?"

"Not my department," Taylor responded in a dismissive voice.

"Then who's riding the county's dime, me or you?" Meeks said again without looking up from his work.

"I don't work for the county, you know that. I'm riding the city's dime to be exact."

"Not surprising no matter who you're working for in my mind." Meeks finally looked up and began to take off his gloves. "Well, the cause of death is blunt-force trauma. The result of being hit by a car driven by an unconfirmed drunk driver."

"Again, not why I'm here, Brian." This back-and-forth between them was normal. Taylor respected Meeks, and over the years this back-and-forth came naturally for them. Today couldn't be an exception. "I need to look in your files for a death certificate. You mind?"

"It's all online. You know that. Why do you need to look into my files?" Meeks asked.

"You know how it is, Brian, computers are great and all, but sometimes you just need to see the original. You do still make hard copies, right?"

"Of course I do." He walked over to the sink and began washing his hands. "Problem with computers is, they are so unreliable. Tech is great until it doesn't work, then what? I like my files."

"No arguments here. Got the key?" Taylor asked.

"Yeah, in the usual place."

"Oh, so hanging in the lock? Real security-minded of you."

"Since when do you care about that? Don't make a mess with my files." Meeks took a clipboard in hand and began writing out his findings on the body.

While he did that, Taylor walked into Meeks's office, and sure enough, the key was hanging in the lock. There were three filing cabinets in the office all arranged in Meeks's unique organization system. The middle cabinet was usually where he stored the files over a year old, so that's where he started. It didn't take long for him to find the

Lawson Pierson file. Sure enough, there it was, the original death certificate, then conclusive proof that the cause of death was in fact changed, and Sidney's story began to ring true. He took his camera and snapped a quick photo of the certificate. He then began to take pictures of the entire file. "You know, if you wanted copies, all you had to do was ask," came Meeks's voice from behind him.

"Had to be sure I saw this with my own eyes first," Taylor said, feeling a little embarrassed for doubting his friend. "Strange things going on these days, and while I didn't think you were involved, I had to make sure."

"Make sure of what?"

"Have you seen the death certificate for Lawson Pierson since you filed it?" Taylor asked.

"Of course not, why would I? My job is to determine the cause of death and file the report. Testify in court if I have to," he said defensively.

"Do you remember how Lawson Pierson died?"

"Yeah, blow to the head as a result of a fall," Meeks responded.

"What about the blow to the back of the head? Was it a fatal injury?" Taylor asked.

"Not directly, no. From what I remember, the victim was intoxicated when he was first struck. Given his state, the blow from... what was it? A, um, scuba tank, right? Cut into his head and may have concussed him, but the skull was intact in that area."

"So what killed him?" Taylor asked.

"Well, he hit the side of his head on another object. That blow forced the skull inward and killed him. Why are you asking? You know all of that."

"Because the death certificate filed in the database doesn't say that," Taylor told him.

"That's not possible. I filed that report myself," Meeks said.

"Take a look for yourself, Brian."

Meeks logged on to the computer at his desk, and sure enough, he found the report on Lawson Pierson's death. "My god, you're right. This report has been changed." Meeks began to rock back and forth in his chair. He was meticulous in keeping his records in good order, so this revelation unnerved him. "Unacceptable," he said, "completely unacceptable."

"Brian, who could do something like this? Who has access to these files that could make these changes?"

"Myself, of course. Maybe someone on my staff, people with access at the police department, or even the DA's office."

"That's what I thought," Taylor said. He didn't want to believe that anyone in the department would purposely file a false report, but if it wasn't a cop, that only led to one conclusion. Someone at the district attorney's office changed the cause of death and was tampering with evidence. It began to make sense why the DA moved so quickly to get a conviction. This wasn't positive proof against the DA, but it did start to point fingers at wrongdoing somewhere along the line, and Taylor was pretty sure where that led. "Brian, I need copies of this file, and whatever you do, don't tell anyone we discussed this. Got it?"

"Yeah, I got it." He sat back in his chair. "Roger, you'll find who changed my records, won't you? Once I file it, that's the end of my part unless there's a trial. I just… I just…"

"I know, buddy. Hit-and-run victim. That's why I'm here, right?"

"Yeah. Hit-and-run victim. Got it."

With that, Taylor departed. He didn't want to say it in there, but he'd suspected for a while that somewhere along the line of people in the DA's office, someone was covering for Leonard Pierson. Too many dead ends, too many cold leads for him not to believe someone was covering for Pierson. Corruption in any system was almost inevitable, but it didn't make it any easier to accept. Now it was time to start putting some pressure on whoever was responsible.

CHAPTER 29

Shelia convinced her television station to allow her to do an investigative report in Seattle on a missing-person case. The case involved an elderly man who went missing six years ago, and she told her producers that she wanted to follow up on a new lead on the case. She half-expected that they would tell her no, but they agreed, and so off to Seattle she went. The real reason she wanted to go was to find one of the girls that Lawson had sex with on the missing flash drive. How she came by the name was a lot of subtle investigating, talking to some of Lawson's former friends at some of their hangouts. Most of them were not very helpful even with a few drinks in them. She was beginning to feel frustrated with her lack of results.

All that changed when she met James Vaughn. He was one of the people on the yacht the day Sidney was arrested. James was a college friend of Lawson and was a part of his inner circle. He also was a heavy drinker and tended to talk too much when he drank. Shelia tried to find him since the first days of her investigation, but he proved elusive. When she finally found him, he was already drunk, but she was able to cozy up to him, and soon he got to talking and began to give her names of some of the ladies he and Lawson had been with over the last couple of years. She used her resources to look up several of the names he gave her. Shelia decided to try some of the names James was most enthusiastic about. The name that stuck out the most was a woman from Seattle named Jamie Carter. James told her all about how and where Lawson met her. It was not much, but without the flash drive, it was all that she had. Shelia would be in Seattle for five days at the most, so she had to make the most of her time, and since there were multiple Jamie Carters in Seattle, she decided to spend her time in the places James mentioned. Her biggest break was that Lawson had sent him a picture of her at one of the local bars, so she would start with that.

It took three nights of waiting and fighting off half-drunken bar goers before her search paid off. Jamie walked into the bar in the company of two of her friends. Shelia decided to try and wait until she was without her friends if possible before making her move. It didn't take long before that happened, so Shelia made her approach. Shelia took an empty seat next to her target and ordered a drink. She made eye contact with Jamie, who didn't seem very interested, and gave her a nod. "What are you drinking tonight?" she asked her to try and strike up a conversation.

"Look, honey, you're not my type," Jamie responded indifferently.

"I'm not here to pick you up," she responded. "Just trying to be friendly."

"Yeah, well, I got friends, so if you'll excuse me," said Jamie as she started to get up and leave.

"You knew Lawson Pierson, didn't you?" Shelia asked her.

"What did you say?" Jamie responded, stopping herself as she was turning to go.

"I asked you if you knew Lawson Pierson. From your reaction, I take it that you did."

"Yeah, I knew him, all right? So what?"

Shelia knew she had the woman's interest now. "Just want to ask you a few questions about him, that's all."

"Look, I don't know anything about his death. We were together a few times when he came to Seattle, that's all," Jamie responded.

"Hey, I'm not here to judge. I just want to know some answers."

"Like what?"

"Like how did you two meet, for starters?" Shelia asked her.

"We met on a dating app. A hookup site really. He seemed nice, so we had some fun."

"How many times?" Shelia asked her.

"Three or four. He was a lot of fun, at least until I caught him videoing us. I mean, the nerve of him."

"Wait, you caught him videoing you?" Shelia asked her.

"Yeah, we were hot and heavy into a great make-out session when my phone rang. I thought I turned it off, but I got up to answer it, and that's when I saw he had set up a hidden camera in his hotel room. I was pissed off."

"And how did he react?" Shelia asked her.

"He tried to blow the whole thing off, but then he got mean about it. Told me there were dozens of girls like me. Then he—" Jamie stopped suddenly. "Look, I need to get home."

"Wait," Shelia said, grabbing Jamie by the arm. "What did he do?"

"I've said too much. I need to go," Jamie said as she grabbed her things and started for the door.

"Jamie, wait." Shelia followed her outside. Jamie was dialing her phone when Shelia caught up with her. "Jamie, you have to tell me. What did he do?"

"Why do you care? What does it matter to you?" Jamie said with fear in her eyes.

"Because if there are others like you that he used and mistreated, then that needs to be told. Even if he's dead, he shouldn't get away with that." Shelia looked her in the eyes and asked her, "Did he hurt you that night?"

Jamie's eyes filled up, and a tear ran down her face. "He slapped me. Then called me a stupid bitch and a whore. He said if I ever told anyone, he'd find me and hurt me."

"Jamie, he's gone now. He can't hurt you."

"What does it matter? What good could it do?"

"It matters to a young woman who has been hurt by him too. She's sitting in prison now because he hurt her too, and I'm trying to help her."

"I hope you do," Jamie said. "Okay, I'll tell you what I know." The two women went back inside, and Jamie recounted the story to Shelia again. After recording the information, Shelia thanked her and gave her a business card. Jamie also gave Shelia her phone number. She told Jamie not to tell anyone about their conversation but that she would be in touch again soon.

The next day, Shelia booked a flight back home. She now had proof that Lawson was recording his sexual exploits, but that was not enough to help Sidney. It also wasn't enough to tie any criminal activities to him or his father. This information was a start. It gave truth to one of Sidney's claims. There had to be more to find, and as soon as her plane landed, she would tell Roger what she found. Then it was on to the next task.

CHAPTER 30

As the weather began to turn cooler, a noticeable change began to take place. Last year, Sidney didn't really notice it because she was still overwhelmed by her change in circumstances. This year as October turned to November, she began to notice the inmates were on edge more than usual. There were a few more fights than normal, and people were a lot shorter with one another. Even Jillian was more withdrawn, speaking less, and going to sleep earlier than usual. The thing about holidays in prison was that everything remained the same. Inmates still performed their duties. The food stayed the same with the exception of turkey loaf, corn bread, and pumpkin pie on Thanksgiving Day and Christmas Day. There were no decorations, no Christmas trees, no carols, and no lights. Everything remained the same. In fact, you would not know it was a time of holiday at all. Cells were undecorated, the halls and offices were undecorated. Everything looked like it did the day she arrived.

It's a depressing feeling to know that while everything inside was the same, on the outside your friends and family were celebrating the holidays. Last year, she didn't think about that much, but now the realization was sinking in. The people she called friends had mostly forgotten about her. Her mom and dad were getting together with the family and friends and would certainly visit before Christmas, but on Christmas morning, she would not see them. That realization began to sink in right after Thanksgiving. Just as expected, Christmas Day began just the same as every day before it. The difference was that most people without a job that was essential to the functioning of life inside the prison had the day off. Things were quiet for the most part. Those with children quietly talked to one another about what they thought their kids were doing, while others made conversation about life on the outside and what they would do to celebrate the holiday. While some laughed and tried to make light of their situation, most were content to quietly, for once, pass the time.

Sidney found Jillian on her bunk staring at what looked like a photograph. "Stupid question, but are you okay?" Sidney asked her. Jillian did not look up at her at all. She continued to stare blankly at the picture. "May I sit down on your bunk?" she asked quietly.

"Go ahead. Mi casa, su casa," Jillian responded without her usual cheerfulness.

"You want to talk?" Sidney asked her.

"Not really, no."

"Okay, then mind if I do?" asked Sidney.

"Can't stop you, I guess."

"Last year, I didn't really get the mood around here on Christmas. I guess I was self-absorbed and too busy throwing myself a pity party to notice everyone else."

Jillian kept looking at the picture, pretending not to listen.

"There's a lot of people in here that are missing family time, children, husbands, and all. My parents and I always waited until Christmas morning to get up and open presents under the tree, like when I was a little girl. Now this is the second year without that."

"Life sucks all around, huh?" Jillian said.

"Yeah, it does. It could have been a lot worse for me though. I'm one of the lucky ones."

"How do you figure that?" Jillian asked without looking up.

"Because of you, girl," Sidney said.

"Oh gosh, you're not hitting on me, are you?" Jillian said with a little more life. "I told you from the beginning, I'm not into that."

"You know better than that," Sidney said as a smile began to crease her face. "I couldn't have made it in here without you, at least not like I have. Things could have gone so much worse for me if not for you. I just wanted to say thanks."

Jillian finally looked at her. "You're welcome. I'll be honest, at first I didn't think you'd make it, but I was wrong. I'm glad you walked through that cell door."

"So it makes you happy that I'm in prison?" Sidney asked.

"What? Yes, I mean, no. You know what I mean."

Sidney laughed. "I know. You can't be the only one who makes stupid jokes."

"My jokes aren't stupid. They're carefully refined based on observation and wit," Jillian said as the mood lightened. "It's just hard this time of the year. Josh and I were going to get married the weekend before Christmas, but instead, I got arrested on the Monday before Thanksgiving. We put off the wedding until after my trial. When I got sentenced, he swore he'd wait for me. That lasted all of about six weeks before he dumped me."

"That's the guy in the picture?"

"Yeah. This is the only time of the year I really miss him and think about what might have been." She sat up and held the picture in her lap. "I had it all, Sidney. I worked at a bank and was on a fast track to the top. Truth is, I hated my life. I was so unhappy that I started taking small amounts of money from the accounts. I don't know why I did it. I didn't need the money, but it gave me a thrill. I thought I covered my tracks so well. After a while, I realized what I was doing hurt people and stopped. I tried to put it all back, but it was too late. Cops showed up and arrested me as I walked out of my home. I lost everything. All the stuff I lost doesn't bother me. I didn't deserve it anyway. Josh was different. He's the only part of that life I really miss."

Sidney listened to her friend's story and felt sympathy for her. "You know, I try not to think about Lawson. Kind of hard not to when you spent two years, seven months, and five days with a guy."

"Dear god, Sidney, you really remember how long you two were together like that?"

"It's stupid, I know, like I'm some high-school girl crushing on her first boyfriend. But I do."

"You've never told me much about him other than the whole cheating and killing thing," Jillian said.

"Never talk about your case," Sidney said. "You know what the worst thing is? Despite everything he did to me, I still love him. Isn't that the most messed-up thing you ever heard? After all that

126

happened, the lies, cheating, I still love him. I guess that makes me crazy."

"Or human. We're all a little messed up inside," Jillian told her.

"Oh, hey, I almost forgot. I got you a little gift," Sidney said, again breaking the mood.

"A gift? Sidney, you shouldn't have done that."

"Look, it's not much. I used some of my canteen money to get it for you." Sidney pulled back her blanket and revealed a small package wrapped in toilet paper. "See, practical all the way around. You get to keep what's inside and the wrapping paper too."

"You're so silly," she said as she began to open to package. Inside was three packets of soup and two strawberry Pop-Tart packets. "Sidney, these are my favorites. How did you get Pop-Tarts?"

"Don't ask. Just enjoy them," Sidney said.

Jillian got up and opened the storage locker she kept under the bunk. "Here, take this."

"Jillian, you love honeybuns. I can't take this."

"Like hell, you can't. Take it, or I'll force-feed it to you."

Before she knew it, Sidney reached out and embraced Jillian. "Thank you, girl. This means a lot."

"Don't mention it. Merry Christmas, Sidney."

"Merry Christmas, Jillian."

CHAPTER 31

Jim Cooper was in his typical bad mood that morning. His only solace from the cares of the day was the cup of coffee and Danish roll he ate every morning. The elevator in the building was slower than normal that day, and his temper only grew shorter as the ride got longer. He stepped off the elevator and then walked down to his office. He threw open the door when Myra Pope, his secretary, tried to tell him something. "Not now," was the only thing he said as he opened the door to his office. Sitting there was Roger Taylor waiting for him. "Taylor, what the hell are you doing in my office?" he asked, feeling the annoyance growing in him.

"Cooper, I need to have a word or two with you, and it's not going to make you happy.," said Roger as he continued to sit in the chair across from his desk.

"Myra, hold my calls. I don't care if it's the governor, understand?" He sat down at his desk and situated his stuff to his liking. "All right, Taylor, spill it. Why are you here so early? What is so important that it can't wait until later or never?"

"Lawson Pierson. That's what."

"Come on, Taylor, that case is closed. Why are you wasting your time with that?"

Roger shifted in his seat and produced a copy of the death certificate. "This is why. Take a look at it."

Cooper took the document and glanced over it quickly. "It's his death certificate, big deal. I've seen this a hundred times. Old news."

"Really? How close did you look at it? You see something bothered me about this whole thing, and I couldn't quite understand why. Usually, even in the most airtight cases, there's a thorough investigation, just in case, but not this one. Sidney Lewis is denied bail, takes a plea, and gets shipped away all nice and neat. Problem is, nothing is ever that clean." Roger could sense that Cooper was starting to worry like he had hit a nerve. Now for the fun part. "That's when it hit me, so to speak. Take a look at this now."

Cooper took the second document from Taylor's hand and saw that it was another copy of Lawson Pierson's death certificate. "It's the same certificate, so what?"

Taylor looked at him with piercing eyes, the same kind of eyes he used to stare at the criminals he helped put away. Something was different about him. "No. Take a closer look," Roger said. Cooper did, and that's when he noticed the difference. "That's the original death certificate, or I should say a copy of it. You see, Dr. Meeks is like me, old-fashioned. In this computer age of electronic files and whatnot, he still keeps a paper copy of death certificates." Roger made his move. He got up and rested his hands on Cooper's desk to stare him in the eyes. "In my notes, there were two head wounds. One to the back of the head, the second to the side of the head, just behind the right eye. There, on his temple. The coroner's report confirms it. It also confirms that Lawson Pierson died from the blow to the side of his head when he fell, not the wound to the back of the head."

Cooper began to squirm in his chair. He began to think about how he thought he'd been so careful in changing that report. It never occurred to him that Meeks kept a paper copy of the death certificate. Meeks was a crazy old man who should have retired years ago. Now that old man had put him in a box, and Taylor was closing it shut. "What are you trying to prove here, Taylor? You trying to accuse me of something?"

"Not yet, I'm not. When did Pierson get to you, Cooper? I always knew you were an ass, but a criminal too? Was it easy for you to lock that girl away? Ruin her life? That easy for you just because a scumbag like Leonard Pierson tells you to? Is that it?"

"You know damn well the evidence against her was solid," Cooper said in an angry voice. "Whether she meant to or not, she killed him. What does it matter if it was directly or indirectly?"

"What does it matter?" Taylor said, raising his voice and standing to his feet. "You're a district attorney. You tell me why it matters.

This isn't some game we get to play with people's lives here. The truth matters. Justice matters. And it matters to me. I stood back and watched this investigation fall apart. I stood there and let things go and said nothing. That's my part in this. I have to live with that."

"Look, Taylor, that's why she had a lawyer. It's not my fault he couldn't make a better deal. At the end of the day, a guilty person is where she belongs, case closed."

"But it's not, Coop. You suppressed evidence and made up evidence, and you colluded with a criminal to win a conviction. Makes me ask what else have you done for him. How many others have you done this to, Coop? So I'll ask again, when did he buy you, Coop?"

"You got nothing, Taylor. Whatever I did or didn't do, you can't prove a thing. So you can just take your accusations and your righteous indignation and walk out of this office while you still have your badge, and don't count on that fact for much longer."

"You're right, Coop, I've got no hard proof that links you to this, but I'm looking. This certificate alone, though, throws serious doubt on the integrity of your office. Don't worry, you're safe for now, but don't get too comfortable. I'll be back." Taylor let himself out the door. As he walked to the elevator, a smile crossed his face. He knew he'd rattled him. Now he just needed Cooper to go crawling back to his boss. It shouldn't take too long for that to happen.

Cooper was, in fact, on the phone that very minute. "Yeah, I need to speak with Mr. Pierson immediately. We've got a big problem."

CHAPTER 32

Though the three of them were working on the case together, this was the first time they had all met as a team. Luke arranged the takeout meals he bought for the group, almost like he was hosting a party. It felt strange to him having the three of them together in the same room. It was a risk he knew but one he thought worth taking. It was doubtful that anyone was watching the office, but it couldn't be completely ruled out. Detective Taylor by now was checking the outside area to see if there was anyone suspicious outside, just in case. Shelia was one her way down and would be there any minute. Satisfied that it was safe, Taylor made his way into the law office. The two shook hands and took a few minutes to catch up. "Detective, I don't think we've actually spoken about the case since I was last in the police station with Sidney. I'm glad you're doing this, but I have to admit I'm not sure why you're doing this." He had to be sure. There was too much on the line to take a risk now.

"To be honest, Mr. Brady, I'm not sure myself. When I questioned her, I could just tell there was something different. Then everything moved so fast, and they killed the investigation. I guess there are just too many loose ends, and I guess there must be something more. And just maybe, I believe her."

Luke thought for a moment. He knew that Taylor had a reputation as a shrewd investigator and not someone who was corrupt. Brady needed allies, but he had to be careful who he trusted. Pierson could not be trusted to keep his word, and while it might be difficult to get to Sidney while she was in prison, it was not impossible. He had to be careful with every move. "I think you're right about loose ends," Brady replied. "I've filed a number of legal briefs to the court, trying to keep the case moving, but without hard evidence, it's slow going."

"How is she holding up?" Taylor asked.

"Pretty good so far. I think she got a cellmate that she gets along with, so that's good. I still warn her every time I see her not to talk about the case even with her cellmate. So far as I can tell, she hasn't."

"That's good," Taylor said. "Luke, I need to talk to her. She may know more than she thinks."

"No. She needs to be kept as much as possible in the dark about this investigation, and if Pierson finds out you're investigating—"

"She's screwed," said Shelia as she walked into the office, placing her purse to the side. "Oh, you got takeout? How sweet. How's it going, boys?"

"You know, you could have announced yourself before just barging in," Taylor said as Shelia took the seat next to him.

"Well, if a bad guy did barge in here, you would both be dead since you left the front door unlocked. You sure you're a cop?" she chided Taylor.

"You're in a good mood. I hope that means you have good news," Brady interrupted.

Shelia spent the next few minutes recounting her recent trip to Seattle and meeting Jamie Carter. She also told about how she had dug into some of the leads she had on other women Lawson and friends spent time with. She believed from the conversation with Jamie that other videos existed and that Leonard Pierson was doing his best to keep secret any evidence of the videos. None of this came as a big surprise to Brady. Sidney told him in one of their conversations that Leonard Pierson, on the night he visited her, said as much. Yet the point of this was not to simply ruin the reputation of Lawson Pierson but to find a way to get Sidney out of the situation she was in as quickly as possible. Taylor was the next to speak. He told about finding the original death certificate, which verified at least part of Sidney's side of the story. What he said next, though, was the most concerning. He told about confronting Jim Cooper over the false certificate and how he promised to expose his part in falsifying the cause of death and tampering with evidence. Brady looked worried.

"You've both done a great job, but I don't think it was wise to provoke Cooper. If he really is in league with Pierson, he's probably told him everything you two discussed," Brady said.

"Luke, that's what we want. We have to turn up the heat so that they get nervous. That's when they will make a mistake," Taylor said.

"Yeah, and what if that mistake is killing Sidney? Can you live with that? I sure as hell can't," Brady said almost yelling at Taylor.

"Okay, boys, let's bring this down," Shelia interjected quickly. "Luke, he's right. We have to move on what we have, or else we will never get anywhere." She then shot a quick look at Taylor. "And you should have told us you were going to confront Cooper. We are in this together, and if we don't communicate with each other, we are going to get nowhere." The mood calmed, so Shelia continued, "We have to trust each other. No lone ranger stuff. Got it, Taylor?"

"Got it."

Shelia looked at Luke. "Do you trust us to do our jobs?" she asked him. Brady sat down again and let the tension in the room ease. Shelia held her determined face. She knew this was the moment that might make or break this investigation, so she stood her ground.

"I think it's time to put all our cards on the table now," Luke said as he broke the silence. "I have something you both need to see, but it's not here. Let's meet again tomorrow, and I'll tell you everything."

CHAPTER 33

Jim Cooper's mood had not improved over the last few days. He was not the type of man to be bullied into doing things he did not want to do, but today was different. Pierson was out of town when he called him, but now he was back and wanted to see him first thing this morning. Problem was, Pierson's office was not on his usual way to the office, and that meant no coffee and Danish this morning. Sure, he could stop somewhere else, but it's not his usual routine, and the idea of going to his usual coffee shop after meeting with Pierson was just too much of a change. "Mr. Pierson is expecting you, Mr. Cooper. Go on in," said the secretary outside of Pierson's office. He walked in like he had many times before. The office, as always, was immaculate and well decorated. The paintings on the walls were all originals, and the wood used in the walls and furniture was of the finest quality. Cooper thought that he could live in this office just as easily as his house.

"Come in, Coop," Pierson said in a voice too cheerful for a man of his character, "I hope I got the right type of coffee and pastry for you. I took the liberty of sending my assistant here to get it for you since you wouldn't be going that way today."

"Thank you, Mr. Pierson. I appreciate it," Cooper said as he took the cup of coffee and the bag that held the Danish pastry. "This is unexpected."

"Well, I thought I would surprise you today. I have to admit it's not every day you get such monumental news," Pierson said. "Please sit. Have you met Mr. Goldman before? I swear I have so many lawyers I can hardly keep up with them all."

"Yes, we've met before. A few years ago when that driver of yours got caught with that shipment of Xanax."

"Oh, that's right, I remember now. That was a close one, wasn't it?" Pierson responded.

Cooper began to shift nervously in his chair. He could sense something was building, and he knew it would explode any minute. This was a game of cat and mouse, and he had few illusions as to what part he was playing. He needed to find a way out of this somehow. "Look, Mr. Pierson, I—"

"You know, I thought I understood our relationship here, Jim, I really did," Pierson cut in. "Whenever investigations get too close to me, you fix them. That's pretty simple, right, Jim? In return, you never have to worry about if you'll have enough money to retire on. Simple."

Pierson got up from his chair and walked to the window. He slowly closed the blinds in his office. "I like simple in business arrangements. I really do. So explain to me how this gets complicated. You were supposed to keep all the details about Lawson's death quiet. A misguided girl goes to jail to pay for her crime, and justice is served. I must say, you did a fantastic job. To a point." Leonard turned around and slowly, menacingly began to walk toward Cooper. He stopped just a few inches from Cooper's feet.

"Mr. Pierson—"

But Pierson stopped him by raising a finger to his lips. "Shhh. It's time to listen, Jim. Time to listen very closely." Pierson held his finger to his lips a few seconds more. "You know, I really didn't think it would be so hard to make a guilty girl look guilty. You were supposed to put her away for life. You really blew that part, didn't you?"

"Mr. Pierson, there was no way I could push for first-degree murder. There just wasn't enough. I did what I could."

"Of course you did, Jim. Of course, you did. I guess I'm partly to blame too. What can I say? I just love a pretty face, and well, she did try to change my wayward son. Pity can be such a weakness at times, can't it?" Pierson leaned down and rested his hands on the chair's arm rails. "Isn't that really where this went wrong, Jim? We pitied someone we should have crushed. But you know, it shouldn't have mattered. No one likes a criminal, not even a pretty one. Unless..." He paused, letting the tension of the room continue to build. "Unless there's a reason to doubt their guilt."

By this time, Cooper, in spite of the air-conditioned office, began to sweat. Pierson was in full villain mode now. He'd seen him like this many times, but never directly at him. What worried him more was that Goldman's gaze had fixed on him, and he held it like a statue. Now Cooper could feel his heart in his throat, and his breath grew rapid.

"How careless of you to leave the original death certificate in the coroner's office like that. I know. Who keeps paper records these days, right?" Pierson said almost happily. "An old-fashioned fool like Meeks. That's who keeps paper records. In a world of high-tech everything, you should have known an old fossil like Dr. Meeks would still keep a paper record."

There it was. The sudden flash of anger he knew was coming.

"And then there's Taylor. A true do-gooder trying to ride to the rescue, like he's Wyatt Earp," Pierson said as he finally rose and backed away. "You got sloppy. Left too many bread crumbs. Now Taylor thinks he's got a case. You should have known that a Boy Scout is always going to be a Boy Scout. Now he's trying to reopen the case." He walked back to his desk and sat down again. "So how do we fix this, Coop? How do we fix this?"

"I, um, I think…maybe…" Cooper could not seem to get out of his own way to respond.

Pierson was out for blood now, and this large cat was ready to pounce. The ease in his voice and the relaxed posture left no doubt he was in charge and was in full intimidation mode. "Well, spit it out, man. What the hell are we going to do?" Pierson burst forth suddenly. "This is your mess. Now how do we clean it up?"

"We could kill the girl," was all he could come up with.

"Kill the girl. Damn, Goldman, why didn't we think of that?" Pierson said. "Oh, that's right, there's the flash drive you still haven't found. You want to try something that doesn't bring the feds and every other agency down on our heads?"

"Then what about Taylor? He could be gotten rid of easily enough. Perp with a gun takes him out on a case, and this all goes away," Cooper said.

"Well, an idea on the table. I like it, but there's a small problem. Mr. Goldman, tell him what you found out."

Goldman produced a file and handed Cooper a picture. "This is Shelia Lee, a crime reporter and ex-lover of Roger Taylor." Cooper looked at the picture, and it didn't take him long to guess what was happening. "She's been looking into some of the women Lawson had…" He paused and looked at Pierson. In response, Pierson gave a slight nod. "Relations with. We think she may be working with Taylor."

"Got complicated, didn't it, Jim?" Pierson added. "All because of some bread crumbs and a pretty face." Leonard got up and walked back to where Cooper was sitting. "Take care of the detective. I don't care how, but take care of him. We'll handle the reporter."

"Mr. Pierson, I will. I swear I will make Taylor sorry he ever laid eyes on that girl. I just—"

"You thought you may never walk out of this room, didn't you, Jim?" Pierson said with a smile on his face. "Jim," Pierson said as he rested his hand on Cooper's back, leading him toward the door, "you don't get to where I am in life by going around killing people. That's what he's for," Leonard said as he cast a quick glance at Goldman. Then he laughed and slapped him on the back. "I'm kidding, Jim. Don't look so nervous. Do your job, or next time I won't be kidding," he said as he opened the door, pushing Cooper through it. The door closed, and Jim Cooper left Pierson's office feeling lucky to be alive. On the other side of the door, Pierson turned around and fixed his gaze on Goldman. Gone was the happy demeanor he showed just a second before. "I have a new assignment for you, Goldman."

CHAPTER 34

Today was a special day. It was Jillian's birthday, and Sidney wanted to make it as special as she could. The routine of the day was the same as any other, but once the day's work was done, she planned to have a few ladies over for a get-together to celebrate as much as they could before lights out. After dinner that night, a handful of inmates came by wishing her a happy birthday and bringing small gifts. Jillian seemed surprised by all the festivities. "Did you set this up, Sidney?" she asked after all had left. Her face radiated happiness a little too much for Sidney. Jillian was acting weird, and Sidney wanted to know why.

"Are you okay? You're acting strange," Sidney asked Jillian.

"Look, I didn't want everyone else seeing this, but I got us something to help celebrate. Well, okay, it wasn't to celebrate originally. It was for me to have a little pity party on my birthday."

"Jillian, you don't have a bag of weed, do you? If they find you with it…"

"Sidney, no, I don't have weed. Gosh, I'm surprised you even know what that is."

"Hey, give me some credit here. I'm not that sheltered," Sidney said defensively.

"Okay, fine, just keep your voice down." Jillian looked around to see if any guards were near. "I had Susie make this for me." Jillian pulled out a twenty-ounce soda bottle that was obviously filled with something besides soda. "This is for us."

"Jillian, that's hooch," Sidney said, surprised that Jillian would take such a risk. "You can't have that. If someone sees you, they'll throw you in the hole."

"Well, they will if you keep talking so loud," Jillian said, trying to calm Sidney down. "Calm down, Sidney. Look, it's fine. We'll just drink a tiny bit and toss the rest of it if that makes you feel better."

"We? Jillian, this could get us in trouble," Sidney said, trying to keep her voice down.

"Sidney, we're in prison. How much worse can it get?"

"Of course it can get worse. Get rid of that," Sidney told her.

"No way, you know how much this costs? Didn't you ever sneak drinks in high school?" Jillian asked.

"What do you think?"

"Tell me you had some fun in college at least?" Jillian asked her.

"I drank a few times," Sidney said defensively, "when I wasn't the designated driver, which was like almost every time."

"And you ended up here. Yeah, I can see that. Said no one ever," Jillian said sarcastically.

"Gee, thanks. So are you going to drink that or what?" Sidney said.

"No, we are going to drink it. Right?" Jillian said.

Sidney stared at Jillian with a disapproving look. "Fine, okay, but just a little."

"Hey, trust me, a little is all you will need," Jillian told her.

Jillian opened the bottle and sniffed the opening. "Oh man, that's strong." She took a drink and nearly retched. "Oh god, that's awful. Here, have some." Jillian passed the bottle to Sidney. She took the bottle and studied it suspiciously.

"You sure about this?" Sidney asked her. She really didn't want to drink the elixir, but Jillian looked at her with a "Come on, Sidney" look. With a moment's hesitation, Sidney took a long draft out of the bottle. The taste and burn of the liquid nearly made her spew it out on the floor. Somehow she managed to keep it down, but it made her cough uncontrollably. "Oh man, that's wretched," she managed to finally utter between the coughs.

"Here, let me have it, and I'll pour it out," Jillian told her as she reached for the bottle.

"Pour it out, ladies?" came a voice from outside the cell. "Why I wouldn't hear of it. Pass it over here, why don't you?" Both Jillian and Sidney were taken by surprise by the sudden appearance of Officer

McConnell, a tall, well-built woman of color. She was known as a no-nonsense but fair correctional officer. The inmates respected her and knew that she wanted to do her job and do it right, but that meant if you broke the rules, there would be consequences. They were both about to find that out. "All right, let's go. Outside the cell." Both Sidney and Jillian walked out of their cell. Jillian handed her the nearly empty bottle, and Officer McConnell sat it on the floor. "Contraband, ladies? I expected better of both of you," she said to them. Sidney felt like she was sixteen and had gotten home after curfew. "All right, both of you, turn around. Hands behind your backs." Both did as they were told, and McConnell cuffed them.

Sidney was more embarrassed than anything, but there was a part of her that really wanted to hurt Jillian at that moment. "I told you to pour that out," she whispered to her as they walked down the cellblock. Jillian, for her part, tried not to make eye contact with her. Sidney could not see her face well, but she could tell she was turning red with embarrassment. Sidney knew she couldn't stay mad at her for long, but she was not happy with her.

"I'm sorry," she whispered back. "I'll take the blame, Sidney, I promise."

"Quiet, both of you," Officer McConnell said.

She led them to the officer in charge for the night, which happened to be Sergeant Ferguson. McConnell ordered them to sit on a small bench outside of his office. They sat there several minutes before he came out. "Okay, both of you, inside." They walked in, and he told McConnell to remove the cuffs. "So what's this about, McConnell?" She related the story to him as he turned his gaze back and forth to the three women in his office. When she finished, he sat for a moment, as if considering what he would say. "So what are we going to do about this, ladies?" he asked them.

"Sir, it was my fault," Jillian answered. "Sidney tried to talk me out of drinking the hooch. I take full blame. It's my birthday, and I wanted to celebrate."

"Oh, you take responsibility, do you?" he asked. "So I'm just supposed to ignore the fact that Lewis here participated too? Is that the way you see it, Lewis?"

"No, sir," Sidney answered, "I accept responsibility too."

"I should put you both in seg for a week. That what you two want?" he angrily said. "You've both been model prisoners, and you do this? Just what got into you?"

Neither of them said a word. It was obvious they were both ashamed of what they did or at least for getting caught. Sidney hated trouble. Most of her life was spent avoiding trouble. Now it seemed to find her at the worst times. In high school, she was only sent to the principal's office one time, and that was for being late for class too many times. This felt worse because Ferguson was not a principal, and this was not high school.

"Since this is your first time, I'll go easy on you. This time. Mostly because I don't want to fill out the paperwork this late at night. So your yard privileges are suspended for two weeks, and you'll have early lockdown for two weeks. So after dinner, you both get locked in for the night. Got it?"

"Yes, sir," they both said in a low voice.

"Great. Goodbye. McConnell, return them to their cell, and make sure it's noted in the guard report that they are to be on a two-week lockdown."

After they were locked in, the two sat in silence for several minutes. Jillian finally broke the silence. "Okay, you're mad at me. I deserve that. I just wanted to mark the occasion for once."

Sidney sat there not saying anything. She felt her anger going away, but it wasn't gone just yet.

"Are we okay?"

"I'm so mad at you right now, but yes, we are okay."

"Look, I owe you, okay? I'll do some of your chores around here."

"Some of them?"

"Fine, all of them. Really, Sidney, I'm sorry. Are we really okay?"

"Yes, girl, we are okay. We better be if we are going to be locked in here for two weeks, right?"

"Yeah. Hope you like cards," Jillian said.

"Lucky for you, I do. Still mad at you, but I'll get over it," Sidney said. "Was kind of fun while it lasted."

With that, Sidney laid back and closed her eyes. Jillian did the same, and soon they were both asleep.

CHAPTER 35

Jim Cooper shut the door to his car as he searched his keys for the one to his front door. Jackie was probably finishing dinner, meaning she ordered takeout for the millionth time. Days like this made him wish that he hadn't quit smoking a couple of years ago. He spent the day going through several drug cases, another hit-and-run, and an identity theft case involving elderly patients in a nursing home. He still had not found the time to deal with the whole Detective Taylor problem. The detective was trying to rattle him into making a mistake because if he really had proof that he had changed the death certificate and falsified evidence, then he would have made his move by now. Pierson was worried for nothing. So he made a mistake or two, but Taylor had nothing. Even if he did, Cooper would see that it got buried so deep it would never see daylight again.

"Jackie, I hope you ordered something remotely good 'cause I can't take any more healthy food," he said, walking through the door. He hung up his coat and set down his briefcase near the couch in the living room. "Jackie, what did you order, huh?" he asked again. He walked to the bathroom in the bedroom but found no sign of his wife. It was strange because she usually was here when he got home. Maybe she was out with friends. He walked back down the hall toward the kitchen. "Jackie, are you—" He stopped suddenly as he entered the kitchen. His wife was lying face down in what looked like a pool of blood. Cooper dropped the file he was carrying at the sight of her.

"You screwed up, Cooper," came a voice from behind him. It was the last thing he ever heard.

CHAPTER 36

It was after 11:00 p.m. when the three of them were able to get together again. Taylor was the first to arrive as usual, and Shelia arrived shortly after. Luke knew this would be an important meeting tonight. He hoped he wasn't making a mistake. He thought back to the many times that he spent at the Lewises' home after he and Todd played a round of golf. He watched Sidney grow up and knew this was killing both of them. He met Todd in college after his discharge from the Navy. They were friends from the first moment they met. He owed this to him. After making small talk for several minutes, Luke got to the point of the meeting. "I'm afraid I've not been completely honest with you both. Please understand I have to think about my client and her family, but I don't think was can go much further until you know this." He took a deep breath as both Taylor and Shelia shifted uncomfortably in their seats. "You both have proven that you are committed to this, and I thank you for it. Sidney's a girl I watched grow up, and I've known her mother and father for years. Her safety is my greatest concern. That why I never told you," Luke said.

"What didn't you tell us, Mr. Brady?" asked Shelia.

"The missing flash drive is not missing at all. I've had it the whole time. There I said it."

Neither of the others could believe what they heard. "You had the flash drive the whole time?" Taylor said as he stood up. "Why didn't you tell us that in the first place? You know how long I've been spinning my wheels trying to find leads on this case?"

"Not to mention all the time I spent trying to find some of those women. I had to spend time with that creep friend of Lawson's to get just one name," Shelia said as she also stood up.

Luke began to fidget in his chair as both of them continued to argue with him about a lack of trust and other accusations. "Okay, okay," he said through the other's raised voices. "Damn it, I said enough." Both Shelia and Taylor finally quieted down, but they were far from finished, he could tell. "I didn't know if I could trust either of you. We are up against arguably the most powerful man in this area. Not to mention he has influence in both the police department and the district attorney's office. What was I supposed to think?"

"So what's changed, then? Why trust us now?" Shelia asked him. She suspected he knew more than what he let on, but this was a shock. As a reporter, one always wanted to know the truth, and one developed ways of telling when someone was not being honest or leaving things out of a story. This revelation surprised her more than normal.

"Because it's been over two years, and I can't do this alone. So if I'm going to help her, I need you both to know the truth." The tension in the air continued to hang there as everyone calmed, but Luke could tell that there was still a lot of frustration in the room. "Look, Taylor, you think she got a bad deal, or you wouldn't be here. Shelia, you want a big story, right? You both want to take down Pierson, so here's your chance."

The three of them sat in awkward silence for several minutes that to Luke felt more like hours. "So why all the secrecy? What really happened between the time Sidney was arrested and the sentencing?" asked Shelia. It was time for answers, and she resolved not to leave until she got them.

"She told me where she hid the flash drive when I talked to her after her arrest. I went to her apartment and retrieved it, and to say the least, it was revealing. It had about twenty sex videos on it, and she was only in five of them. One video was dated a day after the last one she was in. So yes, all of that is true, and none of it made it into the record." Luke could see he had their attention now. Taylor was taking notes in a small pocket-sized notebook as Shelia sat and listened.

"The reason for the secrecy is obvious, considering who we are dealing with, but there's more. Sidney told me that before she accepted the plea, Leonard Pierson himself visited her in her cell at night. He threatened and bullied her into taking Cooper's deal. He even changed it himself while he was talking with her."

"How can he do that?" Shelia asked.

"Because Jim Cooper has been shielding him for years," Taylor said. "I always believed he was working for Pierson, but I could never prove it."

"Well, this time he messed up," Luke said. "Lawson didn't just put videos on the flash drive. He put documents as well. I agreed to give the flash drive to Pierson in return for him leaving Sidney alone."

"You gave it back to him?" Taylor said, feeling the anger well up in him again.

"No. I gave him a copy of the original. He thinks I gave him the original, but I also told him I had a copy made that would be sent to every law enforcement agency and news organization in the country if he harmed either Sidney or myself."

"But now he knows what's on the drive. By now he must have changed things up or deleted the documents that were on it. The information is probably useless now," Shelia said.

"Well, not exactly," Luke said in a confident voice. "You see, I didn't give him an exact copy of the drive. I left a few very nice documents off his copy."

"How many and how nice?" asked Taylor.

"Enough to make the both of you very happy and keep you very busy."

CHAPTER 37

In some ways, being on early lockdown was as bad as solitary confinement. Certainly, it was better than being locked up twenty-three hours a day, and it allowed her time to continue working her job. However, when all that was done, Sidney and Jillian were locked in their shared cell for about an extra five hours a day. What made it worse was that they could see the other inmates milling around outside their cells, but they could not interact with them. Occasionally one of the other inmates would venture over and strike up a conversation, but it usually didn't last very long. "This reminds me of the county jail," said Jillian a few nights into their confinement. "They made us stay in our cells most of the day. The only difference was, I had three other girls in there with me."

"Why was that?" Sidney asked while playing a game of solitaire. She thought sarcastically it was a fitting game to play in her situation. She was more or less over being mad at Jillian. She really couldn't be mad at her too long anyway considering all Jillian had done for her. It reminded Sidney of a spat she had with her best friend in high school. She didn't really remember what it was about now, but it had been silly, and she did not stay mad at her for more than a week. Prison was not high school, and the friend had not written her back after she sent a letter about a week after arriving in prison.

Jillian walked to the back of the cell and stood near the combination toilet and sink they shared. "It's mostly because of the lack of staffing. I guess no one grows up wanting to work in a jail," she said as she ran her hands through her hair. "This is not what I pictured doing when I was growing up either," she said in a more hushed voice.

"What did you grow up wanting to do?" Sidney asked her. She avoided discussions like this with people on the inside, but she let her guard down this time. It's hard to know who and just how much to trust someone on the inside. Luke Brady warned her about telling too much or asking too many questions. Hopefully Jillian was a true friend, but she could never be too certain. Even if she was, it only took one slipup to the wrong person, and there could be trouble. Tonight, though, it seemed a good time for this conversation.

"I wanted to be a singer in a country band. Silly, isn't it?" Jillian said as a small smile came to her face. "You know, I don't even like country music that much. It just seemed like a lot of fun to sing about love and romance and having fun down home and all."

"Would you wear a cowboy hat?" Sidney asked her.

"You better believe I would. I love the look, but the music is not really my thing," she said as she began to pace back to the closed cell door. Jillian did not talk much about her life outside. She let on a few secrets here and there, but she mostly stayed focused on things on the inside. "I used to sing in my church's youth choir. Even did a couple of solos. People said I was good, but you know, most of those people are pulling for you. It's not like singing for people who don't know you and aren't afraid to let you know if you're terrible."

"I bet you were a good singer. Why don't you ever sing around here?"

"I don't know, Sidney. Guess I'm afraid to find out if I really can sing. What about you?"

"Me? No, I can't carry a tune in a bucket. I only sang in youth choir because they needed me to. I think they turned off the microphone in front of me when we performed."

Jillian laughed. "No, they didn't. Stop lying."

"I'm serious." Sidney laughed. "My youth minister was too nice to tell me I was bad, but I could tell by the look on his face when we performed." That made Jillian laugh again. "It's true, why are you laughing at me?" she said, giggling.

"I just caught a mental picture of you singing into a dead microphone with some guy looking at you with a scrunched-up face." Jillian couldn't help it. Now she was fully laughing. "I'm sorry. I'm sorry." She finally made herself stop. "I've said I'm sorry to you a lot these last few days, haven't I?"

"Jillian, it's okay."

"No, it's not," Jillian replied as she sat down on her bunk. "I messed things up again. I've messed up a lot over the last several years. I thought I was so smart back then."

"Jillian, you don't have to tell me this."

"Yes, I do," she said. "I just want you to understand who I am. She motioned for Sidney to come down and sit by her on her bunk. "I worked at a bank for about five years after college. I got promoted and got to learn the ins and outs of the job. I thought that I could skim money off the top and fix it in the computers. I thought things were going well, but one morning as I was walking out my front door, there were cops there waiting for me. They handcuffed me right there in my driveway in front of my neighbors." She drew up in a ball and leaned against Sidney's side. Sidney put her arm around Jillian's shoulders in response.

"Honestly, I don't even know why I did it. I didn't think anyone would catch on because it was in such small amounts. I got greedy and threw away a promising career, lost my fiancé, my home, everything I'd ever worked for just gone." A small tear ran down her cheek, which she quickly wiped away. "Look at me now. Locked up, crying away for doing something so stupid." She laughed to herself again. "I didn't cry one time in the county jail, not once. This is one of the few times since I got here. Just so stupid."

"That's not the Jillian that I know," Sidney told her. "Everyone here has done something stupid to land themselves here. I mean, look at me. I stayed with a guy who made secret videos of us while we were, well, you know."

"He really did that to you?" Jillian asked.

"Yeah, he did. I found the videos of us and several other women too," she responded, "and I still thought we could work things out. I keep asking myself what I could have done differently so that he wouldn't have cheated on me. What did I do wrong?" She stopped and composed herself, seeing Jillian had stopped crying. "Then I realize there was nothing I could have done. That was just the way he was, and I couldn't change him. I could have done more on that night. Heck, I shouldn't have even gone to his boat, but I did, and now here I am." She took a deep breath and slowly exhaled it. "I guess we all make stupid mistakes, some worse than others."

"Yes, we do, don't we?" Jillian said. "One last time, then. I'm sorry, it will never happen again. I swear."

"We're fine, girl. You're one of the last friends I have in the world, so you're stuck with me," Sidney said.

"Yeah, for a long time to come," Jillian said with a smile coming back to her face. Sidney smiled back, and they continued to talk into the night.

CHAPTER 38

The day started simple enough. Taylor had a number of cases back-logged as it was, but these late-night strategy sessions with Luke Brady were beginning to take a toll on him. He followed a few leads before and, as usual, led nowhere. Now armed with the files found on the flash drive, Taylor was sure he had enough to finally go to his friend in the FBI. The feds would be reluctant to look at anything obtained by a convicted criminal even if she did so without knowing. However, just the few files he had time to go through were convincing pieces of evidence. Still, he had to be careful in balancing his time between his current caseload and the investigation into Pierson. Taylor wanted more than anything in regard to his secret investigation to talk to Sidney Lewis. He was convinced that she knew more information about the operations of the Piersons than she realized. Even something that seemed trivial might prove useful in an investigation. In fact, two nights ago when the group last met, he argued for a meeting again. Brady was steadfast, though, in his refusal. Taylor knew that he could always talk to her without his permission if he wanted, but she was likely to not divulge anything, and the opportunity would be lost. Better to keep trying to get Brady on board first before driving two hours in a waste of time.

Taylor began to flip through one of the files on his desk. It was a break-in at a local electronics store. Several computers and high-end pieces of computer equipment were stolen, and Taylor had only begun interviewing suspects and potential witnesses. He doubted that anything would ever turn up, but one had to make the effort at least until what happened next. "Taylor, drop what you're doing and come on. We got a homicide," said Chief Butler. That news roused him out of his malaise.

"What do we have, Chief?" he asked as he got up from his desk. The chief seemed on edge as he passed by Taylor's desk. "Chief, you all right?" The look he got back told him the answer to that question. "It's Jim and Jackie Cooper. They were both killed last night in their home. The housekeeper found them about an hour ago. You're with me."

Jim Cooper is dead? he thought. As he fell in behind the Chief, he wondered secretly what this meant for his investigation into Pierson. He also wondered if Pierson decided to take out a loose end, or was he sending a message? It's also possible that this was completely unrelated, but the timing of it was just too coincidental. Taylor confronted him just over a week or so ago, and now Cooper was dead? No, it had to be Pierson. Cooper got sloppy, and he paid the price for it. It had to be the reason.

They arrived at the home after about a twenty-minute ride. Uniformed officers had secured the home and were asking a few routine questions to the housekeeper. Taylor and Butler walked in and received a briefing from one of the uniformed officers. Butler looked over the scene. He noticed several things were missing: the television, Cooper's laptop from his briefcase, the jewelry from Jackie's body, and Jim's watch. To most, it looked like a robbery gone bad, but things didn't add up. It was too perfect, too placed. The things missing were the obvious things a thief would take, but there were no signs that whoever did this was in any other part of the house. The kitchen door was also kicked in as if the thief forced entry, but the body of Jackie lay facedown as if killed from behind by surprise, not after being startled.

"What do you think, Taylor?" asked Chief Butler as he knelt over the body of Jim Cooper. Most of the time, the chief didn't get so personally involved. He trusted his people to do the job he hired them to do. This case was going to be different. A district attorney killed in his own home was a major case, and Butler wanted to be more hands on with this one.

Taylor could feel the tension in Butler's voice as he surveyed the scene. "Something's not right, Chief," he said and pointed at the kitchen door. "Scene's laid out wrong. Kitchen door is kicked in from the outside, but the Coopers are shot from behind. As if someone was waiting for them already on the inside, like an ambush."

The crime-scene team was still taking pictures and documenting what they saw. Dr. Meeks was late in arriving, so they would have to wait on an approximate time of death. Butler fidgeted nervously as he looked over the scene. "I think you're right," he told Taylor. "Someone went through a lot of trouble to make this look like a robbery. Just in case, let's check the pawnshops in the area to see if anything shows up. We need Meeks here."

Taylor's attention was drawn to a blue van pulling up to the curb. "Speaking of the devil, he just got here." He walked outside to talk privately with Meeks. "Glad you could make it. You stop for coffee?" Taylor asked him. The usual joke felt more deadpan than his usual banter, and Meeks seemed to pick up on it.

"Traffic was backed for an accident on the highway. Got here as fast as I could," Meeks told him.

"Have you gotten any suspicious phone calls or seen any usual vehicles in the parking lot?" Taylor asked.

"No, nothing," Meeks told him. "You think this has anything to do with the death certificate?"

"Too early to tell right now, but it's more than likely that it does," Taylor told him.

Meeks concluded that the Coopers were killed sometime around 8:00 p.m. last night. He also said that it was possible that Jackie Cooper died first by as long as thirty minutes to an hour before her husband. The information reinforced the theory that this was a hit made to look like a robbery. While any of the literally hundreds of people he had prosecuted over the years could be responsible, Taylor knew it had to be on the orders of Leonard Pierson. It made sense considering how recently he confronted Cooper. Of course, getting the man killed was not in the plan. In fact, it, in some ways, made his job much harder. Taylor hoped that he could have squeezed him for more information. It also made proving his accusations against Cooper more difficult now as well because there could be no confession. One thing that did work in their favor was that Pierson had to react. He now knew that the heat was on, and that could lead to him making a mistake. Killing the Coopers could be Pierson's first mistake, but linking the murder to him would be difficult. Still, Pierson had blinked, and Taylor was going to take full advantage of the opportunity.

CHAPTER 39

Leonard Pierson was in the middle of a business call when Jonathan entered his office. Jonathan spent the last couple of days in Chicago on business trying to negotiate the last details of a contract with a new client. He motioned to his son to sit while he finished the call. Leonard was glad to see him because he had a lot of things he needed to discuss with him about the family business, some things that Jonathan probably did not want to hear, but it was far too late for his reluctance. He finally finished the call and hung up the phone. "I swear that man would go on about anything just to hear himself talk," he said, turning his attention to his son. "How was your flight back?" he asked, shifting his weight in the chair. "Did you get everything done in Chicago?"

Jonathan relaxed his shoulders and allowed some of the stress he had felt over the last several days to drop away. "Yes, everything went as expected. The contracts are signed, and we can start our deliveries early next month. The flight back was uneventful thankfully." He gazed at his father with mistrustful eyes. "I guess you heard that Jim Cooper is dead."

"Yes, I heard that. Murdered in his home. His wife too. Terrible," Leonard said, trying to sound sympathetic.

"Yeah, a real tragedy. You have anything to do with that?" he asked point-blank.

"Just what are you accusing me of, son? You think I had anything to do with this?"

"I think you know what I'm asking, so let's just stop playing games. Did you or did you not have him killed?" Jonathan asked, barely able to keep his voice down.

"You know I've built a business that ships cargo across the world. I have made more money than several states, not to mention gave

154

you and your brother a more than a good life, and provided you with a job that will one day see you run this company. So how about a little less questioning and more gratitude." Leonard calmed himself and managed to keep his temper down. One of the few good things he could always say about Lawson was that he never questioned where his good fortune came from. Jonathan was completely different.

"That's not an answer, Father. Are you responsible for Cooper's death?" Jonathan asked again, not willing to let it drop.

"No. I am not. Are you satisfied now?" Pierson again felt anger rising in him. "Why is it so hard for you to accept that we have a business to run and have no time for such distractions?"

"Because of all the other things this business is doing. My god, Father, where does it all end?"

Pierson had all he could take. They had this conversation before, and it always ended the same way. "Son, you are all I have now. Your brother is gone. If this business is to survive, I am going to need you to learn all you can and try to understand our operations." This was an exercise in frustration for him. Jonathan's moral compass was admirable, but Pierson knew that business did not succeed on morals but sound decision-making. While Jonathan might not agree with the decisions he made, his son needed to understand what they all stood to lose if the business went bad. "You also need to understand that there are people we move things for that do not deal well with change."

"Father, you know that I want nothing to do with that. You promised that you would end your association with the cartels years ago." In his heart, Jonathan doubted that his father would ever end the relationship with the drug cartels. He also knew that the cartels often moved people using his father's company. The whole thing made him sick when he thought about what his family had done. "I'm not Lawson, Father. I can't lead a criminal organization. I have a wife and child on the way to think about."

"No, you are not Lawson. You are a much better businessman than Lawson was ever going to be, but he did have one advantage over you. He would do anything to succeed and had no problem with doing what had to be done no matter what it was. You both could have done well together, but that can't happen now thanks to that Lewis girl."

"It's not right what you've done to her either," Jonathan said. "You could have just left well enough alone. It would have all blown over within a few weeks."

"Oh, just stop it. I've heard so much about her these last days that I'm ready to kill her just so I can stop thinking about her. Who would have thought a poor girl from a nowhere town would cause me so much trouble? Now I've got at least two investigations going on in her name and on her behalf. I should have just killed her, but I can always fix that."

"No, Father, enough is enough. Just let it go. Let all of this go. It will cost us a lot of our profits, but we have more money than we need. Just let it all go. Why not use your influence to let the girl go too? You could do that easily with all of your contacts. That would end all of this. Then we could all move on and be done with this for good."

"You can't be serious? She killed your brother. No matter what he did to her, she killed him, and that has to be answered. She has to pay a price. If not, we look weak, and that can be not only dangerous but also fatal. No, she will rot where she is if I don't take care of her first, flash drive or no flash drive. I would think you would understand that since he was your brother."

"I loved my brother, but I knew what and who he was. I know how he treated her. Don't get me wrong, Father, she deserved to be punished, but planting evidence and suppressing evidence and using the DA's office to get what you wanted? It's just wrong. Why not just let justice play out?"

"Because he was my son," Pierson erupted at last, "my flesh and blood. He was supposed to continue my legacy, and you were to make sure he didn't screw it up after I am gone. You were supposed to be a team. Now it's just you, and you want to back out of all that I have built."

"I'm not a criminal, Father. I never wanted to be in charge of a criminal empire. I will run this business, but I will not break the law."

"Fine, son. Fine. If that is what you want, then so be it. Now if you will excuse me, I have work to do. Go home and rest up. I will see you tomorrow."

"Father, I—"

"Tomorrow, son. I have a business to attend to."

With that, Jonathan rose to his feet and left his father's office. Leonard seethed over the exchange again as he had the time before. It wasn't anger that took hold of him, but it was a disappointment. Neither of his sons had lived up to his legacy. He had high hopes for Jonathan, but he just wouldn't give up on this Boy Scout routine. Leonard considered his options and eventually came to a decision. Perhaps it was time to sell the company and retire. Jonathan could continue running the perfectly legal side businesses the family controlled while the less-than-legal businesses could be someone else's problem. There was just the problem of loose ends that needed to be taken care of sooner than later, the first of which needed attention was a certain reporter.

CHAPTER 40

Sidney was working behind the counter in the library when the librarian, Karen Russell, walked over to her. She was in her late thirties and about five feet tall with short brown hair. Corrections work was not something that she ever thought she would be involved with after she graduated college with a library science degree. Karen went through a basic course on corrections work, but it was far less than what an actual corrections officer would go through. "Sidney, when you get a chance, I need you to help clear out that area where the magazine rack is."

"Sure, is something going to be put there?" she asked Karen. Since she started work in the library, Sidney had gotten to know Karen fairly well. All the library workers seemed to have a good opinion of the new librarian, and since she was not an officer, there was a more relaxed atmosphere in the library. When Sidney got put on lockdown, somehow Karen had found out and chided her on it almost like a big sister would do, telling her she should have known better.

As she looked around for a pen to write with, Karen told her that the library was going to get some computer stations. Inmates were going to be issued email addresses and pin numbers and allotted opportunities to go online with a lot of restrictions and monitoring, of course. It turned out that Karen came up with the idea and lobbied the prison administration for the computers. She cited evidence that other institutions experienced success with the program, so after months of lobbying, the prison officials agreed. Personally, Sidney was not too excited about it. She had social media accounts and all, but more than likely, those were not going to be allowed. Her parents were also not the most tech-savvy people on the planet. Her dad used

158

a computer for his work at the printshop, but he was not the type to use one in his personal time. Her mother used some social media but mostly to keep up with her friends from high school and college. Then again, if they could communicate by email, that might encourage them to send her messages online.

The two of them spent most of the remainder of the day making room for the computers. Plans were for an actual computer room with about fifteen or twenty computers. Priority for their use would be for educational purposes like GED and online college courses, but there would also be designated hours for personal usage as well. To start with, though, there were only going to be six computers along the wall where the magazine rack stood now. Karen assured her that more were on the way in the near future. Sidney did not say it out loud, but she doubted it would really be any time soon. Jillian was more excited by the news than Sidney thought she would be. While Sidney had not heard much from any of her friends since she was arrested, Jillian still kept in contact with a small number of people she knew on the outside. The prospect of being able to use a computer to communicate with friends and family lifted her spirits. It was going to be a while before the computers were ready for use, but good news was always welcome.

Life behind bars was like that though. Any time something positive happened, no matter how small, it was a plus. The routine of life on the inside was often one of repetition and boredom broken by moments of fear, joy, sadness, loneliness, contentment, and other emotions. It was hard to believe that one could be content in prison, but it was possible. Sure, Sidney could think of a thousand places she would rather be. She missed the beach. She missed scuba diving and surfing and just lying in the sun. But those things were still nine years away, so she tried to find contentment in the small things as much as possible. That night, as she lay awake in her bunk after lights out. She thought back again for the thousandth time on the night Lawson died. She thought about what she should have done differently and about how uncaring he was when she confronted him about those videos. Then she remembered the look on her mother's face as the bailiffs led her away and about the odd way she and Jillian had met, and she wondered if things had been different, would they have ever met and become friends.

There was still a part of her that could not believe that she was in prison. When she heard the judge say that she would have to spend twelve years of her life away from everything she had ever known, it was the worst feeling she had ever felt. She had been locked away now for three years, and while it might have gotten easier, it still was not easy being away. There were still nights like this where she became introspective of her situation. Maybe she deserved to be there, but that didn't make it easier to take. She didn't want sympathy, good thing since very few felt any for her, but she hoped someone would at least understand why she did what she did.

While she lay there, she didn't cry. She had done enough of that. Honestly, she spent the first several months to a year feeling sorry for herself. It didn't help, and she was through with that. She accepted the fact this was life for a long time to come and that in many ways she deserved what she got. *No more excuses, girl,* she thought. *You messed up, and you have to pay for it.* Hope was something that was dangerous on the inside. This place devoured it routinely. Luke Brady told her every time before he left to not give up hope, but after three years, that was hard. It was better, she thought, to accept her situation and try to make the best of it she could than trust in a vague hope. What she could not know was even as she lay there thinking over her situation, things were changing on the outside in her favor.

CHAPTER 41

The phone charging on the nightstand rang in the middle of the night. Frank Simmons tried to ignore it, but too many years of training wouldn't let him. He grabbed the phone, looked at the number, and cursed under his breath before answering it. "This better be good," was what came out. In the back of his mind, he knew it must be if he was getting a call this late, but it was after midnight on his day off, the first he had in weeks.

"Nice to hear from you too, old friend," came the voice on the other end.

"Roger, do you know what time it is here? Do you?"

"Yeah, sorry about this, Frank, but I need to talk to you. Is this line secured?" Roger Taylor asked him, trying to be cautious.

"Secured? What do you think this is, the CIA?" came a sarcastic reply from Simmons.

Roger and Frank went way back. They had both been in the military together, and both wanted to go into law enforcement when they got out. Frank joined the FBI shortly after his discharge, while Roger joined the police force and became a detective in Philadelphia for a few years before relocating to California. The two stayed in contact over the years and had helped out on a case or two here and there. Roger hated to bother him at such a late hour on the East Coast, but it was important.

"Look, Frank, I hate to bother you, but I got a case you may be interested in."

"Roger, you know there are proper channels for this. I'm not supposed to take cases off the books."

"I know, but listen for a second, all right? You sure no one can hear us?" Taylor asked.

"As sure as I can be. Now will you tell me what you want so I can say no and go back to sleep?" Simmons asked him with even more sarcasm than before.

"Frank, it's about Leonard Pierson. I think I got some hard evidence this time that can bring a solid case on him."

Simmons sat up in bed and turned on the lamp on the nightstand. His wife, Gina, who was hard to wake up on the best of mornings, grumbled about the light being on. "Give me a second, will you?" he spoke into the phone. He gathered himself, grabbed a T-shirt near the bed, and walked downstairs of their home. Upon reaching the couch, he said, "Roger, what did I tell you last time you brought this up? We've been looking for years, and nothing is there. I believe he's a creep, but—"

"I've got info on him now, Frank. I've got delivery schedules, cargo listings, locations, names, everything to blow an investigation wide open."

"What?" Simmons asked in surprise. "How did you get all of that?"

"You heard his boy, Lawson, got killed, right?"

"Yeah, one of his little playgirls killed him or something."

"She wasn't a playgirl. She was his fiancée, and I think she may have been acting more out of fear and self-defense than the record shows. Anyway, he left a flash drive at her apartment one night, and her attorney found it. Frank, it has everything. This could be a game changer."

Simmons started to look around nervously out of pure reflex. "Roger, slow down. I've not heard you like this for years. Look, if this is so good, then take it to the California Bureau."

Years ago, the FBI started an investigation into Pierson's shipping company. It was a case that he and Roger got to collaborate on since it involved interstate commerce, and Roger was the lead detective on the local level. He kept up on the Piersons from time to time but had long since given up.

"Frank, I can't do that. You are one of a handful of people I can trust on this. Can you come to California?"

"Oh yeah, sure, let me just hop on the FBI's plane and get right out there."

"Frank, please, this is important. I'm sure there are good agents at the California office, but you would know that better than me. We can do this, Frank. We can finish what we started years ago. Don't you want that?"

"All right, Roger, fine. I'll see what I can do. This better be good though."

"Trust me, this is good information."

Simmons hung up the phone and sat back on his couch. His thoughts ran heavy as he remembered several years ago how he had hit one dead end after another. It wasn't that he didn't want to help bring down Leonard Pierson, but it wasn't his office, and it wasn't his investigation anymore. It would be a hard sell convincing his superiors to allow him to fly across the country on the word of a local cop, even one that he'd known for so long. He had some vacation time that he was long overdue in taking. Maybe a trip to California was just what he needed.

CHAPTER 42

It had been months since the Lewises went out on anything like a date night. Sophia wouldn't admit it, but it seemed an odd thing to do while her daughter was incarcerated. Yes, she agreed to go on that cruise a while back, but it took a lot of persuasion. Life had to go on though, and she decided dinner and a movie wasn't such a bad idea, so she and Todd went to see the latest comedy release at the matinee. They followed the movie with a nice dinner at a local steakhouse. The couple had a lovely evening and decided that they would call it a night. They joked around with each other about how their younger selves would laugh at them calling an end to a date before ten o'clock at night. It was true they were going home early, but that didn't mean that the date was over. They were not that old after all.

That night, Luke and his investigators were meeting again. Taylor began by telling them about the investigation into Jim Cooper's murder. It was still early in the investigation, but he had a few leads that he was going to follow up on. Shelia, for her part, found some patterns in the shipping records on the flash drive that seemed to point to suspicious activities. Taylor agreed to investigate them by the end of the next week, but Shelia said she would look into it herself. Taylor told her to leave it to him. He also told the group about contacting his FBI friend in Washington, DC. While they were discussing various aspects of the case, Luke's phone rang. He excused himself and answered it in the hallway. When he returned, he had a blank expression on his face. Shelia and Roger fell silent at the sight of him. "There's been an accident, and I've been called to identify the bodies."

"Oh god, Luke, who was it?" Shelia asked him.

"It's the Lewises. Said they were hit by an eighteen-wheeler that ran a red light. Driver has been arrested on suspicion of driving under the influence." Luke looked as if he had gone into shock. Todd Lewis was his oldest and closest friend. Suddenly he started to lose his balance, and Shelia and Roger were quick to stabilize him before he fell.

"Luke, let me drive you," Taylor said. "You are in no shape to drive. I'll go with you."

"Thanks," was all he could muster. Together, they made it to the car. Luke did not speak the whole way to the hospital. He thought about all the times they shared on the golf course. He thought about their college days, then how he talked to them about their daughter's case. He stayed there for hours at their home, answering questions about why he let her take that plea. He promised Todd he would keep fighting for her no matter what. It was a promise he meant to keep.

When they arrived at the hospital's morgue, there was no doubt it was them. Taylor talked to the traffic investigators who were at the scene while Luke identified the bodies. After several minutes, he walked out and found Taylor. He explained to Luke that the driver was in custody, and while it would be several days before the blood test results were known, he did fail the field sobriety test and Breathalyzer test. Luke nodded and walked back to the car. Taylor followed at a respectful distance.

Saturday started as every day did in Helen Palmer Prison. The weekend routine differed very little from that of the weekday routine. Weekends did mean visitation day for a lot of inmates. Sidney was in her cellblock playing checkers with Nora Venable, a young Caucasian woman serving time for drug trafficking. Just before lunch, Officer McConnell came in and told her she had a visitor. Sidney thought it was strange that she wasn't taken to the usual visitation area but the area where she met with her attorney. Sure enough, Luke Brady sat there at the table, waiting for her. She smiled and said, "Mr. Brady, I wasn't expecting you today. I thought it would be next month before we met again."

"Sidney, sit down. I need to tell you something," he said in a weak voice. His expression was that of a man who had to do something that gave him great dread. Sidney sat down, preparing for the worst. "Sidney." He paused and swallowed hard. "Sidney, last night, your parents went out to dinner. They didn't make it home. A large truck ran a red light and hit them. Sidney, they both died at the scene."

She sat there in stunned silence. Did he just say that? Was that really what she just heard? "Which?" she began fighting back tears. "Are they both…" The brave face she had learned to wear quickly dropped. She ran both hands through her hair, but she couldn't decide what she should do. "Are you sure it was them? Are you really sure?" she asked as she began to lose her composure.

"Yes. I viewed the bodies late last night. I'm so sorry, Sidney." Luke was finding it harder to hold it together as well. He tried to put on a brave front for her, but he was afraid it was an empty gesture. Somehow they managed to compose themselves enough to go over some essential legal business. After that was done, he told her that he had to return and help with funeral arrangements in the estate's name and to coordinate with the family. "Sidney, I swear I'm not going to let them down. I promised them I would help you every way I can, and that's what I'm going to do. I have people working on getting you home as soon as possible."

She nodded as she stood up. "Thank you," was all she said and told the guard outside she was ready to leave. She felt as if she were out of her own body. it was as if she were only a shell, empty inside as she walked back to the cellblock. Her mind raced with memories of her parents and the times she shared with them. It was too much to take in that her parents were both gone.

When she arrived back in the cellblock, she walked by everyone without saying a word. She walked straight to her cell and rested her head on her top bunk. Not long after, Jillian walked in. "Hey, I was thinking that maybe…" She stopped midsentence after seeing Sidney turn to face her. "Are you okay?" she asked her.

"Jillian," was all she could say as she rushed to embrace her as the emotional dam she built broke. Jillian guided her to her bunk, and together they sat down.

"Sidney, what's wrong? Tell me, what happened?"

"They're gone. My parents are gone."

"Oh no, sweetheart, no. Oh, girl, I'm so sorry."

"They died last night in a car crash. They're not even going to let me go to the funeral. I can only go to the funeral home if my lawyer hires a deputy to transport me. Otherwise, I can't even say goodbye to them."

"Is he going to do that?"

"Yeah, he said he would. I let them down, Jillian. I failed them. I was supposed to give them grandchildren, do things to make them proud, but I failed them."

"No, girl, you didn't fail them. They were proud of you. I know they were."

"How could they be proud of a daughter in prison? What have I done but screw up? Now I'll never get to make it up to them."

"They knew you weren't perfect, and they knew you made a mistake, but that didn't change the fact they loved you. When this is over, and it will be over, you can spend the rest of your life being the woman they knew you are."

"How do you know that? How do you know?"

"Because it's what my dad tells me every time he visits. I never met them, but they sound like people who wouldn't want you to beat yourself up over, whether they loved you or not. Love is not based on your mistakes. They loved you no matter what."

Sidney continued to sob. Jillian was right though; her parents wouldn't want her to think they didn't love her or weren't proud she was their daughter. The rest of the day, passed by in a haze. Several inmates came by and wished their condolences to her, which she thanked each one in return. It was a long and sleepless night, but somehow she got through it.

Shortly before lunch, as Sidney sat on her bunk composing a letter to be read at the funeral, Jo came by to see her. "May I come in?" she asked. Sidney looked up and invited her in. "Just wanted to let you know how sorry I am to hear about your parents. You need anything, you ask me, no strings attached." She called for another inmate who waited outside Sidney's cell just out of sight. The woman walked in carrying a makeshift basket of packages and foods of various types. "The ladies and I put this together for you. I hope it helps."

"Thank you, Jo, that's very kind of you. Thanks to everyone."

"I told you we family in here. We take care of our own. You all right, girl, and you one of us. Some of us, this all the family we got. We don't always get along, but we are still family." Jo reached out and embraced her and turned to go. Sidney felt better, and shortly after lunch, she was interacting again with the others. Tomorrow she was scheduled to travel to the funeral home with the deputy Brady hired.

In some ways, she was glad she couldn't go to the funeral. It saved her the embarrassment of being seen in shackles during the service. She would also be spared the looks of all the others there judging her. Many of the people who would be there had turned their backs on her, so maybe it wasn't so bad. At least she could have time to say her goodbyes without the judgmental looks of those around her. So there was a bright side to it, then. Either way, tomorrow would be a long day.

CHAPTER 43

Just after breakfast, a guard came and took Sidney to catch her ride to the funeral home. After she was searched, she was shackled hand and feet, but they did not attach the customary belly chain. The guards led her out to a smaller gate where a marked sheriff's car waited for her. The uniformed deputy signed a form and opened the rear door and helped her inside the car, fastening her seatbelt. He shut the door, and shortly they were on their way for the just over two-hour drive to the funeral home. This was the first time in over three years that she had ridden in a car, much less a vehicle with air conditioning. She couldn't remember if the route to the funeral home would take them by her parents' home. She doubted they would, but just being back there was a strange feeling. It would also be a temporary feeling too because the prison officials told her that she would be back that day. As they drove through the gates, she felt a strange sense of relief. Her mind drifted to the last time she drove through the gates, only this time she was leaving prison. This relief was tempered with the thought that it was only for the day.

They had driven for only a few minutes when the deputy finally broke the silence. "Good morning, Ms. Lewis. Do you remember me?"

It took her a few moments to place the voice, but she couldn't see the man's face. She tried to see the man's face in the rearview mirror, and for a second, she worried it might be someone from Leonard Pierson there to torture and kill her.

The man gave a sympathetic laugh and removed his hat. "I didn't think you would, what with me in uniform. The last time we talked, I had a shirt and tie on. I'm Detective Roger Taylor, the investigator who talked with you when you were arrested." His voice was strangely reassuring. Over the past few years, she had come to distrust anyone in uniform. Her mind went back to him insisting on getting her a lawyer and how he seemed to want to help her in her situation.

"Detective Taylor, yes, I remember you," she said, trying to sound confident. "I didn't get to talk to you much after Mr. Brady took my case.

"That's true, Ms. Lewis, and for what it's worth, I'm sorry about that. It's not standard police procedure, but neither is taking a plea so early in the legal process."

She swallowed hard, remembering what Leonard Pierson told her that night back in the city jail. "I was guilty. I told you that when you arrested me." A nervous feeling began to seize her. Sidney was told many times to not get too close to those in uniform and to not talk about her case to anyone without Mr. Brady present. "Why are you the one escorting me? Isn't this something a lower-ranked deputy would do?"

"Usually, yes, and I'm not technically a deputy. I'm a city cop, but I volunteered for this job and pulled a few strings to talk to you." Taylor relaxed in his seat. He worried that she wouldn't talk to him, and this would be a long drive with an awkward silence. "I've been working with Luke Brady on your case. I've got a few new leads, but I need you to help me."

"I can't do that. Mr. Brady said not to discuss my case."

"Yeah, he said you'd say that. Look, I believe your story, and I think you've been set up to take a harder fall than you should. I want to help you, but you need to help me."

"Please, Detective Taylor, I just want to see my parents. I can't talk to you about this."

"Listen to me, I can't promise to get you out, but I want to bring down Leonard Pierson. If that's who you are afraid of, then help me put him where he can't hurt you."

"I'm not afraid of him anymore. I don't trust people in uniform. You might have been the only one who wanted to believe me and actually hear my story, but you disappeared, and I had to deal with that Cooper guy."

"He's dead," Taylor said more coldly than he intended.

"What?" Sidney responded in disbelief. "When did he die?"

"Couple of weeks ago. Murdered in his home along with his wife. He changed Lawson's cause of death to multiple blows to the head from that scuba tank. No mention of how you feared for your life or that Lawson shoved you against the boat railing, among other things." He stopped to let all that information sink in. Taylor could see her face change and that she was taking in the information. He also sensed that she didn't trust him either. He couldn't blame her for that. She's spent the last three years learning not to trust cops, so it had to be hard to trust one now.

"I'm sorry. I don't think I can help you. I made my choices and did what I thought I had to do so that I didn't have to spend the rest of my life in prison."

"Okay, Ms. Lewis, I understand, but think about this. My team has interviewed some of the women Lawson slept with, and we have several new leads. We also have the flash drive. Believe it or not, there are people who are trying to help you."

She fell silent, and Taylor stopped trying to persuade her. Brady warned him that she probably would not want to talk. He had to try, of course, but he could tell after years of learning to read body language that she was thinking about what he told her. The information was something she would have to consider, and maybe she would decide it was worth talking about.

They arrived at the funeral home, and only a handful of cars were there. Taylor opened her door and escorted her into a rear door. Once they were let inside, she was led into a hallway, and he pulled her into a side office. He took out his keys and took her by the wrists and unlocked her handcuffs and then took off her leg shackles. "I'm going to trust you to not run off. You got about thirty minutes, and then we'll need to get back on the road."

Sidney smiled weakly and gave her promise not to run. Honestly, she didn't know where she would run to in the first place. She followed a member of the funeral home staff to the visitation room, where her parents were lying in state. Seeing them brought the tears back. No matter how much she tried to prepare herself, she wasn't ready to see them like this. She tried to remember the last time she had seen them alive. It had been about two weeks before, and it brought to mind that this past weekend, they were supposed to come see her. Now this would be the last time she would ever see either of them.

"They talked about you all the time," came a familiar voice from behind her. Sidney turned to see Luke Brady walking through the doorway in the company of a middle-aged Asian woman and Roger Taylor. "You know, I would have to stop your mother from talking about you so many times when I would go over there to tell them about developments in your case. They never gave up hope."

Sidney put her arm around his waist as he embraced her with his left arm.

"They never stopped loving you, and they were making plans for when you got out."

She could see a small tear roll down his face. She knew her father and Luke went way back and that he was hurting too. "I've missed them so much. I can't believe they're gone," she said, fighting through the tears. "I let them down, didn't I?"

"There's never been a child in all of history except one who didn't, and he was all God and all man at the same time. They never stopped being proud of you no matter what you did or where you were. That's the kind of people they were."

They stood there several more minutes, then Taylor told them it was time to go. She said her final goodbyes to them and turned to surrender herself back to Detective Taylor. He motioned for her to follow him back down the hallway. To her surprise, he led her to a room with a small table. At one end sat the Asian lady she saw with Mr. Brady. Taylor told her to take a seat at the table. A few moments later, they were joined by Luke Brady.

"I'm sorry to do this here, Sidney, but we really need to talk to you," Brady told her in an attempt to calm her down. "Detective Taylor probably told you he was working with me on your case. I told him you wouldn't talk without me, and I was right."

Taylor mumbled a response, which drew a sarcastic smile from Brady.

"This is Shelia Lee, a veteran crime reporter and ex-girlfriend—"

"Fiancée," Shelia interrupted.

Luke chuckled. "Fiancée of Detective Taylor here. She rounds out our little team."

Sidney studied them all closely. She was feeling a range of emotions as she sat there. "Why are we doing this now?" she asked. "I just said goodbye to my parents, and you want to do this now?" She was trying hard to not lose control, but the timing could not be worse.

"We know it's terrible timing, but we only have a small window to speak together. I'm sorry it has to be now, but this is important," Luke told her, trying to sound reassuring. He really didn't approve of this plan when Taylor suggested it to him, but he had to admit this was probably the only way to talk with her unobserved.

"Ms. Lewis, you have to know something about Lawson and his dealings. Whether you realize it or not, he was into some really bad things. I wanted to question you more before, but Cooper took over the investigation and pressured you into the plea. That officially closed the investigation, and I couldn't go forward then," Taylor said.

Shelia added, "I have interviewed several girls in the last few weeks. They're all scared. That means the Piersons are intimidating others similar to you."

"Similar to me?" Sidney said, her frustration growing. "Those girls are not in prison. I am."

"Yes, Sidney, you're right," Luke broke in. "They were deceived by Lawson, just like you were, and they have been threatened, just like you have. But unlike you, they didn't know Lawson like you did."

"I didn't know anything about any criminal activities. He never discussed that with me."

"Yes, but he could have told you about some of the people and places he went. Maybe some names that kept coming up. Anything, no matter how small, might led to a break in the case," Taylor told her. He was beginning to think this was a waste of time.

"Sidney, please," Shelia said to her in a calming voice, "I can't imagine what you've gone through or what it's like to not trust anyone around you. I don't blame you for not trusting any of us. In some ways, I guess we've all let you down. But we are trying to help you. If you can give us anything, no matter how small, that could go a long way to ending this nightmare."

Sidney thought for a minute. Pictures of her mother and father ran through her mind. She remembered her mother's smile and how her father was always there for her when she needed him. He trusted Luke Brady. Now maybe she needed to do the same. "He told me that he was going to meet with someone important once. Sullivan. I think his name was John. No, it was George. That's it, George Sullivan. I remember Lawson talking about him a lot now that I think about it. I heard him on the phone with him a bunch."

"George Sullivan? Are you sure?" asked Taylor with excitement in his voice.

"Yes. I asked him who he was, and he told me it wasn't important."

"You know this Sullivan guy?" Shelia asked Taylor.

Taylor took a deep breath to calm himself. "Yes, he's an investigator at the department. He was the detective that first met with Sidney on the yacht. Do you know why he wanted to talk with him?" Taylor could feel anger building inside himself. He and Sullivan worked side by side for years. This was a man he thought he knew so well. It all started to make sense now how Pierson could always stay a step ahead of him. How did he not see this before? Maybe he just didn't want to believe it was true.

"He just told me it was about several shipments that were going out, that's all," Sidney said. She seemed to realize that what she just told them was very important. "I'm sorry, I stayed out of his work life. Gosh, maybe I should have asked more questions."

"It's okay, Sidney, you did good," Shelia reassured her. "Roger, just how deep does this go at the department?" Shelia asked.

"I don't know. Is there anyone else you can think of, Sidney?"

"I'm sorry. Other than his friends, I don't know anything."

Luke Brady took her hand. "No, Shelia's right. You did good, kid. This helps to prove our case." He looked at Taylor. "How are you going to proceed? You going to question Sullivan?" This was the break they had possibly been waiting on, but it was also a dangerous time as well. If things went wrong, Sidney could be in great danger.

"Yeah, I'll press him. I think I know how to approach him. Always thought Sullivan was a good cop. I put my life on the line with that guy so many times."

"Just be careful. If he talks to Pierson, it could backfire," Shelia added. "I can squeeze some of Lawson's friends for more information. I also found a couple of names of Pierson executives that appear more than a few times on various documents. I can follow them and see if anything turns up."

"Shelia, leave the police work to the police," Taylor said, lecturing her. "These people could be dangerous."

"I can take care of myself, Roger."

"I know that, but you are not a trained cop. We don't need you taking chances."

"I'll be fine. Besides, eventually, we will have to take risks."

Taylor rose from his seat, checking his watch. "Look, I have to get her back. We'll talk about this later." He motioned for Sidney to stand up and told her to go use the restroom before they left. When she finished, he cuffed and shackled her again. Luke and Shelia walked out with them and assured her that the investigation was going well and not to worry.

On the way back, Taylor stopped at a fast-food joint and bought her a burger. It was the best meal she had in a long time. She couldn't help but laugh to herself at how something so routine three years before was something she missed so much. A couple of hours later, they were driving through the gates again. Before walking her back to the intake area, Taylor reassured her one last time and promised he would do all he could to help her. Back in her cell that night, Sidney felt a small feeling of hope, and she slept well.

CHAPTER 44

The police station was the usual hustle and bustle it always was at midmorning. Phones rang nonstop, while people went in and out, some there to report a crime, some there because they committed a crime. It was a busy day, which was typical for even a small-town police station. George Sullivan, a detective on the force for six years, was in his forties. He served in various cities before settling in Warrenton. To him, it was close enough to a big city and the beach but far enough away to avoid a lot of the problems of a larger city. The place had its problems, but that was fine, if for no other reason than job security. He just hung up the phone and picked up a new case file when a uniformed officer, Johnson, he thought, came up to him saying there was a suspect in a case he was working wanting to talk to him. Sullivan thanked the officer and walked to the interrogation room. When the door opened, he was immediately grabbed by the man waiting for him inside. He grabbed for the man's arms in an attempt to fight him. That's when he saw the face of the man who had attacked him.

Roger Taylor was in a bad mood. He hardly slept that night after driving Sidney Lewis back to prison. What kept him up was the knowledge that cops in the department were dirty and doing the bidding of Leonard Pierson. He asked Officer Johnson to get Sullivan to come to the interrogation room, where he would confront him. It was not his original intention to grab him and slam him on the table, but after the lack of sleep and the anger over the corruption, it just felt right. "How long have you been working for Pierson, Sullivan?"

"What the hell are you talking about, Taylor? I don't work—"

"Don't hand me that crap, Sullivan," Taylor interrupted him with a growl in his voice. "I know you've been working for him. I want to know when he got to you and why you altered the crime scene on Lawson Pierson's boat?"

"I didn't change anything. I—"

"Lie to me again, Sullivan, and you'll lose teeth. I know you met with Lawson, and you are the only other investigator from the department to analyze the crime scene. I read your report. Want to compare notes and see who remembers how it was best?"

"Okay, look, you know how it is. Long hours, low pay. I got behind on—"

"That's bullshit, and you know it. Why did you alter the scene? Talk."

"Okay, okay, Taylor, I admit it. I called the man that I report to Pierson through. Said that they needed me to doctor the scene to make it look like the girl killed him during an argument. He said that he needed to get attention away from Lawson and that the girl simply lost it."

"This man got a name? Answer me."

"Goldman. Bernie Goldman."

Taylor released him and ran a nervous hand through his hair. "You're sure it's Goldman?" The revelation sent a chill through Taylor. On the one hand, this was the first time that anyone linked that close to Pierson was named in connection to the case. On the other hand, Goldman was a trained attack dog, and he knew that Pierson unleashed him on anyone that posed a problem for him. Sullivan was in deep if Goldman was sent to him.

"Look, Roger, I didn't want to set the girl up that way. She seemed like a nice kid and all, but Goldman said that it was important that Lawson stay clean in all this."

"So you decided to ruin someone's life for the Piersons?"

"Ruin her life? Roger, she killed the guy. She would have gone to prison anyway."

"You don't know that. To hear her tell it, she was afraid for her life after he tried to push her over that rail. Did you also know he was carrying the bottle of scotch upside down by the neck? Did you know that? Did you know that he slipped on the wet deck and hit his head a second time, and that's what killed him?"

"Roger, please, I've got—"

"Did you know?" Taylor screamed at him.

Sullivan reeled under the pressure, sweat pouring down his face. "Yes. I knew all of that," he said, breaking under the pressure.

"And you went along with it. That girl has missed three years of her life, missed her parent's funeral for a lie. My god, man, how can you live with yourself?"

"Roger, what are you going to do with this information?"

Taylor nearly decked him for that question. He genuinely wanted to hit him square in his cowardly face. "We're going back into that squad room, and you are going to give me everything you know about Pierson and his interests. Then you are going to help me dismantle Pierson one part at a time until he's sitting in one of these cells. Lastly, you are going to get me the name of every cop on his payroll. After that, I'll talk to the DA, and maybe you'll just lose your pension."

"Roger, please, I can't—"

"You will, or I might just ride you up to the Pierson's front door and thank you for all of your help and useful information."

Sullivan's face went blank. He knew Taylor well enough to know that he wasn't bluffing. Now he was in an unpleasant situation where he might be a dead man one way or the other. Goldman wouldn't care about his situation or how the tables were turned on him. "Where do you want to start?" he said, resigned to the idea that if he were a dead man, better to be a dead man with a chance at redemption.

After a long talk, the men emerged from the interrogation room. Roger felt that finally things were going in the right direction. If this didn't get his FBI buddy here, nothing would. That's when Officer Johnson approached him again. "Hey, Detective Taylor, we just got a call on the Cooper murder case. A lady said she saw a guy coming out of their home around the time of the murders." Today just got a whole lot better.

CHAPTER 45

After the evening meal, Sidney sat in the commons area, watching whatever was on the television. She wasn't really into the show. She just more or less wanted the distraction that the program offered. Conversations struck up here and there, and she even decided to sit in on a game of checkers, anything to keep her mind off her parents. One of the worst parts about prison was the loneliness, but what made this worse was the knowledge that there was not going to be a reunion with her parents when she got out. Not for the first time, she began to wonder what she would do when that day did arrive. A few minutes before lockdown, she walked to her cell and situated herself on her bunk. Jillian was already there writing on what looked like a form. She didn't ask what it was at first. In fact, Jillian had remarked on how withdrawn she had been over the last couple of weeks since she got back from seeing her parents. It was true. Sidney just didn't feel like herself. The feeling went beyond the usual unhappiness at her situation. She felt low as if life had lost a lot of its meaning. She prayed a lot, but that emptiness remained.

The sound of the cell door slamming shut roused her out of her malaise. In a couple of hours, it would be lights out. Jillian popped her head up and checked on her, asking if she was doing better. She said she was without really feeling it was true. Jillian asked her to come down and look at something with her, and Sidney climbed down. That's when Jillian handed her the form letter. "I've been wanting to talk to you about this, but with your parents and all, I didn't want to trouble you anymore," she told her in a way that reminded Sidney of her best friend in high school. Back then, they had planned to go to the same college. But late in the summer of her junior year, she told her that she was going to another school out of state instead. It strained their relationship over senior year, but Sidney understood, and the two made up. "I've just gone over the halfway mark of my sentence, so I'm applying to the parole board to have my case reviewed for early release."

"Jillian, that's great news. When will you know?"

"I'm not sure. I'm sending this in the morning, and they are supposed to let me know when I will appear before them in a few weeks."

"I'm happy for you, girl. I really am. I wish you would have told me sooner though."

"I know, but I just didn't want to hit you with this with all you're going through. Please tell me you aren't mad."

"Of course not. Jillian, this is your chance to start a new life. How could I be mad about that?"

"I know, but I don't want to get my hopes up too much. They may say no."

"You know, I'll help you. We need to practice. Practice everything you will say, how you act, all of it. I'm so happy for you."

"Hey, again, it's not for sure." Jillian stood up and paced back and forth. "Maybe I shouldn't. Maybe I should just stay another year and get ready."

"Jillian, no. You need this. If anyone in here deserves a second chance, it's you. Now you get that paper to where it needs to go, or I'll pick you up and carry you there myself."

"Yes, ma'am," Jillian replied and gave Sidney a big hug. "Will you be all right if I do get out?"

"That was always going to happen," Sidney replied in a soft voice. "I've always known you'd leave before me. I'll be all right. I promise. Go be happy."

The two embraced again. She was putting on a brave face, but the reality of living without someone she regarded as the only friend she had in the world frightened her. Still, it was selfish of her to want Jillian to stay. It was a strange feeling. She wanted very much for her friend to be happy even if life after prison would be hard. She also would miss her very much, and who knew what kind of cellmate she would have next. Still, the news made her happy in a way she could not describe. Maybe this was a sign of things to come. Even if it wasn't, she wanted to help her friend, and that's what she was going to do.

CHAPTER 46

Shelia knew that being out here was dangerous at best. She followed up on a lead she got from an informant about a warehouse in the business district that was used to load illegal narcotics onto trucks. She cross-referenced the names, and sure enough, more than a couple of them led her right to Pierson's shipping business. It was nighttime, and she used the cover of darkness to slip into a spot unobserved near the warehouse in a small wooded area. She brought her camera, but as of yet, there was nothing to see. Taylor often told her that criminals did not often keep regular hours, and now she knew what he meant. She had been there over an hour and was ready to give it up for the night when a semitruck pulled to the loading dock. Nothing too suspicious since trucks were loading and unloading all the time day and night. This one was different. The first man that came out was in what looked to her like a light-brown uniform; no surprise there. However, the next two guys that came out were carrying what looked like automatic weapons. She couldn't be certain if they were really automatic, but that would not matter if they spotted her.

Suddenly she heard voices behind her. She could not hear exactly what they were saying, but she could clearly tell they were getting closer. Quickly, she got down behind a tree as the footsteps grew louder. "Yeah, I swear I thought I saw someone moving over here," she heard one of them say. She stayed still as humanly possible as the voices grew louder and slowly passed on by. Relieved she wasn't seen, she decided to snap a couple of pictures, then leave. She got her photos and quietly began to make her way back to her car, which she had parked several feet away. As she made her way out of the wooded area, she heard the voices grow louder again. Had they seen her after all? She'd made up a story about being a lost hiker, but the more she thought about that, she realized no one would believe her. She hid behind a small group of trees and then made a break for it right into the arms of a large man not five feet from her. She tried not to scream, and since he put his hand over her mouth, it wouldn't have mattered anyway. "Just what the hell are you doing here?" the man asked her as if he, too, was trying to keep his voice down.

"Look, you see, I was trying to find my way back to the interstate, and my car broke down and... Roger, is that you?"

"Yes, it's me, but why are you here? You were supposed to stay away from the police work."

"Roger, I told you I can take care of myself. What are you doing here?"

"About to raid that warehouse. Those other voices you heard are some of my most trusted officers."

"God, Roger, you scared me to death. Why didn't you tell me you were raiding this place?"

"Because it's police business, that's why. Now stay here, or I'll have Murphy put you in the van."

His radio crackled to life, and the voice on the other end said, "We're in position. Will move on your mark."

Roger activated his radio. "Copy that. We're almost in position. Wait for my signal." He gave her one harder look and then made his way down to the front of the warehouse, unseen. "All right. Go," he said into his radio as the team started to move on their targets.

"Police department. Everybody, freeze," he said as he made his way into the building. Few of the men inside stayed put. One of the men with the automatic rifles opened fire, just missing Roger. He let loose three shots, putting two into the man who fell in a heap on the floor. The other man armed with an automatic rifle ran square into an officer and never got a chance to fire his weapon. Those trying to escape out the back were cut off and caught without a struggle.

"All right, round everyone up. Make sure to read them their rights," Roger said, making his way to a newly opened container. Inside was a number of boxes marked Fragile. He opened one and found what looked like computer parts. He pulled several of them out, finding the exact same thing each time. A sense of doubt began to come over him until he looked at one of the twelve people in custody who had a nervous look on his face. That's when he saw the box that looked as if it had been opened. He reached into the crate and picked it up. Sure enough, the weight of the package was off. He opened it and found a large bag containing a white powder.

"Get me a test kit," he said. Sure enough, the chemicals inside the kit turned a brilliant blue for cocaine. "Hot damn." Suddenly he caught sight of a man hiding under a desk toward the back of the room. He walked his way over there, but it was clear the man was not trying to escape but cowering in fear. Taylor found the man visibly shaking under the desk, so he reached down and pulled him out and onto his feet.

"I want a lawyer," the balding middle-aged man said.

"Yeah, I bet you do, Mr. Gaddis. I bet you do."

Shelia waited just out of sight as the police processed the scene. Taylor came out after nearly an hour and found her impatiently waiting for news. He took her back to the car and told them what took place, and they caught an important target, although he didn't tell her who he was. She could tell Taylor was more excited than she had seen him in a long time. Roger Taylor was not a man who showed his emotions, but she knew him long enough to know when he was excited about something. "Now will you please let me handle this?" he asked her as they walked up to her car.

"I told you I can take care of myself, Roger. I don't need a babysitter."

"I know you can, but these are dangerous criminals. Hell, one of them took a shot at me tonight. I'm the cop, and you are the reporter. I promise to keep you in the loop."

Shelia fished for her keys and, when she found them, opened her car door. "No promises. What's the next move?" She could tell he was frustrated with her, but this was her best way to stay involved in the investigation. She smiled at him in that disarming way she did while they were dating all those years ago.

Taylor shifted on his feet and exhaled a response, "I have an interview with a witness to the Cooper murders tomorrow morning. You can tag along if you want, but no names in the media. You got it?"

"Got it," she said as she shut the door and waved goodbye to him before driving off. He watched her drive away and shook his head.

The next morning, the two meet up at a local restaurant for breakfast before driving to the witness's home. The message said to arrive precisely at nine that morning and not after ten thirty because she had a luncheon at her senior's group. In spite of their best efforts, they arrived at ten minutes after nine. The home was located across the street from the scene about two houses down and belonged to a Phil and Amelia Goggens. When Taylor knocked on the door, he and Shelia were greeted by a lady in her late seventies. "Yes, how can I help you?" she asked. He flashed his badge, and she opened the door to let them in. She chided them about being late to which Taylor responded that police business wasn't always able to keep a time schedule. Shelia nudged him hard on his arm as they were shown into their sitting area.

Amelia spoke with a definite German accent to which she explained that she was not German but Austrian. "My family came to America before the war because we did not want to live under that terrible man. After the war, my mother and father went back to try and reconnect with our family. I was actually born there and lived in Austria for several years in the American zone. We came back to America when I was thirteen, and I've lived here ever since then." She asked them to sit as she took a seat on a glider rocker across from a small couch. Taylor and Shelia took their seats and declined an offer of coffee.

"Mrs. Goggens, you said that you saw the person who may have killed the Coopers. Could you describe him for me?" Taylor asked.

"Oh no, I'm sorry, I can't."

"Why not? You said you saw a man coming out of the Cooper's home the night of the murder," Taylor said, trying to keep his temper in check.

"Well, you see, I didn't see him that night. I have this camera on my front door that my grandchildren just insisted I get a few years back. About once a week, I watch the footage from the camera before I delete it."

"Wait a minute," Shelia interrupted, "you watch all the footage? That takes hours."

"Well, no, I fast-forward through it. And that's how I saw that man. Would you like to see the footage?" She took them to her desktop computer and called up the footage from that night. She explained that she really didn't like computers, but her grandkids showed her how to use this one and how to watch the footage from the camera. Soon she found the video from that night and pointed to a man walking down the sidewalk to a waiting car. "That's the man. Never seen him here before, and he was the last one to come out of their house before morning." The video was of good quality, but it did not give a good image at the distance from the man in the video. He asked if he could have a copy of the video, and Mrs. Goggens said that he could. Shelia produced a flash drive and saved a copy of the video. Taylor couldn't help but think how ironic it was that a flash drive was what started this whole thing and a flash drive was what could solve it.

They left the Goggens's home at about ten twenty-five because she let them both know how important her senior group was to her. They wasted no time leaving the home. "So what do we do now?" Shelia asked as they got in the car.

"We take this to a guy I know and see if he can do some computer magic with the video after I make a copy or two of it." He dropped Shelia off back at the restaurant they ate breakfast at and then drove to the station. After making a few copies, he made a call to a computer guy that he knew across town. They met up after lunch at the man's home.

Tavon Garrett was a twenty-six-year-old black man and ran a small computer business in Warrenton. Taylor met him a few years ago while investigating an identity theft case. Since then, any questions he had involving computers he trusted to Tavon. That afternoon, he took the copy of the video to his shop to see if he could enhance the footage of the man leaving the Cooper's home.

"Yeah, I should be able to do something with this. Come back tomorrow and I'll have it ready," Tavon told him.

"Can you get it sooner?" Taylor asked him.

"Come back in a couple of hours, and maybe."

"What about now?" Taylor pressed him. "Come on, Tavon, I need it."

Without saying anything, Tavon started working on the video. Taylor didn't know the ins and outs of computer work, but he knew

Tavon would do his best. An hour and a half later, Tavon told him he had something. "That's your guy," he said without taking his eyes off the screen. "You know him?"

"Yes, I do," he responded. "Yes, I do."

CHAPTER 47

It was just after the evening meal that the mail was distributed to the inmates. Jillian found Sidney in the commons area and called her over, holding a very official-looking envelope. The two walked to their cell and sat down on Jillian's bunk. "Sidney, I'm so nervous I don't think I can open this. What if they rejected me?"

Sidney looked at her with a stern face. "You'll never know if you don't open it."

"Here, you open it," Jillian said, trying to force the letter into Sidney's hands.

"No way. You have to do this. Now put your big-girl pants on and open the damn letter."

Jillian was taken aback by her tone. "Fine." She took a deep breath and slid her finger into the small crease of the envelope flap. She tore the top and pulled out the letter inside. Jillian took a deep breath and opened the letter. Silence followed as her expression turned blank.

Sidney waited for a response, but Jillian only sat there in uncomfortable silence. "What did they say?" she finally asked. More silence followed. Jillian gasped for air as if she could not catch her breath. "Jillian?"

"They granted my parole," she finally broke the uncomfortable silence. "I'm going home. Oh my god, I'm going home." The two embraced each other in an expression of joy and relief. Sidney told her how happy she was for her and wished her well. "I'm not leaving for another month, but I've got so much to do. I have to tell my parents, I have to find work, I've got to—"

"Jillian, calm down. You're going home. That's the important thing. I am so happy for you, and I know you are going to do well. You've got support on the outside, people who care for you."

"I know, I know, but what if I screw it up again? What if I'm right back here in six months? You know how many girls end up back here?"

"You won't. You learned your lesson, and you won't be back. I know it," Sidney said, fighting back a tear. "I'm going to miss you, girl, but you deserve this."

"Are you going to be okay, Sidney?"

"I'm going to be fine, and I have you to thank for that."

"I'm going to miss you. I promise I won't forget you, and I'll keep in touch."

"You better. Hate to have to come and find you."

On the first day of the month during the morning count, a guard came to the door. "Porter, let's go roll up your stuff." Jillian was surprised they were releasing her this early. She looked back at Sidney in disbelief, not knowing what to say. "You want to stay here longer, Porter? Let's go."

"Come on, let's get your stuff," Sidney said as she gathered up Jillian's belongings.

"No, wait," she said, "give away my stuff. Tell the others." She paused as she felt a lump growing in her throat, and her eyes beginning to sting. "Tell them, just tell them something from me, okay?" The two embraced one last time. "I really suck at this. I don't have the words."

"You don't need them," Sidney whispered.

"Let's go, Porter. Last call or your ass can stay here."

Jillian let go and walked out of the cell door. When she heard it close, she looked back with tears streaming down her face. Sidney smiled and waved to her. Then she mouthed the word *go*. With that, Jillian waved one last time and followed the guard down the cell block. A few hours later, she walked down a sidewalk to a gate that led to the outside. The guard opened the door and looked at her. "Get out," he said. "Good luck and don't come back."

She walked through the gate and took her first breath of freedom in four and a half years. Waiting in the parking lot was an older couple waving for her to come over. Her parents didn't wait for her to walk to them. Her mother ran to her with her father right behind. After an embrace that seemed to go on forever, she finally said, "Let's go home." A few hours later, they arrived at her parents' home.

CHAPTER 48

Thomas Gaddis sat in the interrogation room, sweating nervously. His lawyer kept trying to calm him, but it was no use. He knew what happened to those who betrayed the Piersons and sometimes what happened to those who were compromised. In his best guess, he was in a no-win situation. So he sat there nervously waiting. The police had interviewed him several times, but they could hold him up to forty-eight hours without charging him with anything. Taylor knew that too, and he decided to make him wait and sweat it out for a day before interviewing him personally. Now he was ready to make his move. He entered the room and laid a file on the table. Taylor sat down, put his hands together, and stared blankly at Gaddis and his lawyer. He knew he had a winning hand, but he had to be careful not to tip it off too quickly. "This is a pretty unique situation you find yourself in, isn't it, Mr. Gaddis?" he began. "So how does it happen that an executive vice president at Pierson Shipping show up in the middle of the night to a warehouse full of cocaine? What dumb luck is that?" He could see Gaddis and his lawyer exchange glances.

"Are you going to charge my client or what?" the lawyer said, barely able to control his anger.

"Oh yes, we sure are, Counselor," Taylor responded, "we sure are, but I thought we'd give your client here a chance."

"What kind of chance?" Gaddis blurted out before his lawyer could stop him.

"The kind that saves you a lot of time and that 'whole dealing with Leonard Pierson' kind of chance. You talk now, and we can offer.you some protection. If not, well, you can take your chances with your boss."

"Just what are you offering my client, and what is it you want to know?" asked the lawyer, clearly getting tired of the game.

"I want you to talk to a friend of mine." Taylor got up and opened the door, and another man walked into the room. "I'll let him introduce himself."

"I'm Frank Simmons, FBI," the man said as he showed his badge. "I think you have some explaining to do about why you were in a warehouse full of drugs. Is that where we are, Detective Taylor?"

"Yep, that's where we were. Mr. Gaddis was about to make a choice to tell us or his boss what he was doing there. Which is it going to be?"

"Wait a minute," said the lawyer. "Why is the FBI here?"

"Because that truck was scheduled to drive to Reno, Nevada," Simmons said. "That's called interstate commerce, which means the bureau is interested. Honestly, where did you get your law degree?"

"Point is, this goes deeper than just you," added Taylor. "Time to choose how you want this to go down. Are you an informant willing to testify, or are you a loose end that, for the last day and change, has been talking to the police?" Taylor could tell that Gaddis was getting nervous, and he became more and more convinced that the man was not a martyr for the cause of Leonard Pierson.

"We want protection and a solid deal," the lawyer commented after an odd silence.

"Depends on what your client has to say, so let's hear it," Simmons told the man. Within a few minutes, Gaddis began to tell his story. Taylor believed that the walls built to protect Leonard Pierson were finally beginning to fall.

CHAPTER 49

Almost a month had passed since Jillian was released. For several days, Sidney felt empty inside. She felt guilty for that because she knew her friend was happy now. In the meantime, she got a new cellmate. Her name was Lisa Burnette, who had just arrived on a drug conviction and was sentenced to three years. She was a slender, blonde woman with shoulder-length hair. She wore eyeglasses all the time and was a few months younger than Sidney. The two got along fine, but she was no Jillian. Lisa spent most of her time with other inmates and basically used their shared cell to sleep. Sidney tried to keep busy and make new friends as much as she could, but she never could feel the same level of trust she had with Jillian. She missed her and wished she knew what was going on in her life and that she was okay. Time seemed to drag by more than before with each day passing by slowly. It had been a while, but she was really feeling the strain of life behind bars.

Several more days passed with no visitors and no word from the outside. Mr. Brady was scheduled to visit her in a couple of weeks, but he was the only one. She was starting to feel sorry for herself again. It wasn't that she didn't like the other inmates. At least she liked most of them. It was the fact that she just wasn't bonding with them like she did with Jillian. One day after the evening meal, she was sitting in the commons area playing cards when the mail came. To her surprise, the guard called her name out. At first, she didn't respond, thinking it may be someone else, but he yelled out her name again and practically threw the letter at her when she got up to retrieve her mail. Looking at the envelope brightened her mood considerably. Sidney ran to her cell and opened Jillian's letter. It was the first mail she received in months. She pulled out the contents of the letter to find it contained a number of pictures.

Sidney,

I hope you are doing all right. Sorry I haven't written before now; this month has been crazy. I got a job as a waitress at a local restaurant. My dad pulled a lot of strings for me with the owner of the place, so he agreed to hire me on a probationary basis. How's that for you? I'm on parole and probation. I also met with my PO recently. Nothing too important to tell about there.

Did you look at the pictures first? I bet you didn't. Knowing you, they got set to the side so you could read the letter first. So predictable, Sidney. I put a picture of me and my parents on top, but you should really see the others. I remember you always talked about going to the beach and surfing and scuba diving. You know, I never really went to the beach that often before I went away, but I decided that it was time. So I took these pictures for you. They're not very good, but I never said I was a photographer. I got another surprise too. Make sure you check your email when you get to the library.

This is my way of saying thank you for all you did for me. I know you won't believe me, but you saved me from myself. I wanted to stay out of trouble because I knew you would be disappointed in me if I didn't. When I got there I was angry at the world but mostly angry with myself. You helped me to get through that. Now don't sit there being all sad and lonely. Get out there and live the best you can. And don't forget to check your email.

Jillian

Sidney flipped through the pictures, and sure enough, they were of the beach and ocean. The last picture was a special one. It showed Jillian standing next to a surfboard with a strange attachment. After a closer look, she recognized it as a small mountable camera on the end of the surfboard. She realized that if she couldn't go surfing herself, then Jillian had done the next best thing and, in a way, brought the ocean to her.

That night, she could hardly sleep with anticipation of seeing the video Jillian had shot. After breakfast and a lukewarm shower, she arrived at the library. She logged on to the computer, using the information given to her by the prison. It didn't take long to find the video. "Bout time you checked your email, girl," said the video image of Jillian. The wind blew across the microphone, making it a little hard to hear her, but she managed. "Just to warn you, I've never done this before, so don't expect to see a lot of fancy flying." She grabbed the board and ran toward the ocean. Sidney wanted to yell to her that she hadn't attached her safety line to her ankle. Right as she hit the water, Jillian remembered to attach the line. "See, told you I've never done this," she said into the camera. "Okay, this is for you, girl," and she began to paddle out into the water.

She wasn't kidding. She really was bad at surfing. Sidney could not help but laugh at each wipeout. Each seemed more painful than the next. She caught herself trying to coach Jillian, forgetting at times it was a video. One particular wipeout made her cringe. It seemed to last forever even though it was only seven minutes long. Finally, a beaten and battered Jillian made it back to shore. "Well, I hope that you enjoyed that oceanic beatdown of my body. Got to go. Love you, girl." With that, the video ended. A shadow seemed to lift off her. She felt happier than she had in weeks. Jillian was right. She had been feeling sorry for herself, but that had to end. There were people out there that still cared for her. She had a life to live even inside the confines of this place. It was time to join that life again.

CHAPTER 50

Shelia was staking out another name on the list from the flash drive. She knew Roger and Luke would not approve, but when she got word from a source that a high-ranking Pierson executive was on the move, she couldn't wait for permission. She followed him to a small office building across town and watched him go inside. She decided to walk to the glass doors and peek inside. To her disappointment, there was a security guard sitting at a desk. She decided to wait and return to her car and see who all came out of the building. It occurred to her that there was probably at least another entrance to the building. Still, it was a risk she decided to take. An hour passed and the executive came out of the building and drove away. Although tempted to follow him, she decided to wait and see if someone else came out. A half hour passed and no one came out. They must have exited the building from another door. Disappointed, she decided to call it a night. Roger Taylor told her many times that sometimes police work was like that. One could wait and wait, and nothing would happen, and you had to call it a day. Reporting was like that too. Time spent on a lead for a story went nowhere, and you had to start back at square one. It's frustrating but a fact of life in her line of work.

Parking her car outside the small garden home, a thought crossed her mind that things had gone very well for them over the last several weeks. Taylor had brought in his FBI friend, and they were getting workable information from Gaddis. They were also able to prove that Luke's client had evidence both suppressed and planted in an effort to make her look far more guilty than she was. If nothing else, she was confident they could get her a reduced sentence for her cooperation. Walking through the door, she felt the day's concerns start to melt away. She was carrying tension in her shoulders that certainly came from the workload she put on herself. *Time for a vacation*, she thought, but she knew that wasn't likely. It was late, and she wanted to finish up a report and go to bed.

She had just finished putting the finishing touches on her story and sent it to her editor when she heard glass breaking outside. The sound jolted her, and she sprang to her feet to find out the cause of the noise. Instinctively, she grabbed a small statue off an end table as she walked by her couch. Shelia searched around the house but didn't see any signs of broken glass. She made her way to the kitchen door, but it, too, was closed. Opening it, she flipped on the lights. Suddenly a shadowy figure jumped at her. She recoiled in terror to see her neighbor's cat at her feet. Looking on her back porch, she saw that a couple of broken wine bottles lay on the concrete floor. "You scared me to death, kitty cat. Knew I should have put those bottles in the trash can." Relieved, she walked back inside. She shut the door, locking it. As she turned around, she walked straight into a large man who put his hand over her mouth before she even had time to scream. There must have been something in his hand because she could feel herself getting light-headed. Without the least amount of resistance, she felt the world go dark.

CHAPTER 51

On visitation day, Sidney was excited to see Jillian waiting for her. The two quickly embraced and sat at a nearby table. It was the first time since her parents died that she received a visitor that wasn't her lawyer. From time to time, a church group or some other organization came in to visit or give encouragement or some type of goodwill, but it was different when someone came specifically to see you. Jillian was visibly uncomfortable in these surroundings after being away for so long. This was the first time she had returned since her release and even then had to get special permission to visit. It surprised her that the powers that were allowed it, but they did so here she was. Sidney looked happy to see her again. Jillian knew that it was a lonely place on the inside. A small feeling of guilt passed through her mind that she had not gotten here sooner. Being back here brought back a lot of memories, many of which she did not want to remember. Maybe that's why she wanted to return so badly to see the woman that she came to regard as her best friend. She also knew that a lot of people once released never had anything to do with those left on the inside or those she knew while locked up. Sidney was different.

After sitting down, it was Sidney that spoke first. "How's life on the outside?" she asked. There was a genuine curiosity in the question. Being cut off from the rest of the world was a strain in and of itself. She craved any news from what was going on beyond the walls around her.

"It's still taking a lot of getting used to," Jillian said, trying to be as honest as she could. "The first night home, I couldn't sleep because it was so quiet. I swear I got up and couldn't bring myself to walk past the room door. Good thing my bedroom had a bathroom, or I might have been in trouble."

"Come on, girl, tell me, how is your job? What's it like to be able to eat what you want when you want? I want to know," Sidney said while smiling, but there was a desperation underneath that really wanted to know those kinds of things. She couldn't help but think how one could forget how things like that worked in the real world outside.

"I've had to relearn how to relate to people. Working as a waitress, you get disrespected a lot. Well, if that happened in here, those are fighting words, but at work, you have to say 'Yes, sir' and 'Yes, ma'am' and learn to take it, or you'll get fired quick."

Sidney laughed at that thought. "It's hard to picture you in a waitress outfit." She knew that statement had a lot of meanings. Jillian was college-educated and had a good job at a bank before she went to prison. Now she worked as a waitress at a local restaurant for less than minimum wage plus tips. "Are they treating you all right? Giving you good shifts?"

"Yeah, the owner is friends with my dad. He was a little reluctant at first, but Dad won him over to the idea right before I was released. They are good people, so I try to work hard for them. Enough about me. How are you? Everything going good? As good as they can at least?"

"I'm fine, Jillian, I really am. Things are different now, but I'm making it. The pictures and videos you sent me have helped a lot. Thank you so much for doing that."

"Hey, look, I'm not that good, but being only an hour or so from the beach, I thought, why not? I knew you loved going to the beach, but surfing is kicking my butt."

"You don't have to surf just for me, you know. I love the videos, but you don't have to do them."

"Would you just let someone do something for you for crying out loud?" Jillian said, trying to keep the mood light. "Seriously, I want to do this for you. It's fun too once you get past the bruises and nearly broken bones."

"You're so silly." Sidney laughed.

"Listen, Sidney, there is something I need to tell you," she said in a quiet but serious voice. "I didn't want to tell you in a letter or email unless I had to, but." Jillian stopped in midsentence, not knowing what to say next.

"Jillian, tell me. Are you in trouble?"

"Well, maybe."

"Jillian, please tell me you're not getting sent back here."

"What? No, no, not that at all. No, nothing like that. Jeez, really? No. Sidney, I'm getting married."

"You're what?" Sidney responded in a voice that drew a look from a guard. "Jillian, that's great. Why were you afraid to tell me?"

"I didn't want to seem to brag. Believe me, it's not something I wanted to happen."

"Well, who is he? How did you meet? How long have you dated?"

"Whoa, slow down, chic, slow down. His name is Steven Byrd. He's a guy I knew in high school. I'm kinda embarrassed about it, but I hardly knew him because he was a little on the dorky side, and I was a cheerleader. I didn't even recognize him when I first saw him. He started coming into the restaurant and sitting in my section several times a week. He asked me out, but I turned him down. I guess he wore me down, not in a creepy stalker kind of way, but he was sweet, so I agreed."

"You two couldn't have dated that long though," Sidney said. "Did you tell him about where you've been?"

"I told him on our second date. Funny thing was, he already knew I'd been in prison. He said he liked the thought of dating a dangerous woman." Sidney repeated the word *dangerous* and couldn't help but laugh. "No, girl, it was cute. Look, it's not like we're a couple of teenagers. We just fit together. I can't explain it, but we just work."

"What does he do for a living?"

"What are you, my mother?" she kidded Sidney. "He's an insurance adjuster. And yes, before you ask, he's a churchgoer, and I've been going with him. He really is great."

"I'm happy for you, girl. Really, I am. I wish you both the best. When is the wedding?"

"Well, we want to wait until this spring or June. It's going to be pretty small." Jillian paused for a moment. "I want you to be my maid of honor."

"Jillian." Sidney got quiet. She didn't know what to say. "You know I can't do that. They would not even let me go to my parents' funeral. There's no way I can be at your wedding."

"I know, but Steven will have a best man, so I want you to be my maid of honor even though I know you can't be there. So there will be three bridesmaids but no present maid of honor. There's no one I would rather have, so in the pictures with the wedding party, there will be a space between me and the bridesmaids for you."

"Jillian, you should have someone there with you."

"No. There's no one who could take that spot but you. Whether you are there or not, it's yours."

"Thank you, girl," she said, wiping a small tear. "You really are crazy though."

A few minutes later, their time was up. They embraced one more time, and Jillian promised to write and send more videos soon. Sidney promised to write back as well. As she walked back to her cellblock, she went through all the memories of her time with Jillian. She was happy for her, but a part of her couldn't help but wonder if she would ever find love again. After Lawson, she wasn't sure she even wanted to, but never was a long time. However, first she had to get out, but that would be a long time from now. Still, she thought, maybe.

CHAPTER 52

He got a call on his way to the station that morning to meet the crime-scene techs at a small park. This was never a good situation and probably meant someone was robbed, beaten, kidnapped, or killed, which was going to be the beginning of a long day. Taylor arrived at the scene in about twenty minutes. He asked one of the uniforms where the location was, and the man pointed him in the right direction, a wooded area of the park's walking trail, never a good sign. Taylor spotted the crime scene techs and called one over to him. "What have we got?" he asked, taking out a small notebook he kept in his shirt pocket.

"The deceased is a female, probably in her midthirties. Might be an immigrant because she appears to be Asian. No identification was found on the body or sign of sexual assault from what I can tell just by looking at her. She was shot once in the head and three in the back, and that's your cause of death. Jogger found her this morning."

Taylor spotted the body down a small hill from where they stood. Carefully he made his way to where the body lay. She was still lying face down on the ground, and he could easily see the three gunshots. "Has anyone taken pictures yet?" he asked the tech who followed him down.

The tech said they had and were waiting for him to get there before they rolled her over. When they did, Taylor nearly fainted. Shelia's eyes were still open and seemed to stare at him accusingly. The technician was caught off guard by his sudden reaction. "Detective, are you okay?" Taylor didn't speak. He just stared blankly at the body of Shelia Lee. "Do you know her? Hey, we need an officer down here right now." Taylor felt weak and nearly fell. "Here, sit down before you fall. Can I get someone down here now?"

It only took a few seconds to get several officers to where they were, but it seemed much longer. "Taylor, hey, look at me, man," Officer Barnes said, trying to bring him back to reality. "Talk to me, man, what's wrong?"

"I know her. That's Shelia Lee. We just…oh god, we just talked the other night. I just talked to her."

Barnes called for backup and medical help. Another officer was saying something or another to him, but he couldn't hear him. Taylor kept replaying the last time they spoke in his mind. Since they reconnected a few years back, he held out some hope that they would get back together as a couple. She even left that door open recently. Now there she was, and all of that was gone. He warned her not to go off on her own. Was that what happened? She went out again, only this time, the bad guy found her. He didn't have any evidence, but then again, he didn't need any to know this had Leonard Pierson's fingerprints all over it. He also knew that this meant that the gloves were coming off, and no one was safe now.

"Taylor," came the voice of Chief Butler, "Taylor, talk to me."

Paramedics started to take his vitals. The activity around him continued to whirl as he continued to sit there with a blank stare. What eventually brought him back to reality was the mentioning of putting him in an ambulance. Slowly he felt blood rush back into his brain. "Chief. Chief, I'm fine."

"Like hell you are. You're going to the hospital."

"No, Chief, listen. I know her. Chief, you got to listen to me."

"I will as soon as you are checked out. Get him in the ambulance."

The paramedics started to put him on a gurney, but Taylor insisted on staying. Chief Butler told him that if he refused to go to the hospital, he would place him on administrative leave. He also promised to listen to what he had to say as soon as he was checked out. Taylor acquiesced and walked to the ambulance. He knew he had to get in touch with Luke Brady and warn him that suddenly the game had changed.

Taylor regained his senses by the time they arrived. He also managed to get in contact with Luke Brady, who agreed to meet him at the hospital. With his police training starting to kick back in,

Taylor began to form a likely scenario of what happened to Shelia. She was not dressed in running clothes, so she wasn't ambushed on the track. Her clothing suggested that she was taken either from her home or from outside her television studio. *Did she try to go out on her own again?* he wondered. He needed to focus, push back the pain of losing her, and focus on the job now. His life and that of Luke Brady and Sidney Lewis might depend on it.

The doctors finished their examination by the time Brady arrived. They had only begun to talk when the chief walked into the exam room. Over the next several minutes, they filled him in on their investigation. To his credit, Chief Butler let them tell the whole story without asking a lot of questions or giving in to the anger that he could feel welling up inside him. When Taylor and Brady finished, he sat there in silence for a couple of minutes, not really knowing what to say. When he broke the silence, it even surprised him that he was able to keep his temper in check. "So let me get this straight. The three of you were conducting an investigation off the books on Leonard Pierson's involvement in the murder case of his son? You've brought in the feds and managed to get a district attorney killed and now a well-known TV reporter also killed. Did I miss anything?" He knew that he was going heavy on the sarcasm, but honestly, it seemed appropriate. Butler knew that Taylor kept track of the Piersons over the years, but this crossed a line.

"Chief, we all knew what we were getting into. This just seemed like the perfect time to go after him. The information we got from Brady's—"

"Oh yes, the second-rate lawyer that got his client locked up without a fight. Yeah, tell me again how you were protecting her by sticking her in prison?"

Brady shifted uncomfortably on his feet. "Pierson has compromised your police department, district attorney, and who knows what else. Was I really supposed to turn her safety over to you when I didn't know who could and couldn't be trusted?" He also felt more than a little anger welling inside him. "Shelia approached me and was quite willing to do it alone without my help. Everything we did was within the boundaries of a private investigation."

"You're lucky I don't have you locked up for obstruction of justice."

"There's no obstruction if there is no official police investigation," Brady replied back to the chief.

"That's not the point. A woman is dead while on an unsanctioned police investigation. And what made you think that it was okay to call in the feds without letting me know? I should fire your ass right here and now, Taylor."

"Chief, we didn't know who we could trust, and if Pierson got wind of Brady's involvement, it could put a lot of people in danger. We uncovered at least one dirty cop that is willing to testify against Pierson, we've linked him to drug trafficking, and we know that Goldman was at the scene of the Cooper murders at the time of the murders. We've got him now. Shelia's murder proves just how desperate and dangerous he is."

"You talk like the death of Shelia Lee is just some unrelated fact."

"No, let me stop you right there, Chief. Don't you question what I'm feeling right now. Shelia and I were once going to get married. Her death is tearing me up inside, but this is what Shelia would want us to be doing right now. We have probable cause for a warrant to raid his office, and the feds now have a reason to investigate as well." He paused, out of breath as he picked his words more carefully. "It's over for him, Chief. We've got him."

Butler gave Taylor's argument some thought. The detective had gone about this all wrong. A man of his experience should have known better. When this was over, there would be hell to pay. In the meantime, Taylor was right. It was time to get a warrant to search Pierson's office and computers and all. He also needed to see the information on the flash drive as well. "Fine. Get the warrant. I want this to be airtight."

CHAPTER 53

Leonard Pierson's day was not going well. Over the last week, several shipments were intercepted by the FBI, DEA, California Highway Patrol, and God only knew how many other agencies. Profits were down, and his suppliers were starting to doubt his ability to deliver their product. Goldman had also finally dealt with the Lee woman, but according to some of his sources, Goldman was compromised. He was ordered to lie low, but Pierson knew Goldman might be a loose end that needed to be dealt with as well. His intercom buzzed, bringing him out of his thoughts. "Mr. Pierson, the police are here, and they say they have a warrant." The bad day just got a lot worse. Before he could answer, the door opened, and Detective Taylor walked into the office. He had a smug smile on his face oddly curious since his ex-girlfriend just got killed.

"Mr. Pierson, I have a warrant to search your office and take your computers in for a very long and thorough search. Hope you had something you were working on that will delay you in, oh, everything."

"Detective Taylor. How long have you been investigating my company? At what point are you going to give up?"

"Well, I have good news for you, Mr. Pierson. We're almost done here. Oh, and the feds will also be paying a visit to you soon as well. Every agency in the alphabet wants to talk to you. I'm going to let these fine people do their work collecting evidence now, but I'll be back, and when I come back, you and I are going to take a long ride together. It's going to be fun for one of us, at any rate."

Pierson walked out of his office, seething. There was no question the information on the flash drive was being used against him. With Gaddis also turning against him, it was only a matter of time now. It was time to enact his contingency plans before it was too late. The world had shrunk, and there were not as many places that refused to extradite to the United States. Some of those places were not friendly to Americans, but there were still a few he could spend the rest of his days in comfort and ease. It was time to tie up those loose ends.

Goldman knew that the heat was on him. The informants in the department had all but dried up; however, he instinctively knew that something was in the air. In his line of work, it was always a good idea to have a place off the grid to lie low until the heat passed. It had been a while since he last had to do this, but it was a risk inherent in his line of work. He was making ready to leave the state when he got a text from Pierson on a burner phone. Reading the message, Goldman felt a sense of vindication. "It's about time," he said as he closed his message app.

Mail was handed out at its usual time after the evening meal. *Routine, routine, routine,* Sidney thought. She was waiting for this letter with particular excitement because it had the wedding photos from Jillian's wedding. When she saw them, she marveled at how beautiful they were. The last picture was one of the bride and groom and their wedding party. When she saw the picture, she gasped in excitement. There were three people in the picture, the bride, groom, and the best man. In Jillian's hands, instead of her bouquet, was a small sign that simply read "Miss you." The next day, she was surprised to have a visit from Mr. Brady and Detective Taylor. Neither was in a good mood when she sat down across from them. They filled her in on the events of her case and that they believed that sooner rather than later Leonard Pierson would no longer be a threat. As soon as that happened, they could seriously start moving forward on trying to get her case reviewed by the courts. The next part was where things got dark.

"Sidney," Brady began, "I need to warn you that you need to be extra aware of your surroundings. This is a dangerous time for all of us." He adjusted his glasses and sat straight up in his chair. "Shelia Lee was murdered a few days ago. Pierson is taking the gloves off in a bid to stop us. Failing that, he will go for revenge on us all."

"Is there anything else you can tell us about the Piersons?" Taylor interjected into the conversation. "Anything you can remember can be a help even if you think it's not important."

Sidney shifted nervously in her chair as she let the information sink in. She had not seen or heard from Pierson since the card he sent her after she first got to Helen Palmer Prison. "No. Lawson never talked to me about his business. I'm sorry, I honestly don't know anything." She tapped her fingers nervously on the table. "He told me once while we were staying at his family's mountain cabin that he was the go-between of his father's clients and the company, but he never wanted to talk very much about work. It made me mad when he brought work files while we were staying there. He said it was just to keep them safe and not lying in his office."

Taylor's countenance suddenly brightened. "Wait. You said Pierson had a cabin in the mountains?"

"Yeah, we used to go there a few times a year."

"Can you tell me how to get there?" Taylor asked, trying hard to temper his excitement.

A few days later, Taylor and several officers he trusted raided the cabin. Sidney's directions were spot-on. The cabin was not fancy at all but was still bigger than a small house. They made entry and began to secure the scene. Taylor entered the building and saw that there was a half-eaten sandwich in the sitting room on a couch facing the television. Someone had been there recently and had possibly been alerted to their approach. "Officer Barnes, pick five officers and come with me. We may have a runner. The rest of you, secure this cabin. Don't touch anything in here until I get back."

He wished he had a K-9 unit, but there had not been one available, and the cell reception was spotty at best here. The officers spread out through the woods, searching for any sign of whoever it was that was hiding out in the cabin. He knew it was probably a wild goose chase, but he had to try. Suddenly a shot rang out, and an officer called out in pain. Taylor and the others rushed to the scene in time to see a man on a dirt bike take several more shots at them, one hitting a tree near his head. He returned fire, but the man took off. Taylor rushed to the spot and found what looked like an old logging trail. The bike and its rider were long gone, and there was no way to find him. Plus, there was a wounded officer to tend to in the meantime. It took nearly half an hour to get an ambulance to their location. Fortunately, the officer's bleeding was under control, and no vital organs were hit. He would pull through thankfully. Taylor was angry with himself for being taken by surprise like that. He should have known someone might be hiding out there. Once he collected himself, he walked into the cabin. Simmons was there going through some files he found.

"Hey, Taylor," said Officer Barnes, "I found how he knew we were coming. There's a camera monitor and motion alarm set up over here."

Taylor saw that it was pointing down the only road in or out of the area. At least they knew how whoever it was had been tipped off. Simmons called him over to the table in the kitchen. "Look at this. Delivery schedules, cargo manifests, and a ledger with names and amounts of money, all off the books. And here's the kicker, I recognize several of these names as known drug pushers and cartel members. You wanted a smoking gun, Well, here it is. How much do you want to bet my DEA friends can fill in the blanks?" He could hardly contain his excitement. "After all these years, we've finally got him."

"Detective, we got something else too," said Officer Barnes. She handed him a man's wallet. In his haste, he must have left it behind.

Taylor took the wallet and quickly found what he was looking for, the man's driver's license. When he saw the name, a new wave of frustration went through him. "We almost had him," was all he could say. He showed the others the license that belonged to Bernie Goldman.

CHAPTER 54

Over the last several days, Sidney kept more to herself than normal. Changes in habits tended to get noticed in a place where you saw people every day. A couple of inmates asked her if anything was wrong, but she told them that she was fine. The last thing she wanted to do was arouse suspicion in someone who might be keeping watch on her. She tried to keep as normal a routine as she could under the circumstances. Warmer weather allowed them more yard time. She enjoyed being outside on days like this. There was no official walking track in the yard, but the inmates had established one of their own makings. Sidney tried to go at least twice a week to get some exercise. It was a good stress reliever, and goodness knew she needed to relieve some stress.

It was time to return inside, and the inmates began to make their way back. They were supposed to form a line, but often the line turned into a mob near the door, and the guards would bark out orders to line up. Today was one of those days. As they were trying to sort things out, Sidney tried not to get in their way and not mix in with the bunch. She never saw what happened next. She felt a sudden pain in her side as she stepped back from the thinning group upfront. An inmate she didn't know screamed in terror as blood began to flow from the wound in Sidney's side. Before the woman could strike her again, one of the guards wrestled her to the ground. Sidney stood in shock as she reached down and touched the wound on her side. Seeing blood on her hand, she went blank and lost the strength in her knees and fell. Jo, who had stood only a few feet away, rushed to her side. "Look at me, Lewis," she said, taking Sidney's head into her arms. "No, don't you close your eyes. Look at me."

Sidney didn't speak, the color draining from her face.

"Damn it, girl, look at me. Look at me."

Somehow her eyes stayed open, but she didn't speak. Her breath began to grow shallow. The warm day began to grow cold as the guards rushed her away.

CHAPTER 55

Pierson was clearing out his office as he got ready to make his flight. Everything was nearly in order for his getaway. The last thing he needed to do was access the secret floor safe the police failed to find when they searched his office a few days back. Inside the safe were important documents and a large amount of cash. It was more than what he needed where he was going, but it never hurt to be prepared. The urgency for escape was heightened by an ominous phone call he received from one of his suppliers. To say the least, his former business associates were angered at the loss of product over the last several weeks. They were ready to make changes, and that was never a good thing for those on the other side of the change. It was ironic that after such a long business relationship, the people at the top would so easily discard him, as he had done to so many others. Such was the inherent risk in what he had done, and it was the main reason why he was planning on going into hiding.

He was removing the last contents of the floor safe when his cellphone rang. "Mr. Pierson," came a tired and haggard voice on the other end. He recognized Goldman's voice immediately and realized quickly that if he was calling at this time of day, it was important. "Mr. Pierson, they found the cabin."

"What did you say?"

"Sir, they found the cabin. I took what I could, but they got just about everything."

"When did this happen?"

"About three days ago. I would have called you sooner, but I've been on the run, and the cell signal is nearly nonexistent. I've only now been able to emerge long enough to call. I'm going into hiding, and I suggest you do the same if you can."

"Hiding? Your job is not to hide but to do as I tell you, Goldman. Get yourself back to—"

"Sorry, Mr. Pierson, but I believe this is my resignation. Been an honor, sir, but I'm afraid this is it." With that, he hung up the phone. Pierson nearly slammed his own phone to the ground. Three days? This was completely unacceptable.

As Pierson regained his composure, he heard an alarm. Turning to his monitors on the far wall, he saw a line of cars coming into the parking lot of his office complex. Jumping out of the lead car was Roger Taylor. There were uniformed officers and agents from what looked like federal law enforcement from various agencies. It would take them some time to make their way to where he was, but there was no stopping them. He felt like a trapped animal for the first time in his life. Trapped he might be, but that did not mean he was helpless. His whole life he was in control of himself and those around him. Now would be no different. Pierson stood in front of a mirror on a sidewall of his office. He straightened his tie and smoothed the wrinkles from his jacket. When he was satisfied, he returned to his desk and began to neatly rearrange the files and items on the desk.

They were through the ground-floor door and had made their way to the stairwell. Pierson turned to the decanter of scotch he kept behind him and poured a glass full. No need to hold back now. Taking the liquid into his mouth, he savored the richly smoky flavor of his favorite brand. One last drink now. He stared out the large window behind his desk. Outside the parking lot was now filled with police and flashing lights from their cars. He looked at the monitor. They were near to his floor. Returning to his desk, he withdrew from a hidden compartment an old .44-caliber revolver. It had once belonged to his grandfather and then his father before becoming his possession. He hoped to one day pass it on to Lawson, but his son never seemed to take interest in those kinds of things. Pierson's thoughts briefly turned to Lawson and how he placed too much faith in him; Jonathan, the do-gooder who wanted to run a legitimate business from a crime family; and a stupid girl that he couldn't bring himself to destroy when he had the chance. He still had not heard from the assassin he paid, but he was sure by now she was dead. That at least was something.

The police were now on his floor. The door to the office was solid, and it would take several minutes for them to force entry, time enough to do what had to be done. "Open the door, Pierson. This is Detective Taylor. We know you're in there. The place is surrounded. There's no escape."

"You fool, Taylor, there is one place to escape to that you can never bring me back from," Pierson said. He took the revolver into his hand and pulled back on the hammer. "You will never have me, Taylor. With my last act, I defy you one last time." He raised the revolver to the side of his head and pulled the trigger.

CHAPTER 56

The next day, Taylor began a roundup of officers who cooperated with Pierson over the years. In all, fifteen officers were found to be on his payroll. The new district attorney granted immunity to former Detective Sullivan in exchange for his cooperation in rooting out the bad actors in the department and even in the DA's office itself. Frank Simmons joined him in his office later that day. "Well, I guess you were right after all, Roger." Simmons handed him one of the two cups of coffee he carried with him. "It's been great working with you again, old friend. You know, we could always use a good agent at the bureau."

"Not a chance," came the voice of Chief Butler. "We're going to need him to clean up this mess he made of the department and someone to help me run it. There's going to be a lot of questions asked in the coming days."

"Sorry, Frank. I think my place is here, not to mention that Goldman is still at large. Until he is found, this isn't over."

"Well, if you change your mind, you know where to find me."

The two shook hands and then quickly embraced. Simmons left the office and drove the rental car to the airport for his flight home. After Simmons left, Butler and Taylor were alone in the office. There were some things that Taylor wanted to get off his chest. Chief Butler had been a mentor to him, and he regretted going behind his back during his investigation. He wanted to tell him, but Brady had insisted on keeping what they were doing secret for as long as possible to protect Sidney, for all the good that did. "Chief, I want—"

"Save it, Taylor," the Chief cut him off. "You know what you did was wrong by the book. You exposed corruption in the department, corruption in the DA's office, and single-handedly cast serious doubt on several cases prosecuted by Jim Cooper, not to mention the case of that poor girl a few years ago." Butler took a deep breath and slowly let it out. "A woman died during the course of your investigation. There will be a lot of questions to answer for that as well. Officially, this is a giant screwup." Butler crossed his arms and sat on the corner of Taylor's desk. "But you brought down a major criminal organization. Unofficially, good work, Taylor."

"Thanks, Chief," Taylor said, feeling a sense of relief. "So what happens now?"

"We've got a lot to clean up, and I doubt I'll survive it. Gloria's been wanting me to retire for a while now anyway. Now seems as good a time as any."

"Chief, I don't know if that's what you need to do."

"Yes, it is, and I intend to make sure your name is the only one on that short list of candidates. You've earned it, Roger."

"Thanks, Chief, but there's still some unfinished business to take care of for now."

With that, the two men walked out of the office to begin the process of reorganizing their department.

CHAPTER 57

Everything was dark, so dark that she couldn't see her hands in front of her. She felt like she was floating in the air, hovering over something that she couldn't fully see or understand. She saw a small light in the distance, a light at the end of the tunnel, so to speak. She had always heard people saw a light when they died. She was floating toward the light, and it grew ever closer. So this was how it all ended. As she got closer, Sidney began to hear voices. They were ones she recognized. She thought, *Mom, Dad, is that you?* It wasn't clear; she needed clarity. The light grew brighter; she was almost there now. The voices were growing louder. It was time. At last, she drew a breath.

A breath? How was that possible? She began to feel heavy, as if the ground was rushing to meet her feet. Her eyes opened in a small slit. It was all so bright. She could make out two shapes. They were not in the distance but much closer now. Instinctively, she took another breath, deeper this time. The air filled her lungs. It hurt to breath so deeply. Pain? There shouldn't be any pain unless…

Slowly, she tried again to open her eyes ever so slowly. Apparently this time, someone saw her because she heard a male voice call for the nurse. Another voice was calling to her, a female voice, not her mother's but familiar. "Sidney," it called to her. "It's me, girl. Do you recognize me?" It was so familiar. Where had she heard it before? "Jillian," came a weak reply from a voice that sounded almost alien to her. "Yes, girl, it's me," came the response.

The nurses came in and began to attend to her. Behind them walked in an older man. She looked through the haze and came to recognize Luke Brady. "We nearly lost you, my dear. It's a miracle you're still alive."

Sidney tried to sit up, but the pain in her side wouldn't let her bend at the waist. As she slightly moved her leg, she heard the clanking of a metal chain. "Sorry, it's procedure. You're in a hospital, a real hospital. They let us stay here with you for certain hours, but there's a guard outside the room. As soon as you can be moved, you'll have to go back."

"What happened?" she weakly asked.

"You were attacked in the prison yard," Brady told her. "The woman told authorities that she had been put up to it by Pierson or someone who represented him, rather." Even in her weakened, drug-induced state, he could tell she was scared. "Sidney, he won't come for you again. Leonard Pierson is dead. Killed himself a few days ago."

She tried to move, but she felt too weak, and her head was heavy. "Dead?" she finally managed. "Is it over, then?"

"Not yet. There's still the manner of your conviction, but we can start moving forward now much faster. Don't worry about that right now. You just rest."

Jillian took her hand and said, "I have to go home soon, girl, but I wanted to be here when you woke up. I've got more pictures and more videos to send you. Get better for me, okay?"

Sidney gave them a small and weak smile and closed her eyes again. She hated to go back to sleep with them still there, but she was exhausted. Slowly she drifted off to sleep. A sense of safety swept over that she had not felt in a long time. Pierson was gone now, so maybe this nightmare would also soon be over.

The wheels of justice moved ever so slowly. It had been almost a year since the attack, and very little had been done with her case. Jillian was true to her word. She regularly sent videos and pictures to her, about two or three times a month. Sometimes it was less, but she did what she could to keep her connected to the outside world. Luke Brady returned finally with news on her case. "I've been in constant contact with the court," he told her. "I'm afraid it's not all good news. The court refused to completely set aside your conviction. They said since you took the plea bargain, it was an admission of guilt that they could not ignore. They have ordered a negotiation with the new district attorney." Brady looked down at his files with a depressed expression on his face.

She considered what he just told her. It was disappointing, to say the least. "So what does that mean?" she asked him.

"It means that you're not likely to get out anytime soon. When I meet with the DA next week, Detective Taylor is coming with me to tell him about the information you gave to help his case against Pierson. Hopefully, the DA will take that into consideration along with all the other irregularities in your case. At the very least, I think we can get your sentence greatly reduced."

She gave him a smile and said, "Well, that's something, I guess." It was more sarcastic sounding than she meant it to be, but after four years of being locked away, she had lost some of her courtesy. Brady looked as if he had lost his best friend, and in fact, he had. Her dad was his best friend, and she tried to remember that her parents trusted him with her case.

"I'm sorry, Sidney," he said, "this is my fault. I should have taken your case to trial. Maybe I could have done more for you if I had."

"You did the best you could with what you had. Mom and Dad would be proud of the job you've done. So am I."

Six weeks passed before she saw him again. When he returned, he had news about her case. "I'm afraid I have mixed news on your case," Brady began. "The DA has agreed to reduce the conviction to first-degree manslaughter. They have offered a six-year sentence with credit for time served. That means you have eighteen months left to serve. However, he agreed to allow you to spend the last six months on parole. If the court agrees, you should be out next year. You'll have to appear in front of the parole board, but that should just be a formality."

The next several months passed by to her as a mixture of fast days and slow days. Eventually, the day came for her to appear before the parole board. She answered their questions and told them about her plans for life after her release, the things she had learned from her experience, and how she planned to never break the law again. As expected a few weeks later, Sidney received their decision to grant her parole on the last six months of her sentence. On her last night,

Sidney began to give away her things. She began saying her good-byes to the inmates she had known over the years. Sidney thanked Jo again for saving her life a year ago. That night, she made her way back to her cell and heard the door close, locking her in for the last time. After tonight, she hoped to never hear that sound again. She didn't sleep much with the excitement of knowing tomorrow she would leave this place.

The next morning, she got up quickly, hoping that like Jillian, they would come for her early in the morning. She was not disappointed. Shortly after the head count, Officer McConnell came to her cell. "Lewis, roll up your stuff. Let's go." Sidney turned to her cellmate and wished her well. The door opened, and Sidney began her walk to freedom. As she walked down the cellblock, she said goodbye to some of the inmates she knew on her way out. After they walked through the door to the cellblock, McConnell told her it would take a few hours to get her released. "For the record, I'm happy you're going home. Just do me a favor and don't ever come back here." They arrived after a while at the processing area, where she was told to have a seat and wait her turn. She was there about an hour before she was admitted to start signing papers—sign here, initial there, all so formal and exacting paperwork. Once completed, she was directed again to the waiting area, where the clothes and personal items Luke Brady brought for her would be brought out. She sat there for over an hour, waiting for her belongings. Finally, they brought them, and she was directed to a changing area. Even upon release, a guard watched her undress and dress. It seemed ridiculous to her that they would search her one last time on her way out, but after so many searches over the years, she just did it and got it over with.

Finally, she began the long walk to the freedom gate. A male guard walked beside her down the long sidewalk. She seemed to walk forever before they finally arrived at the gate. The guard quickly turned the lock, and the gate to the outside opened for her at last. He wished her good luck as she walked out through the gate. Sidney took in her first breath of freedom in over six years. Almost before she knew it, Jillian ran to meet her and threw her arms around her.

Sidney dropped the bag she was carrying and returned the embrace. They stood there for what seemed like forever, with tears streaming down their faces. She looked up and saw Luke Brady leaning against the front of his car. She smiled at him as he waved at her from the car. Linking arms with Jillian, she said, "Let's go home."

CHAPTER 58

He had chosen his spot carefully over the course of several weeks. He kept watch, observing where people coming out of the facility were being released. Goldman had found the best spot where he could observe unseen and have the best vantage to finish one last task. He watched and waited with his binoculars until he finally caught sight of his target. There she was, the girl that had caused so much trouble. Goldman hated loose ends. He could have just as easily let this one go. Pierson was dead, but if he had listened to him and killed the girl, he would still be alive, and things would have continued the way they were. It was revenge then. Petty revenge perhaps, but he just couldn't let this go. He put down the binoculars and picked up the suppressed scoped rifle resting next to him. Slowly he gazed through the scope and found his target. *Ah, there you are*, he thought. A red-haired woman ran up and embraced her, blocking his shot. "Come on, red, move out of the way," he muttered under his breath. He could just as easily kill them both. It wouldn't matter that much more to him. He then spotted the girl's lawyer leaning on the front of a car. The body count was getting higher, but no matter. After all he had done for Leonard Pierson, three more bodies would not make a difference.

Goldman again placed his crosshairs on the red-haired woman. When the two broke their embrace, he had a clear shot at Sidney. "How nice of you to step aside, red. I'll be with you in a moment." He had a clear shot at Sidney now. He placed the middle part of his finger on the trigger. Goldman took a deep breath and exhaled half of it. His aim was true, and he slowly began to put pressure on the trigger. Slowly the pressure increased, and then a shot rang out. Goldman did not see where the shot landed because he felt a searing pain in his left shoulder. He moved his right hand to take the concealed pistol in his shoulder holster. Rolling over, he pointed his weapon from where the shot came from. Roger Taylor placed his second shot in the center of Goldman's chest. His breath became shallow, and his body began to grow colder.

Detective Taylor walked over to Goldman's body and kicked away the pistol. Looking down at the dying Goldman, he said to him, "That's for Shelia, you son of a bitch." Picking up the binoculars, he saw that Brady and the ladies seemed nonetheless aware of what had just happened. He made a note to himself to tell Brady about this next time he saw him. After they drove away, he put the binoculars down and called in what he did to the state police.

The search for Goldman had gone cold after he disappeared in the woods about a year or so ago. Taylor began to think that maybe he would try something like this when Sidney was released. He looked around a few days ago and found the spot he was standing on now. The giveaway was several footprints around the best vantage point overlooking the gate where inmates were released and what looked like an improvised rest for a rifle. He hid just out of view from the spot and waited until Goldman was distracted with lining up his shot. The plan worked. Now he could begin to close the book on Leonard Pierson once and for all. After the state police finished with him, he began to drive back to Warrenton. He stopped at a small cemetery outside of town. He placed a bouquet of flowers on Shelia Lee's grave. "We did it, Shelia," he said. A few minutes later, he made his way back home.

Sidney arrived at her parents' house that afternoon. Mr. Brady and Jillian stayed with her for a couple of hours. Brady bought them all a pizza for dinner. Sidney so looked forward to having real pizza for dinner. Not long after they ate, they all said their goodbyes. For the first time in years, she was truly alone. That night, she found it hard to sleep. The mattress was much larger and far more comfortable than what she had been used to in recent years. What got her the most was how quiet it was at night. She was used to sleeping with people all around her screaming, laughing, and shouting at one another, toilets flushing, body noises, and other sounds at all hours of the night. It was also far darker than she remembered at night.

Though she wanted very much to sleep in the next morning, Sidney found herself awake at around five thirty in the morning. She got up and used the bathroom and made up her bed. The door to her bedroom was shut, and she found herself sitting on her bed, waiting for someone to come and unlock it so she could go to breakfast. Eventually, she made her way to the kitchen to make herself breakfast. It amazed her that she still remembered how to do that. Mr. Brady made sure that the kitchen was fully stocked for her when she got home. Tomorrow, Mr. Brady would come by so that they could sign legal documents signing the estate back over to her as well as various other legal documents. Today, though, she wanted to spend time in her parents' home, now her home, and enjoy her first full day of freedom. She busied herself trying on the clothes from her apartment. Surprisingly, most of them still fit even if they were probably well out of style.

After lunch, she went into the backyard. Memories came rushing back to her as she strolled around. Her mother's flower garden would need a lot of work, she noticed. Her father's grill was just how he left it, in pristine condition. They loved being outside working in the yard or grilling burgers and hot dogs and other meats. She could almost picture them now as they went about their day in years past. She returned inside and started flipping through some old photo books. Her parents' wedding photos, pictures from her childhood, and even her high school graduation photos were all there. Next, she found a more recent photobook. In it were pictures of her from college. Near the end of the book, she found a picture of herself and Lawson. Sidney hardly recognized the seemingly happy couple staring into the camera. Her first instinct was to tear the picture to pieces. She stared at it as a whirlwind of emotions raced through her, but in the end, she decided to keep it as a reminder of times gone by.

She slept much better that night. When she woke up, it was again at around five thirty. Sidney accepted that it might just be a part of her that would never go away. Mr. Brady would be there to pick her up around ten that morning. He called her around nine on the cellphone he got for her, another thing she had to put in her name, telling her that he was running late at the courthouse but would be there soon. She couldn't wait to get her license back so she could drive again. He arrived shortly before lunch to begin what promised to be a long day. Before they started on all the legal work, there was a stop she insisted on making first. They drove out to the cemetery where her parents were buried. Luke escorted her to where they were interred and then excused himself to give her some time alone with them.

Sidney placed a small bouquet of flowers she picked from the flower garden that morning at the foot of the headstone. It felt strange to be standing there after so long. The wind blew through her hair as she stood there remembering them. Several minutes passed when Mr. Brady approached her. "I have something that I need to talk to you about, and well, this is just as good a place as any," he said, breaking the silence. She turned her head to look at him as he spoke. "As you know, the driver of the truck that killed your parents was drunk at the time of the accident. Once the toxicology report confirmed it, I started a civil suit against the trucking company in the estate's name. Two years ago, they settled with the estate out of court."

The news shook her out of her train of thought. "How much did you settle for?" she asked him.

"Enough to take care of you for a very long time, if not the rest of your life."

It came as a shock to her. She thought something like this might happen, but no amount of money could ever replace her parents. "I can't accept it. I don't care what you do with it, but I don't want it."

"Yes, you do, Sidney," he told her. "Your mom and dad set up a fund for you for when you got out. It's got a couple of thousand dollars in it. They wanted to make sure you would be taken care of and be okay. They're gone now, so this is the last thing they could do for you. They would want you to have this money. Let them do this one last thing for you."

She thought about it for a minute or two. In a way, it didn't feel right to profit from their deaths. The more she thought about it, the more what he said made sense. Job possibilities would be few and far between, so she made her decision to accept the money. "A part of this belongs to you," she told him.

"I'm paid through the estate. I don't need it."

"At a seriously discounted rate. I owe you far more than that. Please, they would want me to do that for you."

He reluctantly agreed. They grabbed lunch and began the long process of signing documents giving her ownership of her parents' estate. After they had finished for the day, he drove her home, and she asked him if he would like to come inside. He accepted, and they walked in and began to unwind from the day. "I have something else for you. Almost forgot I had it." He reached into his pocket and produced a flash drive. "Recognize this? It's yours now. Don't worry, all the important documents have been saved, but the videos are still on it. Check and see if you want, but trust me, they are still there. I think I got all the ones Lawson had and deleted them. These should be the last. I think you know what to do with it."

She took the flash drive from him. It was hard to believe something so small caused her so much trouble. She turned it over and over in her hand, thoughts rushing through her mind of the last years of her life. Getting up from her chair, she walked into the kitchen. Inside was a tool drawer where her dad kept a small hammer and several screwdrivers along with other small tools. She placed the flash drive on the chopping block and began to smash it to pieces. Luke had followed her and watched as she destroyed the flash drive once and for all. She turned and hugged him and thanked him again. With that, he told her good night. That night, she had yet another good night's sleep.

In May, Sidney planned a trip she had been waiting to take for over six years. She stepped on the sand with her bare feet, relishing the sand between her toes. She began waxing the new surfboard she bought, eagerly anticipating hitting the water. "You think you can still ride that thing?" came a familiar voice from behind her. Sidney turned to see a bikini-clad Jillian behind her.

"It's just like a bike. Once you learn, you never forget," Sidney replied. "Besides, I've been waiting a long time for this."

"Yeah, well, I still haven't gotten the hang of it yet. Looks like I would have after all of those videos."

"Come on, girl, the idea is not to be a champion surfer but to have fun and enjoy the water and sun."

"Sure, as long as you don't end up with water in your eyes, ears, and nose. Not to mention all the bruises on my body."

"Jillian, you're so silly. Let's do this."

The two made their way to the edge of the water, where Sidney paused momentarily. She looked at Jillian, smiled, and rushed into the water. It didn't take too long before she was riding the waves. It made her feel alive in a way she hadn't in years. To Sidney, it was as if the ocean was washing away the stress of the last several years. She began to feel whole again as the ocean washed over her. Finally, she could start to put the events of the last several years behind her.

EPILOGUE

A year passed since Sidney left prison. Since then, she started to work at a small company as a secretary. What she did not know about it was that Mr. Brady had paid a visit to Jonathan Pierson to remind him of the promise his father made to him before Sidney went away. Jonathan sent word to Sidney's employer to remind him of a favor that he owed him, and that was how she got her job. After he hung up the phone, Jonathan told Luke that this small deed was a start in reforming the Pierson name. Luke decided to keep that information secret.

Sidney began going to church again a few months after her release, but she couldn't bring herself to attend the one her parents once held membership. She began to go to another church and became involved in the ministries there. She joined a Sunday school class for singles, and it gave her a place to fit in, and no one seemed to mind about her past. She was relieved, but still a long way from beginning to trust people again. One morning, Sidney heard an unusual noise coming from her engine. She called into work, saying that she had car trouble and would be late for work. She drove the car to a local dealership's service center and was met by the manager. She told him what was wrong but had a strange feeling about the man who ran the garage. "I'm sorry," she said to him, "I feel like I should know you. Have we met before?"

He smiled and told her that they had met. "I doubt you remember me since I haven't been there in a few weeks, but we are in the same Sunday school class." He seemed to blush a little. "I'm Jason," he said, pointing to the name on his uniform. "Jason Douglas. I recognized you the second you drove in. Not that I was staring you down or anything." Jason looked away for a moment.

Sidney smiled slightly, not knowing what to say. "Well, do you think you can fix my car today?"

"Well, we are pretty busy right now, but tell you what. I'll take a look at it and see what I can do. Can I get your phone number so I can call you later?" he said. Immediately, his eyes got wide, and he stuttered. "So I can let you know about your car," he finally said.

"Um, yes, I would like that." Now it was her turn to be surprised. "So you can call me about my car, I mean." She thanked him and walked to the waiting area, where she called Luke Brady and told him about the car. He couldn't leave the office, but he sent his secretary to pick her and take her home.

The next day, the car was ready, but when she got there, Jason was not at work. She drove home both disappointed and relieved. *It's too soon,* she thought. *I can't right now. Not yet.* She put the thought out of her mind and went about the rest of her week as normal.

That Sunday after her class, she felt a tap on her shoulder. Turning around, she saw Jason standing there and started a conversation with her. "Sorry I didn't call. I had a lot of cars to work on, and we were shorthanded," he said nervously. He seemed nervous as if talking to her took a mountain of courage.

"Oh, it's okay, Jason, I'm just glad you got it fixed. Thank you."

"Well, I hope we did a good job on it." A silence followed before he continued. "Listen, I don't want to seem creepy or anything, but I was wondering if, um…well, if you would like to have dinner sometime. I know a great little grill that has the best steaks in town."

Sidney felt off-balance. He was being nice and seemed sweet, but she just didn't feel ready. She smiled slightly and said, "Yes, that sounds great." Instinctively, she put her hand to her mouth. "Wait what?" she said, not really knowing where that answer came from.

"I think I asked you out," Jason replied, almost in disbelief.

"Yes, I think you did," she responded. "Look, you seem like a really nice guy, so yes, I will go to dinner with you." *You said it again, what are you saying?* she thought. *You're not ready for this. Just tell him no.* "Is Friday okay?"

"Sure. I'll pick you up at seven. How's that?"

"Sounds great," she said, surprised at what just happened.

Over the next several weeks, the two met for dinners and watched movies together. She told Jillian about what she had done, and she told her she was happy for her. "You deserve someone in your life, Sidney. There's nothing wrong with that. You can't sit around that house all alone."

"I know, Jillian, but I just don't think I'm ready. I'm not sure I can ever be with someone like that again."

Jillian told her to give it time and trust that things would work out the way they should. Sidney promised that she would try.

Jason and Sidney continued to date, going on a couple of months. That February, Jason came over to watch television and hang out with her. In his hands when he arrived was a small box of chocolates. "Oh gosh, Jason, I forgot it was Valentine's Day."

"It's all right," he said as he walked into the house. The two sat on the couch, and she felt him place his arm around her. She flinched noticeably, and he quickly pulled his arm back.

"I'm sorry. I just…"

"It's okay. I kind of thought this might happen. I like you a lot, Sidney. You're a sweet person, and if we are moving too fast, I understand. Even if you don't want to see me again, it's okay. Well, not okay, but I understand."

"Jason, you don't really know me or what I've been through. I've made some really bad choices."

"Sidney, I know a little about you. It's a small town, and people talk. I know where you've been, and I don't care. It doesn't matter to me where you've been or for how long. I just want to be with you."

"How can you say that? You don't know me. I—" She was startled when he quickly kissed her on her cheek. She stared at him and placed her hand on the spot he kissed her.

"I'm sorry, I shouldn't have done that. I just…" He turned his eyes and stood to his feet and started to leave.

Sidney grabbed his arm, stood up, and pulled him to her. "No, what you should have done was this." She kissed him and wrapped her arms around him. Though he was taken by surprise, he took her into his arms. When they parted their lips, she rested her forehead against his. "I couldn't let that be my first kiss since I got out. I guess I still remember how after all," she said and kissed him again.

A year later, they were married in the church where they first met. Jillian's daughter was the flower girl. Jillian also complained that the dress Sidney picked out for the bridesmaids were not made for pregnant women. Sidney told her to pull it together and get dressed. Luke Brady knocked on the door, ready to escort her down the aisle. She gave Jillian one last hug and waited for her turn to walk to where Jason stood ready for her.

A couple of years later on a chilly fall morning, Sidney found herself at the cemetery, visiting her parents' grave. She tried to visit at least every other month. Most of the time, she didn't say anything. She just placed flowers from the garden and left. This time was different though. She felt like she had more to say, so she decided to say her peace. "I wanted you both to know that I'm thinking about opening the printshop up again. There are a few ideas I'm kicking around on how to modernize it. Jason supports me and says we make enough with his job at the dealership to get by while I get it running. That is, if I decide to do it. I wish you could have met him. He reminds me sometimes so much of you, Dad. You would have liked him. He treats me good." She drew a deep breath before she continued, "I wanted you both to be the first to know that I'm pregnant. Just found out for sure a few days ago. I haven't told Jason yet, but he will be so excited. I wish you both could be here. I love you and miss you both."

Minutes later, she arrived home. Jason was already there fixing dinner. As she closed the door, she thought about how lucky she was. Many people who left prison were not nearly as fortunate as she was. *No*, she thought, *I'm not lucky. I'm blessed.* She set her things down and walked into the kitchen to help with dinner. At last, she felt like she was finally home.

About the Author

Chad Spradley is a teacher of US history, government, and sociology in high school and college in the state of Alabama, where he currently resides. He is an avid sports fan with a fascination for mysteries, science fiction, horror, and Westerns. In his spare time, Spradley enjoys traveling around the US and playing electric guitar. *A Long Road to Redemption* is his first full-length novel.

CPSIA information can be obtained
at www.ICGtesting.com
Printed in the USA
LVHW011405010622
720195LV00009B/401